TH
FROM GRACE

TICKERS

MICHAEL RICHARDSON

The Fall From Grace

Tellwell Talent
www.tellwell.ca

ISBN
978-1-77941-707-7 (Hardcover)
978-1-77941-706-0 (Paperback)
978-1-77941-708-4 (eBook)

With special thanks to:

Dr. Mohammed Shurrab.
Also to his assistant: Sarah Heino.
Not only for your technical expertise but also, for maintaining a level of personal care and empathy that makes a world of difference to your patients.

Thank you, with all my "Heart"

PROLOGUE:

THEY STOOD ASSEMBLED ON THE FIELD that morning, in the early mist. The moisture pooled and drained from the men's armor, while they waited in a hushed anticipation of the upcoming battle. Through the early morning fog, the approaching sounds of armored men and beasts filtered through with a rumble. The sun's rays danced dimly through the murky morning air; perhaps a rainbow might break through the gloom, though no one would notice on this day.

While the soldiers readied their weapons, most of them looked between Constantine - the local druid holy man - and Dafyd, the Clan Chieftain, for instructions. Neither man offered any sign of the nervousness they were concealing. This was yet another battle of the savage hordes that they had been warding-off since the colony formed. Battle was becoming almost routine, but still a cause for concern to Dafyd. He realized that, if the colony was to survive, they would have to endure these losses; losses he knew were inevitable.

Unlike the hordes they faced, Dafyd and Constantine had both learned a lesson from the Romans; they had seen the effectiveness of their training and organization, both on and off the battlefield. In his opinion, one of

his army's greatest weapons was their discipline and structure on the battlefield. Both men had endured much ridicule to make sure that their fledgling community would be modeled after the very people they had fought to expel. The Romans may have brought roads and plumbing and government, but they took much more in return. Dafyd and Constantine, like the rest of the community, valued their freedom over anything else.

Constantine's concern ran far deeper. The last few years had brought varying reports of a new threat. Travelers, who had ventured from beyond the Isle of Britain, had reported the new movement of Catholicism. There had even been reports of other, even more-strange religions to the east; all of these threatened their way of life. Raiding hordes had come before, but these believers in Christ, they could destroy the Druid way of life without un-sheathing a sword. Paramount to Constantine were these, Christians. They had survived the Romans, and their many gods, and were heading here. They had not just survived the Romans, but now they come to the shores of this island nation with the very Romans that threatened to destroy them, while they were still considered an obscure cult. The Romans had come to Britain as invaders, conquerors, and now these Christians had even conquered the mighty Roman Empire. Constantine almost laughed when it occurred to him that he might miss the Romans.

Constantine had sent Christian to the wagons at the rear of the assembled ranks. He was to stow his master's cloak, and retrieve a book of prayer. Constantine was, in fact, the boy's guardian, having taken him in after his parents died at the hands of the same clan they now faced.

Christian paused as he approached the rear of the ranks, to take in and absorb the sight their sheer numbers. Their ranks swelled towards the edges of the field in both directions.

Christian was in his sixteenth year but was considered small for his age. He had never excelled at physical feats and had received no training of any kind in the art of war. Instead, he had been educated in reading, and spent most of his time indulging in such pursuits. He was meek, and even considered a coward by some. He stood in awe of many of the soldiers and wished he could be like them. His fear when facing danger kept him from combat.

He could see Dafyd atop his mount, adorned in his finest battle armor, pacing in front of his troops. He proudly carried his broad axe at his side as he inspected the men.

Constantine could be seen slightly ahead and to the side of the ranks, perched on a rock for all to see him. He was dressed in his usual full-length tunic, tied at the waist with his rope belt, from which hung his branch of mistletoe. He held his staff, a simple wooden staff as tall as the man who carried it, crowned at one end with a small green gem embedded in a golden tip. Christian had never seen him wield it in combat but had tasted it's sting when being disciplined. He knew Constantine would never fight unless on behalf of the gods, but if he was ever called to do so, he would be capable of the task.

Christian now made his way through the ranks towards his master. In a moment of inattention, he stumbled into one of the soldiers, knocking himself to the ground, and causing the other to stumble.

"Save it for the savages..." the man started, as he turned to see Christian sprawled on the ground behind him. "Damn it, lad," he started, in a grunting laugh. "I should have expected this of you."

"My deepest sorrows to you, Captain," Christian said, as he covered his head in anticipation of the corrective blow, that never came. Instead, he felt himself being hoisted from the ground by his neck. He opened his eyes and tried to gasp for air through his restricted windpipe. His eyes followed the arm that held him in the air, until they came to rest on the other's enraged face.

"I've told you too many times, boy!" he grunted. "My name is Gabriel. I no longer have rank or title and would advise to take you heed of that fact. I grow tired of your stupidity boy," Gabriel barked, as he casually dropped Christian to the ground with a thud.

"Yes, sir... Gabriel," Christian cried, in the hopes of no further reprisal. Then he lay still, and watched as the large man turned his back to him. Gabriel had, at one time, been friendly towards the boy. He had even offered to train Christian for combat, but Constantine, as his guardian, forbid it. Three years earlier, Christian had been taken prisoner by an enemy clan. Being perceived by outsiders as the son of Constantine, they had hoped to convince Constantine to surrender his clan's harvest in trade for the boy. Constantine refused;

he had to consider the welfare of the clan. He also knew that he could not risk war with this clan, and therefore ordered the matter, and his son, to be forgotten. The Clan Council agreed. Gabriel took it upon himself to rescue the boy. He single-handedly raided the camp one night and made off with the boy. For his actions, or more correctly, for disobeying the council, Gabriel was stripped of his rank and holdings, and reduced to the infantry. He had grown more and more bitter towards Christian over the time since.

Christian lay there another moment in silent shock from the encounter, admiring the utter size of the man, and was thankful that he was more concerned with the up-coming battle than a small boy. He made his way to his feet and collected his things. Instead of continuing forward past Gabriel, he doubled back and took a different route back towards Constantine, giving a wide berth to Gabriel.

Christian had now made his way, without further incident, to the front of the ranks. He stopped for a moment, then could feel his master's gaze set upon him. Without even looking to Constantine, he made his way to his master's position. Upon climbing the rocks, he could survey the entire area, and what was to be the battle ground. Off to the side in the distance, was the ringed, Hanging Stones, the mysterious structure about which his master was instructing him; a sacred place whose builders were long dead, referred to as Stonehenge in the local dialect.

The prehistoric monument always caught Christian's eye and his imagination. The labor involved alone seemed staggering. Surely it was done with magic or technology now lost to the ages. The outer ring of stones stood in a circle, each stone around thirteen feet in height and waying many tons. They had been moved a great distance and each placed with such precision that, amongst other things this sight was used to track the seasons, the sun falling behind the trilithon – two vertical stones with a horizontal one laying on top – perfectly at sunrise on the winter solstice. It aligns directly with the heel stone, the largest stone in the monolithic monument.

Then, at the far end of the field, he could see movement – shadows danced through the mist. The horde was here. They carried no banners and portrayed no semblance of order. In the rising mid-morning sun, their barbarous screams echoed over the land, and sent a shiver down the young man's spine.

Christian wasn't sure why, but the two forces seemed to stand and stare at each other for what seemed like hours. It was easy to interpret his countrymen's purpose: they were hoping that their resolve and size might encourage the invaders to reconsider their provocative course. Although they outnumbered the enemy by a few hundred, the Savages were not easily intimidated.

The massing horde might have been playing a ruse, a distraction, while a larger force came in on the flank, but none of the spotters Dafyd had dispatched indicated any such thing; they may have been attempting to frighten their prey, or they might have been reconsidering.

Then the battlefield grew silent. Christian realized that they would not be that lucky today. Realizing the same, Constantine held his hands up to the sky, offering a prayer to the gods for his people to carry the day, and with a mighty roar from his men, the battle was on.

The silence was destroyed by the screams of warriors, and the pounding of their feet that, in a full charge, shook the ground. It was deafening and horrifying, particularly to Christian. The young man cowered slightly, and watched as the two armies raced towards each other, weapons at the ready. Archers from both sides discharged their burning arrows, the flaming missiles crossing in the air. The burning rounds dropped men indiscriminately on contact. The terrible race ended with a horrid crash as the parties met, stopping, and holding most men in its grip.

The bloodshed was chilling, as men in both warring parties were slashed, crushed, and dismembered. The air became rich with the stench of death, the blood and other parts expelled from a body in the throes of death. Combined with the smoke and smell of seared and charred flesh, the scale of it all was making breathing intolerable.

Amid the fighting, Christian was horrified to watch as Constantine left his post and traveled towards the battle. Some of the fighting had spilled in among the sacred stones, and Constantine would not stand for it. Christian knew his place was with his master, but he was powerless to move against his fear. It took some moments, and many deep breaths, before he found his legs and moved slowly toward his master. As he traveled, he became mesmerized by the carnage of the battlefield. He had feebly marched more than half the distance to the stones before he turned his attention in that direction. Through the fray, he could now see what had really caught Constantine's eye.

Mabus, a former Druid and colleague of Constantine's, stood poised, waiting for Constantine in the center of this contained battle. Mabus had renounced his religion and the teachings of the Druids when he learned that his education brought him power when among those who were lacking. He now "led" this horde, and would want nothing more than to kill Constantine, and any others like him. He had convinced his followers to pursue this campaign for conquest, but his real goals were of a much more personal nature.

Christian now watched in amazement as his suspicions of Constantine were confirmed. His master quickly bested any man who dared get between him and Mabus, all the while the other taunting Constantine on. Once Constantine reached the inner circle of stones, he was alone with Mabus, and they quickly locked in combat. With an unexplainable sense of urgency, Christian increased his pace towards his master. He had to help Constantine, as Mabus was easily his equal.

It was then that Christian noticed he was being pursued. A Savage had broken free from the battle and noticed the young man. He was a good distance away, but with Christian having nowhere to go and no ability to defend himself, he felt doomed. He struggled with the heavy book he carried as he tried to run.

He tried calling out, having seen Gabriel near the edge of the battle. Gabriel was engaged and unable to be of help anytime soon. A cry to his master brought a similar response. Christian continued fleeing and had reached the outer ring of the stones when his assailant caught him, hitting him from behind with his weapon, and knocking him to the ground; he was bleeding badly. As he tumbled, he noticed Gabriel approaching; he had only his dagger, but if attacking from behind, it would be enough. Christian's eyes desperately raced between the savage now standing over him, and Gabriel. The Savage raised his weapon for the last blow, then hesitated, noticing Christian's gaze. At the last moment, without looking, the Savage spun, landing his weapon into Gabriel's chest. The now dead weight of Gabriel crashed into his killer, sending them both to the ground. Christian lay gasping for air, feeling his life being sucked from him through the gash he had received. He tried to drag himself towards his master again, without much success. As he clutched at the ground around him to get up, he noticed it was thick with blood, his blood.

With a gasp, he fell still, looking around from the mass of bodies littering the field to Gabriel's lifeless face, and then to his master. As he watched Constantine and Mabus do battle, his vision was blurred by horror. Before his very eyes, a burst of light blazed from the stones and consumed both Mabus and Constantine. The light was so intense it was bright to him even with his eyes shut. Unlike any other light sources Christian was familiar with this one gave off little to no heat, though the sensation of the light washing over him, and the rest of the field was tangible enough to send a wave of shivers across his entire body.

Christian tried desperately to call for help, though he lacked the strength. He needed to tell someone of what he had seen, as it seemed no one else had noticed. Christian felt cold. He knew his end was near, and yet could only think of what had happened to his master and Mabus. This scene was somehow familiar to him, though wrong, somehow. He felt as though he had failed somehow. He struggled to stay in this world, but despite his efforts, his mind went dark.

CHAPTER 1

CHRISTIAN HAD MADE HIS WAY OVER the rough, treed terrain behind the compound slightly faster than the last time. On his previous reconnaissance mission, he had been, perhaps, a little over-cautious, but it was, of course, paramount that no one knew he had been there. He was now in place at the rally point, found the supplies he had cached there, and this time, this was no recon mission.

The rally point was at the top of a small rock-cut overlooking the compound. He surveyed the target area for movement as he geared up. He had holstered his side arm, was loading the assault rifle, and checked it for damage. He had left it out here for a few days, and wanted to make sure it was still in proper working order. Through his binoculars, Christian could see that there was only the one guard outside the main building, as expected. He scanned the compound for surprises as he switched his radio on.

"Comm check," he whispered into the headset. "In position at rally point. Sam, you got me?"

"Yeah, I got you." Her voice sounded a little strained. "Receiving you on locator tracking, mini cams are up, drone is on station, receiving clean images. Ready

to proceed." Sam had launched a mini drone a few moments earlier, that would be her main eyes over the compound.

Sam was sitting in their mobile command unit, an RV equipped with the latest in computer, surveillance, and communication technology. Christian had set out on foot from there, just over thirty minutes ago. His best time to the rally point, so far, had been forty-three minutes. This time, he figured his good travel time was due to anxiety.

Christian and Sam had been working together for five years. They had gained a reputation as "Cult Busters" in that time; they were good at what they did, but not so good at adhering to all the laws protecting the rights of the offenders. This wasn't their main concern. Christian's focus of each mission was in achieving the goal. He was paid well to do the job, not so much worrying about the welfare of the people behind the "cult". In his experience, they were usually mental cases, suffering from delusions of grandeur or persecution. The followers were usually worse off. Not once had they ever come across any cult that delivered what it promised. Usually, they were just a means for socially inept men to get laid.

It was on Christian's first solo mission that he and Sam had become reacquainted. In fact, she was the person he had been tasked to liberate; Sam had been abducted from a soup kitchen late one night. The people of the cult had assumed she was simply some transient and wouldn't be missed. Sam was actually working there as a volunteer. She and her devoted husband were old friends of Christian. During the rescue mission, Sam's husband was killed while he and Christian were trying to save her.

Christian looked after her afterwards, and her anger eventually turned to resolve. She insisted that the two of them start an organization specializing in rescuing people from cult activities. Christian was becoming disturbed by the fact that their business was always escalating.

"Alright! What's wrong?" Christian asked, having noticed the tone in her voice. She hesitated before answering.

"This is a big one," she started. "These guys are into the sex trade, drugs, you name it. They're well-funded, and totally nuts. I wish you had some back-up on this one."

"I do," he answered calmly. "You."

"I meant..." he cut her off.

"I know, Sam. It's okay. I put a few surprises in the compound for back-up. Don't worry, this isn't my first barbecue."

Sam didn't answer; she wasn't convinced, but didn't want to upset Christian before going in, and he was going in, that much was obvious.

"Show time," he whispered into the headpiece as he chambered the first round out of the clip into his weapon. He vaulted out of his cover, over the side of the rock-cut, and dropped the 10 feet to the ground below.

"Good luck," Sam whispered, making sure to cover her mouthpiece.

Christian landed like a cat and paused only briefly to make sure he was still undetected. He moved with great stealth through the underbrush and emerged at the edge of the compound. The little light from the quarter-moon helped to hide him, and, of course, the compound was poorly lit; they weren't interested in being discovered here.

Christian broke cover and bolted towards the first building. He described himself as compact, being only 5 feet 10 inches tall and in decent shape. The years had taken some toll, however. There used to be a lot packed into his frame; a well-funded private business and a military pension had seen to it that he had gotten comfortable. He continued toward his goal, sliding along the side of the structure.

"Freeze!" As he heard the words over his headset, he froze and dropped into a crouch.

"Got a stroller," Sam warned him. "He's just around the corner, heading your way."

Christian had nowhere to go and readied himself to take this guy out. He saw the man turn the corner and stagger towards him into the shadow. He hesitated, and the man, obviously under the influence of something, stumbled past him, heading towards the bush. He could hear the man barfing as he approached the tree line. He waited another second or two, then took a shot. The silenced round made less noise than the body tumbling into the brush.

"Now I don't have to hide the body," he thought with a shrug, then turned, and moved on.

Sam picked up on the fact that he was moving again. The kill had taken place out of camera range. "What happened?" she quietly spoke into her headset.

"He'll feel that in the morning," Christian replied. "Am I clear?"

Sam scanned the camera feeds to ensure that the area around Christian, the parts she could see anyway, were in fact clear. "Affirmative," she keyed her mic.

His extrication target was thought to be housed in the largest building, in the middle of the compound. This place was laid out like a military camp; a guard tower in each corner, and 3 smaller buildings surrounding the main structure. His last time through, Christian had mapped out the entire place, planted the cameras, and scouted the housing setup.

Although his goal was saving a 14-year-old girl who had been missing for nine months, he had no intention of leaving this place in operation. Her name was Clara, the daughter of a very important person in Washington. Before she disappeared, she was in a choir at school, and loved riding her horse on her dad's ranch. Her dad had been an acquaintance of Christian, and a connection that helped Christian stay off the most wanted list. Clara's dad, a southern gentleman, had taken an interest in Christian's work early on. He was a religious man and felt that satanic cults were a major threat to national security. Although it was never made policy, Christian had been granted a wide berth when it came to his activities. When Clara went missing, and it was confirmed it was a cult that was involved, Christian had been offered nearly limitless resources, but he preferred to work only with his team.

He thought that it was just a local drug gang, until he started to investigate. The leader was renowned for brain-washing younger girls into doing what he wanted. He was using drugs, poor nutrition, and sleep deprivation to convince these kids that he was the prophet of God, sent here to ready them for bliss. What they were getting was anything but. These girls were bought, sold, and traded. They suffered through repeated rape, and other exploitations. Christian had yet to see any of them cry, despite the conditions. But perhaps the most disturbing thing was that these girls acted as though this was normal behavior, almost as if they liked it.

At first, it seemed to just make good business sense for this guy, Quintus, as he was known. Young slave labor was cheap and easy, and as with most cults, the sexual exploits were simply the next step. Christian was amazed at how successful he was. He had seen the FBI file on Quintus, and there had never been a girl escape, or even try to escape from this cult.

Christian broke cover again, sprinting to the side of the main house. There was, as expected, one guard outside. He was foolishly guarding the door, however; Christian had no intention of going through the door.

Because they were situated in the middle of the Florida Everglades, the buildings were all built on stilts to try to keep out the local wildlife. Christian had cut a small hole in the floor of the building the last time he was here, so he could get in undetected. He slid under the house to the trap door, and carefully let himself inside.

As far as he could tell, no one had found his trap door. At least there was no one there waiting for him anyway. He had made the opening in the floor of a small office, the only other room within the building. The rest of the structure was one large hall where the members congregated. He could hear loud voices from the next room. The last time he was here, they were doing some kind of ritualistic chanting; basically, just an excuse for Quintus and the other leaders of the operation to have an orgy with the young girls. Christian didn't stay long, but after seeing this, decided they needed to move fast.

He took out a small fiber optic camera and slid it under the door. There was no one close to the door; his exit was in shadow. In fact, most of the large hall was dark, except for the center of the room. Under the flood lights, he could see Quintus and three other men, surrounded by at least ten girls, none older than 16 years old.

Christian opened the door slowly and crept out into the shadows around the edge of the room; no one had noticed him. He looked around to make sure there was no one else in the room. He could see Quintus standing in the middle of the group. In front of Quintus was a young girl, naked, squatting down, holding a large book from which Quintus was reading aloud. Another girl was in front of Quintus, pleasuring him orally. The rest of the group was otherwise engaged, deep within the throes of an entranced orgy. The men were sodomizing two young girls at a time. The girls appeared to be in great pain but could not resist; they were being held at knife point.

Christian wanted to look away. He felt nauseous, and his first instinct was to simply open fire. His nausea was quickly replaced by rage, and he found it hard to concentrate.

"Mother Fucker," he whispered in disgust.

"Are you in? What's going on?" Sam's voice broke through Christian's thoughts through the earpiece. She had lost visual contact with Christian since he slipped under the building. Hearing her voice helped re-focus Christian on his mission. He wanted to just start shooting but had to find his goal first.

"Yeah, I'm in. Get ready to blow the charges. I'm going now," he answered. He raised his rifle, and took aim on Quintus, but something caught his eye. There she was – the girl he had come to find – Clara. She had walked in from the shadows towards one of the girls near the middle of the group. She had a large knife and held it to the other girl's throat. Christian froze. He knew what would happen if he didn't act, but if he shot her, he'd be killing an innocent victim, and a Senator's daughter. In his hesitation, Clara had slit the other girl's throat; the man who had been sodomizing her didn't even stop as she bled out.

Back in the Command vehicle, Sam was beside herself. In the dark, she had lost visual on Christian. She was used to these operations, but she couldn't remember the last time Christian had sounded as disturbed as he did now. She could still see his red locator dot on the digital map of the compound. He was in the southwest corner of the building. All the cameras they had planted were useless to her now. From the main hall feed, she could only see the activity in the middle of the room, and she had seen enough of that already. She scanned the outside cameras for any sign that Christian had been discovered, then switched the view to infrared.

Even Christian was shocked at what came next. Clara dunked her hands in the growing pool of blood from the girl she had just killed. She reached up and rubbed it on the chest of the man who was still having sex with the corpse. She then took some and rubbed a streak on Quintus's cheek. With a devilish smile, she pulled the knife out and turned towards another girl. Christian took a deep breath, and let it out slowly, trying to calm himself. He aimed carefully and fired, hitting the knife in Clara's hand. The blade shattered as it flew out of her hand. He re-aimed at Quintus, but before he could fire, he was interrupted.

"To your left..." was all Sam could get out. Christian turned without hesitation and fired at a shadow. It dropped to the floor, but they were on to him now. He turned back to the center of the room. The orgy had broken up, and there were now three armed, though still naked men facing him. The girls were still there, just not moving. The two others were in front of Quintus, blocking any shot Christian could take.

Christian had time to fire once, dropping one of the men before bursting into a lateral sprint. The gun fire from the others tracked just behind him as he tore away from where he had been crouched. There was no cover that he could find; he only hoped that they wouldn't start to lead him better.

He blindly returned fire as he ran. Two shots missed their target but were enough to make them move. Christian remembered the girls, and decided not to return fire again, until he could aim better. In the dark, he tripped over a cable, knocking him to the floor. He tumbled to a halt and rolled to his stomach. He fired again, dropping the other gunman. Quintus grabbed two of the girls as human shields, leaving Clara to drop to the ground unconscious. Christian had no shot, and no cover – he figured he was dead. The ground shook, and the room lit up. Through the large window at the other end of the building, Christian could see the explosions; the blast wave shattered the glass, spraying it all over the floor. Sam had detonated the charges when she saw Christian was in trouble. Most of the compound was used for cocaine production, which helped amplify the blast from the charges.

Christian jumped up and ran back the way he had come, figuring if nothing else, he could jump back through his trap door. Quintus was shooting again as Christian ran. A man from the shadows ran into Christian, knocking him down, and knocking the gun from his hand. Christian quickly found his feet and met the immediate threat of the man closest to him. He made quick work of him; three quick punches, then driving his knife into his chest. He turned and ducked while drawing his side arm to once again face Quintus.

"Give it up, Quintus!" he yelled out.

"I don't think so. I have the girls...and the book," Quintus said slowly, as he ran his hand over the book in front of him. Christian realized the girl holding the book hadn't moved yet, but he paid little attention to her.

Christian still didn't have a shot. He knew he was in trouble. He jumped slightly when a shot rang out, but it was Quintus that slumped over the girls, and fell to the floor, dead.

"Sniper! Sniper!" Sam's voice rang in his ears, the voice letting him know he was still alive.

"Where?" he asked, but Sam wasn't sure.

The girls fainted and fell to the floor. Christian was surprised, but relieved. His mind raced through different scenarios; was the sniper from a rival gang, or maybe the police, or FBI. In either case, he wasn't out of the woods quite yet.

CHAPTER 2

THE CELL PHONE RANG AND BEGAN vibrating, dancing its way across the end table. Gabriel fumbled for the light, then caught the phone before it fell to the ground. "Frost," he grunted, as he tried to wake up. He knew it was the field office, and he knew it wasn't going to be good.

"Special Agent Frost, this is Deputy Director Sloan."

"Yes sir," Gabriel answered more clearly as he strained to see his watch. It was early, still dark, but it was sometime around 3:00 a.m.

"It seems someone is messing about in your back yard. We have reports of explosions and gunfire from a suspected cocaine lab out in the Everglades."

Gabriel could feel his pulse pick up.

"My team and I have been investigating a suspected drug ring there, sir. We were planning a raid later this week." Gabriel was concerned now. This had been a big operation, and his first as lead. He didn't want anything going bad on his first time out. This had been a strange case, though. In his experience, investigating drug dealers like this was different. This group was into some strange stuff, almost cult-like. A thought occurred to Gabriel as this all went through his head – he might know who was doing the raid. He hoped he was wrong, but he still figured he should plan for the worst.

"Seems someone beat you to it; preliminary reports suggest this is an all-out attack." Sloan sounded a little disturbed. "If this is a take-over, they'll take what they want, kill who they don't need, and move on, and we'll have nothing until they set up shop somewhere else."

Gabriel was out of bed now, and already getting dressed.

"I'll assemble my team, and get right out there, sir."

"Yes, do that. And Frost, if this Rafeo character is there, I want him arrested this time."

"Yes sir," he answered, and the line went dead.

"Rafeo," Gabriel paused as he said the name out loud to himself. The guy was like an urban legend; he was obsessed with the occult, and notorious for taking the law into his own hands. Gabriel had heard of him while he was coming up through the ranks and was denied the opportunity to read the file on him until he took the lead in this case. The FBI and Interpol didn't have a lot of solid facts on this guy. They usually discovered his handy work, but never the man. If there was a cult operating anywhere in the world, sooner or later this guy would show up and clean them out. He'd leave no one alive, but all the victims would be laid out, covered in incense, and left with some kind of pentagram on or near their body. He was on the most wanted list, but there were never enough clues to get a lead on him. Even worse, it seems that others were following in his footsteps, taking the law in their own hands, and shutting down these cults – a task he believed should be handled by the proper authorities.

Gabriel shook it off and dialed his phone. He was calling his TAC Team Leader.

"Get 'em up." Gabriel said when the line was answered. "We have work to do."

Christian didn't move. He frantically searched for any movement, any sign as to where the sniper might be.

"Talk to me Sam. You got eyes on this guy, or what?"

"I don't see him yet, but I just heard on the scanner that the heat is on us. Local law enforcement and the FBI are coming."

That wasn't good, and Christian knew it. He didn't want to bring Sam in until the area was secure, but he had no choice.

"Get rollin'. We'll have to get the target out, and any other survivors. We'll leave any of the cult members who are left for the feds, but I don't want Clara going with the FBI. I'll try to find the sniper."

"I'm on my way," Sam answered.

Christian decided to move. If the sniper had him, there was little he could do to stop him. He moved towards the middle of the room, checking the bodies for weapons, and seeing who was still alive. A few of the girls began to wake up. They were crying, and looked as though they didn't know what was going on, or where they were. Christian found Clara and took his jacket off to cover her. She looked up at him with tears in her eyes, then down at the blood on her hands. She was terrified.

"Clara, your dad sent me. I'm here to help you." Christian tried to sound as calming as he could. "I need you to stay right here and try to keep quiet." She nodded as though she understood and lay back down on the ground.

Christian got up and began to move around to the others. He came to the girl who had been holding the book. He reached down to check on her; she was unconscious, but alive. The book she had been holding caught his eye. He didn't understand why, but he couldn't take his eyes off it. He moved over, knelt, and ran his hands across the leather cover. The urge to open it was immeasurable, Christian wanted it more than he understood. The markings on the cover, he assumed they were words, were in a language he had never seen before, something akin to Sanskrit, but he thought he also recognized some Egyptian hieroglyphs. As he studied the cover the markings changed before his eyes. The ink moved on the page and the re-formed into words, in English. The confusion and surprise engulfed him completely. So much so he jumped when a voice broke the silence.

"Get away from the book," the voice echoed in the stillness of the hall. Christian turned in the direction of the sound. He didn't have time to raise his weapon before the sniper stepped from the shadows. Christian wanted to play this cool, as he had been caught off-guard; he had been completely spell-bound by the book. He looked at the man, and realized he recognized him.

"Rafeo," he said slowly. "I thought you were in South Africa?"

Christian had met Rafeo when he was a boy on the family's farm. Rafeo was a priest at his church; in fact, it was Rafeo that had convinced him to go to seminary school right after high school. He hadn't seen him since he had started his first case, rescuing Sam.

"I was, but now I'm here." Rafeo explained out of hand, then raised his weapon, aiming at Christian "I won't ask again... get away from the book."

"You're not gonna shoot me, are you?" Christian asked. He slowly stood and moved away from the book; his hands raised in the air.

"If you make me..." Rafeo's voice was cold. "Your eyes are not meant for that."

The two stood staring at each other for a few moments. Christian's mind was racing, trying to figure out if the man before him was the same man he knew as a child, or if he should be worried. Rafeo looked as though he hadn't aged a day since the last time he saw him. Christian found that troubling. His face looked slightly more weathered, a small scar over his right eye, and a long scraggly beard, but the eyes still had the same flare he remembered from his youth.

Rafeo had always been a bit eccentric but being on the FBI most wanted list was new. Christian had moved away from the book in an attempt to resolve the tension he was feeling from the old man, in spite of the book's continuous draw.

"I think the sniper might have moved towards you." Sam's voice sounded panicked over the headset.

"Thank you," was his reply to her. "Sam says 'hi'," Christian said to Rafeo, and loud enough for Sam to hear it over the radio.

"He's there, isn't he!" Sam screamed into her mic. Christian calmly turned his radio off to avoid being deafened by her screams; he also needed to concentrate.

"You shouldn't involve her here; it's not safe," Rafeo said as he lowered his weapon as well. He moved to the book, closed it without looking at it, and slid it aside with his foot.

"So, are we just gonna stand here, or are you going to tell me what's going on?" Christian asked, sheepishly. He still felt out of sorts, having been caught without his weapon ready.

Before Rafeo could answer, Quintus burst to his feet. Any sign of the bullet wound he had sustained was gone. He moved like lightning, firing a gun he must have had hidden somewhere. The bullets scattered blindly, but both Christian and Rafeo had to duck and weave to avoid being shot. Before they could react, Quintus was gone.

They both found their feet and sprinted to the shattered window through which Quintus had leaped. They saw no trace of Quintus but there were sirens in the distance. Quintus was gone, and without any further thought, Rafeo turned back, walked over to the book, and picked it up. He wrapped it in an old cloth and turned back towards the window. Christian still stood by the window and watched Rafeo.

"Raf. What's going on? Are you going to tell me, or what?" he asked, feeling frustrated now.

The old man walked past him, paused, and turned to face him.

"Get the girl and get out while you still can."

Just then, Sam came busting through the front door.

"We've got company. We better get moving..." She stopped and stared as Rafeo jumped through the window frame and ran into the fading darkness.

"Was that really…?" She didn't finish her sentence.

"Yeah," Christian answered plainly. "Let's get the girls out of here."

They turned back to the people in the middle of the room. Sam pulled some blankets from a bag she had slung over her shoulder and covered the terrified girls. They both helped the few survivors into the RV, and Sam drove off. Christian figured he'd stay and talk to the FBI.

The sun was starting to come up as Gabriel's car approached the gate of the compound. Smoke hung in the air from a few of the buildings that were still smoldering. He could feel himself start to get angry, knowing that his entire investigation was ruined.

The tactical team had arrived a few minutes before and secured the perimeter. The car stopped at the main gate, and Gabriel jumped out. The field commander met him a few moments later.

"We're conducting a search of the outlying buildings. The perimeter is secure. So far, we haven't seen too many people, alive, anyway. This sure was some kinda cluster-fuck, sir." Gabriel listened while he finished strapping on his TAC vest. He was more and more aggravated; no one left to arrest, nothing to show for his entire investigation.

"All right. Have the teams converge on the main building. I'll meet them there. Do not go in till I get there."

With that, the field commander gave orders over the radio and signaled Gabriel with a nod after getting confirmation of the orders. They took off at a jog towards the main building. Visibility was low from the smoke rising from what was left of the smaller buildings. There was a heavy stench in the air, part of which Gabriel identified as burning flesh.

The others surrounded the building, while Gabriel took the lead near the front door. Before he could kick in the door, it opened.

"FBI... FBI... freeze!" he yelled, as the tactical team closed in to offer support. One man walked out with his hands on his head.

"I'm unarmed." It was Christian. Gabriel recognized him, but he couldn't place where from. Christian slowly reached for his pocket, and was met by more yelling, and guns being shoved in his face.

"ID..." Christian explained nervously. "Just my ID."

Gabriel grabbed it from him. He was surprised to see a government ID, but it was a division he wasn't familiar with.

"And just what the fuck is A.G.A. Division 13, Agent Christian Perditus?" Gabriel asked with disgust. He was pretty sure he had mispronounced the man's last name but could not care less now "I've never heard of it." If it was legitimate, then he was even more pissed that he wasn't notified of another government operation going on in his back yard.

Christian smiled slightly. He knew this wasn't going to go well. "It's a small branch of homeland security. I'm tasked to investigate activities from religious extremist groups or cults," he explained.

Gabriel handed the ID to the field commander to call it in for verification.

"Looking for Al-Qaeda? In the Everglades?" Gabriel asked, with just a little sarcasm in his voice.

"Not exactly," Christian smiled. "I deal with more extreme cases."

The last statement caught Gabriel off guard. "More extreme?" he thought to himself but tried to hide his surprise under his anger.

"Yeah. Cults," Christian said plainly, knowing full well that this is where a lot of law enforcement personal stopped taking him seriously. He could tell from the blank stare he was getting from Gabriel that he was at that point, now.

"ID checks out, sir," the field commander said as he handed the credentials back to Gabriel. Gabriel didn't take them, almost like he didn't want to touch them. Christian calmly took them and put them back in his pocket. They all stood there for a moment without speaking. Gabriel was trying to gather his thoughts.

"So did the Devil do all this?" Gabriel finally asked, not even trying to cover his sarcasm this time.

"Not exactly," Christian answered. He knew he had to keep his temper in check, but it was getting harder to do that. "Why don't we go in here, and take a look around?" Christian offered.

"I'm sure you haven't removed anything from the crime scene," Gabriel said as he walked into the building.

"Not at all." He hadn't lied. It was Sam who took the victims out, and Rafeo who stole the book, so, really, he was telling the truth.

They walked through the door into the main hall. The tactical team members spread out around the room. Gabriel walked towards the dead girl laying in a pool of blood. He paused to look at a pattern on the floor.

"Just 'cause these assholes scratch some pictures on the floor doesn't mean it's a cult. These are drug dealers, trying to scare their employees into staying loyal, that's all."

Christian walked over and squatted down next to the pentagram. He looked over the seen, sighting many different symbols carved into the scene. "This is a sacrificial circle." he explained, pointing to the large symbol drawn around the outside. To the untrained eye it looked like one large image, but Christian knew that each symbol, each image had a meaning and a purpose separate from the whole. Most of the symbols were words of curse, spelled out in a multitude of ancient languages. If combined in a proper order it was believed, by the cult members anyway, that they would complete a spell or incantation.

"These symbols, here, can be traced back to a Mesopotamian cult that was prevalent over five thousand years ago. They were known for massive human sacrifices and thought to have magical powers. The leaders would coat themselves in the blood of their victims in the hopes of absorbing their soul." He paused and stared at the design. There was a symbol – an hourglass that he wasn't familiar with. Gabriel muttered under his breath, but Christian wasn't paying attention. Before he could get a better look at it, there was a series of team members who called out from around the room; they had each made a grueling discovery. The lights from their weapons and the light from the rising sun uncovered more bodies around the perimeter of the room. They were hung on the wall, spread out and nailed in place. Christian hadn't seen them in the darkness when he first came in, but there were ten in all.

"Not just some pictures scratched in the floor, I guess," Christian said as he walked past Gabriel, heading towards the closest body. Gabriel was upset, and chose to examine another body, choosing to avoid Christian for the time being.

The bodies, a mixture of men and women, though the latter seemed more numerous, were hung as if crucified, but upside down. They were emaciated and dirty, probably from being there for a while. Christian stepped in for a closer look. He noticed the hourglass symbol again; it had been carved into the victim's forehead, but it had scared over slightly, indicating it had been done a while before the person had died. He pulled out a small camera, looked around to see if he was being watched, and took a photo of the forehead.

"Sir, I think I hear something...ticking..." One of the other officers reported to Gabriel.

Gabriel had noticed Christian take the picture and turned from the body he had been looking at. "Hey – what do you think...?"

Before he could finish his sentence, the inverted body on the wall leaped from its perch, and tackled Gabriel, knocking him to the ground. Gabriel rolled away, but the body jumped up, and ran towards the other side of the room. Christian was taken by surprise and found himself unable to move for a few seconds. He saw that Gabriel was all right and managed to shake off his shock. He pulled his weapon and paused again. Ticking, he remembered hearing, and a strange thought occurred to him.

"Get down!" Christian yelled to a group of officers near the far side of the room. The seemingly dead body was running towards them, but as Christian already knew, there was no cover to be found. No one dared to take a shot in a room full of people, for fear of hitting their own men. An explosion rocked the building, big enough to knock Christian over from across the room.

It took Gabriel a few moments to get up and fully absorb what had just happened. He saw 2 men down from the blast.

"Clear the room!" he ordered and made his way over to the men who were still down. Christian decided to help Gabriel get them out before he left.

"Okay, that was fucked. Maybe there could be something to your theory," Gabriel admitted, as Christian scooped up one of the officers, while Gabriel had a second in a fireman's carry. They made their way back out the main door into the compound.

"I bet that was painful to admit," Christian said, as he put the man he was carrying down on a waiting stretcher outside. Gabriel decided not to be baited by the comment.

"But how do you explain this? That guy was a corpse, no pulse, wasn't breathing? How the hell did he… uhhhh it, pull itself off the wall and start to run around?"

Christian didn't quite know, himself. This was far stranger than anything he had encountered, but his pride wouldn't quite let him show it.

"Maybe Hell has something to do with it," he said, and could see that this un-nerved Gabriel a little.

They both stood in silence for a moment, and Christian debated whether to tell Gabriel about the girls they had rescued earlier.

"The girls…" He made a connection in his mind and could feel the blood rush from his face. He stepped away, and pulled out a cell phone to call Sam.

"So, are we in the clear?" Sam asked as she answered the call, but Christian cut her off.

"Sam, stop the vehicle and check the girls... are any of them ticking?"

CHAPTER 3

JOHN HAD BEEN A HELICOPTER PILOT in the service of the FBI for fourteen years. He was used to flying over all kinds of terrain. He had been flying a perimeter pattern searching for anyone trying to get in or out of the crime scene area. The Everglades offered all kinds of cover for people trying to evade detection, but both John, and his spotter Terry, had been doing this for quite some time. They knew what to look for.

They were making a pass over the compound from east to west, heading out over the service road, which was the only way in or out of the compound, by car anyway. They headed out roughly twenty miles before starting a turn to swing wide to the north and head back over the compound. As the helicopter traveled through the arc of the turn, Terry was the first to look up and see a column of smoke rising out of the wooded area on the far side of the compound.

"I got smoke!" he informed his pilot through his headset. "Lots of it..."

John quickly spotted the smoke and the two of them exchanged a look of surprise. The chopper continued towards the smoke, allowing the two occupants a chance to see the big picture. There was a wall of fire, spread out

over a few miles, burning everything in its path, and it was heading towards the compound. Without saying another word, John keyed his headset to the ground commander's channel.

"Sir! There appears to be a brush fire, a big one, and it's heading your way, fast."

"Sir! You should hear this..." It was the TAC Team Leader now, running over to Gabriel. "There's a fire moving through the brush this way; apparently it's big and moving fast."

"Fuck me!" Gabriel pounded his fists onto the hood of the vehicle he was using for a table. His bad day only seemed to be getting worse. He hadn't noticed Christian slip away. "Everyone get ready to evacuate!" Gabriel yelled.

Christian's mind was racing. He wanted to get to Sam, but even if he could, he wouldn't be able to do anything. If the victims she was transporting had some kind of explosive planted inside them, he wasn't qualified to do anything about that.

"Check them for scars, surgical marks, anything..." he yelled into his cell phone at Sam, then he paused again, thinking back to what he had seen with the last person who exploded. "Check them for a scar shaped like an hourglass."

He could hear the girls crying in the background, then Sam's voice came back. "Found one, Chris! It's Clara!"

Now, Christian was in a state of panic. "Where are you?" He was now on the run.

"Just about to turn off the service road onto I-75 back to Miami."

"Try to keep them calm. I'm on my way."

Christian jumped into an unattended FBI SUV; the keys were in it, luckily. He fired it up and tore out of the compound. Gabriel noticed this. "Now, where the hell is he going? With my vehicle?"

Gabriel jumped into another car and followed Christian. He radioed the Tactical Team leader. "Get them out of there. I'll check in with you back at the office." He then changed frequencies and keyed the mic again. "So, now you're into stealing government property?"

Christian grabbed the mic; he knew this could get him in trouble.

"Commandeering, really," he said with a smirk, knowing the semantics wouldn't matter. "Sorry about that, but I think I got another body about to explode."

"Damn it! I knew you had removed something from the scene."

"Actually, it was my partner, so I didn't lie... technically." Christian cringed as he said it. Once again, he knew Gabriel wouldn't appreciate his technicalities.

"Well, technically, I'm gonna kick your ass, and then I'm going to arrest you!" Gabriel shouted.

"I'm heading down the service road towards I-75," Christian reported, then hung up the mic. He really didn't intend for this to go as bad as it had. He liked Gabriel, so far, and figured he might need his help. Christian was in over his head. He wasn't sure what, if anything, he could do once he got to Sam and the girls. He also hadn't seen anything like what had happened this morning. Having the resources of the FBI might come in handy, so he really hoped he could smooth things over with Gabriel.

Gabriel was surprised that Christian told him where he was going; at least he was able to give him points for that. "Hopefully, we can get through the fire." Gabriel answered, a little more calmly.

"Fire?" Christian fumbled for the mic again. He hadn't noticed the smoke just yet, but as he heard Gabriel say it, he looked down the road and saw the flames and the smoke. He sighed, slightly frustrated, then pushed the accelerator all the way to the floor.

There was the wall of fire ahead, even stretching across the road. At his speed, he was able to blast through without any real damage to the vehicle. Once past, Christian noticed the scorched earth stretched out as far as he could see on either side of him. Then, it just stopped. The fire had started in a straight line all at once; he couldn't figure out how.

He could see the RV, parked on the side of the road. It came up quickly, and he locked the brakes on, sliding to a stop on the dirt road, right next to the RV. Christian was out of the truck before the dust had settled, and ran to the other vehicle. Sam was standing with the other girls behind her. Clara sat on a bunk, crying. None of them looked like they knew what to do. When Sam's eyes met Christian's, he could tell she had been crying.

Christian walked over and sat next to Clara; she was still only wrapped in a blanket. He was straining to hear a ticking sound but couldn't.

"Clara. Hi," he said awkwardly, then paused to look at the others. "Sam, why don't you take the girls outside, and wait for Agent Frost; he should be along shortly." The girls filed out, leaving the RV still and silent. Christian turned back to Clara. "Sweetie, do you remember ever seeing a doctor while you were away from home?" Clara shook her head negatively.

"I need to see if anyone has hurt you… I'm sorry but I must check." Christian could feel her tense up. He could only imagine what she had been through in her ordeal. He got her to stand up and wrap the blanket around her waist. Her hands were still caked in dried blood. Christian was very uncomfortable with this whole situation. He heard another vehicle pull up, and shortly, Sam appeared back in the doorway. Christian motioned for her to come in.

"Sam, where did you notice her scars?" Sam indicated on her own body by pointing awkwardly at her own chest.

"Oh... I'll be right back." He wanted out of there, away from the poor girl. She had been through enough. The last thing he wanted was to have to check her over while she stood there naked.

He ran outside to see Gabriel loading the other girls into his vehicle. Christian walked over to him. "Look,

I know this looks bad, and I will try to make this up to you."

Gabriel paused for a moment and stared at him. "You owe me a lot," he finally answered. The two men both realized while they were willing to trust each other, that they both respected one another, and Christian did not hesitate to acknowledge it.

"Fair enough." Before either could speak again, Sam rushed outside, and yelled for Christian. They both went towards the RV as other FBI vehicles showed up.

"We need to do something," she said blankly. Christian turned back to Gabriel.

"You got a field surgeon with you?" he asked.

"No. Best I could do is a medic." Gabriel wasn't sure what was going on.

"Get him here. Now!"

"We have a major problem. This girl has had breast augmentation surgery." Richard had been a medic in the military for five years, having served in Iraq. He had been with the FBI Tactical Team for another eight years. In all that time, he had never seen anything like this. Richard was panicked as he stepped down from the RV, having just finished giving Clara a check-over. "The bad news is, they used Symtex instead of saline to enlarge her breasts. She is, literally, a ticking time bomb." On Gabriel's advice, the bomb squad came with Richard, and had helped in his assessment.

"Can you get it out?" was all Christian was interested in. he knew what kind of damage this could do. Semtex is **a general-purpose plastic explosive.** It is used in commercial blasting, demolition, and in certain military applications.

"Here? Now?" the medic sputtered. "I don't know; it could go off..."

"Richard," Gabriel tried to calm him. "You can do this. You must."

Richard nodded nervously, then slowly turned, and walked back into the RV, where they had set up a make-shift operating room. The kitchenette table was cleared off and some tools and saline bottles were spread out on the counter across from it, definitely not ideal circumstances. All around the table stood bomb squad personnel, holding blast shields in case the worst happened. Sam tried to keep the RV ready for anything, they did have some first aid supplies but nowhere near what they really needed for the task at hand, but what choice was there?

Gabriel, Sam, and Christian waited anxiously outside. No one spoke for quite some time before Sam decided to break the silence.

"I'm Samantha, well Sam, by the way," she introduced herself to Gabriel, giving Christian a sideways glance to point out that he had neglected to introduce her.

Christian realized what she meant by the look right away. "Oh yeah, Sam, this is Agent Gabriel Frost with the FBI," he stammered.

"Nice to meet you, Samantha," Gabriel said, as he shook her hand. He took a moment to look her up and down.

Sam was a very attractive woman in her early thirties, a red head, and in very good shape. The look didn't go unnoticed by either Sam or Christian. Christian thought of Sam as a little sister, and his protective instincts kicked in. He wanted to say something but wasn't sure what to do. He also took note of the fact that, suddenly, Gabriel wasn't as angry as he had been, so Christian let it slide. Besides, Sam was a big girl, and could certainly take care of herself.

Sam didn't seem upset to have been checked out; in fact, she returned the look, taking in Gabriel's tall, muscular frame. He was a good-looking man, with Hispanic heritage and becoming dark features.

"So, I guess we messed up a case you were working on," Sam blurted out. Christian almost choked on his own breath. He had been trying to avoid bringing that fact up again, but Sam, in her innocence, didn't think twice about it. Gabriel threw a quick, stern glare at Christian, before he smiled back at Sam.

"Yes, in fact, you did. We'll deal with that later, but I'm just interested in that young girl making it through this." Gabriel didn't sound like the same guy who had been yelling at Christian all morning.

Sam was taken in by his compassion and Christian picked up on that as well and couldn't help but clear his throat. It sounded almost like a warning, but neither of the other recognized it.

"So, what was up with that brush fire? Seems a little too convenient to have been an accident." Christian could see the water bombers overhead. He was trying to turn the conversation back to business at hand, but he was still pretty sure Sam would have a date tonight.

"Yeah," Gabriel said with a sigh. "I mean, yes," he stammered, as he remembered he was still in the middle of a case. He was all business again. "Last report was that the fire swept right through the compound. The water bombers and ground crews are starting to get it under control, but it doesn't look like there's much left back there."

"Did everyone get out safe?"

"Everyone so far, not including Clara," Gabriel answered. He sounded somewhat relieved, but still concerned. "Now, we have to figure out what caused a wall of fire over two miles long, to ignite all at once, and burn that fast towards the compound."

Richard was sweating profusely. The bomb squad techs were trying to reassure him, but with little success. He had managed to remove one of the devices from the left breast so far, but the right one was proving a bit more difficult. He was struggling with the fact that the best-case scenario here was that Clara would live, but she would be horribly scarred, physically and emotionally.

"Easy Richard, just like the last one." The bomb disposal team leader was coaching him through. "No signs of any wires but, wait a second. What is that?" He pulled out a magnifying glass and held it over the implant that was now half-way out. There was a small computer chip on this one that he hadn't seen on the last one. He paused to look at it.

"Does anyone else hear that ticking?" Richard interrupted. The two looked at each other quickly, then scrambled. Richard yanked out the implant the rest of the way and threw it into the bomb box that they had waiting. He dove on top of Clara to cover her as the bomb disposal team ran the box to the door.

"Get down! Get down!" was all they heard. Gabriel, Sam, and Christian had still been talking nervously, waiting for news on Clara's condition. They all broke into a sprint in unison when they saw the bomb disposal tech come running out of the RV. They made it to the far side of the parked SUV where Christian had slid to a stop. Gabriel opened the back door and threw Sam in while Christian dove into the front. Gabriel had just managed to crawl into the back and look out the window.

"Come on; throw it." Gabriel whispered to himself. The technician hurled the bomb box into the field and hit the deck. The explosion blew the windows out of the RV and rocked the SUV. Surprisingly, it's bullet proof windows held up. The technician was rolled over by the blast; his protective suit did its job. The fire ball rose into the air and dissipated.

Gabriel jumped back out of the truck and ran over to check on the technician. He gave Gabriel a thumbs up, and Gabriel moved to the RV; Christian joined him at the door.

"All clear?" Gabriel yelled into the vehicle. They both, finally, let out a sigh of relief when they heard Richard's shaky voice.

"Yeah; I think we're still alive." He leaned down again to check Clara, then looked at Christian and smiled.

"We'll need to get her to a hospital, but she's gonna be fine."

CHAPTER 4

RAFEO NERVOUSLY STRUGGLED TO SLIP THE book into a backpack. He slung the bag over his shoulder and took to the woods as fast as he could. He wished he had more time to talk to Christian, but that would have to wait until later. Right now, he had to get away, lest Quintus was to track him down.

He had stashed a car out near the service road and had to make it there before the FBI found him, or worse. He ran over the rough terrain at a pretty good pace for a man his age. Maybe the excitement of finally having the book again was giving him strength. He had been chasing this for years, all around the world. He had been its caretaker for longer than he cared to remember and thought that he had hidden it well. Having the book in his possession meant always being on the run. Some time ago, he had decided to hide it somewhere safe, but it was only a matter of time until someone found it. It was an extremely powerful and important book. Others wanted it and were willing to kill for it.

He heard a whooshing noise behind him and knew right away that he was in trouble. Rafeo stopped to look around, and soon saw the smoke rising high enough for him to see it through the trees. There was a fire storm

coming down on him, and he knew it would catch him before he made it to his car. He ran, even faster than before. He wasn't sure if the fire was a desperate attempt to catch him, or if Quintus knew where he was.

Rafeo looked behind him as he broke from the woods into a field. Faced with the wall of fire, he stumbled on the uneven ground, and fell, tumbling to a stop. Instead of trying to run, he took the backpack off and pulled the book out. He got up on one knee, closed his eyes and prayed until the fire overtook him.

"What? Are you taking me to church? I thought you were taking me to some kind of headquarters." Gabriel couldn't help but notice the architecture of the building next to them as the SUV came to a halt. They had argued most of the way back into town, Gabriel insisted on seeing Christian's operation and talking to his superiors. Sam sat quietly in the back seat, not wanting to get involved.

"Have a little faith," Christian answered with a grin, as he opened the door and got out.

"Actually, it's both," Sam said as she opened her door to get out. She was trying to reassure Gabriel. "When this little operation was formed, it was decided that we keep a low profile. We found this old church that was empty and moved in. In our line of work, it doesn't hurt to be on sacred ground."

Gabriel raised an eyebrow, smiled, and got out of the truck. They walked through the front door. There were people praying in the pews. It was a fully operational church, complete with priests. No one in the congregation paid any attention to them as they came in.

"Do any of them know what really goes on here?" Gabriel whispered to Sam.

"No," she whispered back, as she dipped her hand in the holy water, and crossed herself. "This way." Gabriel awkwardly copied her with the holy water and followed her through the back of the church and into a door marked 'Rectory.' Once inside, they walked into what looked like a closet. The rear wall moved as they shut the door, revealing a staircase.

"How secret agent of you," he said, as they descended the stairs into a large open basement. There were computers, workstations, and a large glass-walled conference room in the middle of the larger area. Gabriel was impressed by what he saw.

There was a small staff; most of them appeared to be priests, or nuns, by their clothes. Gabriel felt a little uncomfortable, as he wasn't a church-going man. In the conference room sat a man who got up as they all approached. The door to the room silently slid open. Gabriel recognized the man inside as the Chairman of the Senate Appropriations Committee. Now, he was really impressed.

"Senator," Christian said, as he reached out to shake his hand. "Clara is safe. It was a little rough, and she's at the hospital for treatment, but should be fine. We'll be observing her to see if deprogramming is necessary, but I don't think so.

The Senator was quiet for a moment, and then his eyes began to tear. "Thank you so much for saving my daughter. I owe you everything."

"Daughter?" Gabriel blurted out.

"Clara is the Senator's daughter. That's why we had to move when we did," Sam whispered quietly. The Senator heard the exchange, cleared his throat, and turned to Gabriel.

"Yes. I understand that this operation had a negative effect on your first command, Agent Frost. I do apologize."

Gabriel was caught off guard that the Senator knew him. "Yes sir, but..." he stammered.

"I will be calling your director to settle the situation. I don't want this to reflect poorly on your otherwise spotless service record."

"Thank you, sir." Gabriel said and shook his hand.

"I must be going. I want to see Clara," the Senator turned to leave. He paused, and gave Sam a hug, "Nice to see you again, Samantha. Thank you."

"Think nothing of it, sir. Just take care of Clara," Sam answered with a familiar smile.

He smiled in turn, and walked out, leaving the room in silence. Gabriel looked down at his feet and rubbed the back of his neck. He needed a few moments to process what had just happened. In his mind, coming into this, he was in control, but after seeing the Senator, it was hard to argue with Christian's credentials. He looked around at the rest of the facility. There was a multitude of technology in one area of the room and on the other side of the building was what appeared to be a library, containing some very old books. He looked up at Christian but didn't know what to say.

"Quite the place you got here," he blurted out.

Christian smiled warmly. "Thanks." He then paused for a moment. "Look... I'm sorry if it seems like I was trying to play a trump card there. I just thought you wanted to see the human side of what happened. This had nothing to do with jurisdiction or anything political. I just wanted to save that man's daughter."

Now Gabriel smiled. "Hard to argue with that, I guess," he said with a shrug. "So, what else you got on the go here?"

"Well, maybe Sam can give you the tour; I have to go do some paperwork." Sam took Gabriel by the arm, and Christian walked over to one of the rooms on the perimeter of the building; he had some temporary quarters set up here. He wanted to take a long shower and try to make sense of what had happened today.

"This is the library," Sam explained as they approached the bookshelves. "There are some very rare books here, including lost gospels, and early drafts of the Bible. In our line of work, we need to reference this stuff sometimes."

Gabriel was impressed as he ran his fingers over the spines of the books on the shelf in front of him. He read the titles but had no idea what was contained on the pages within.

"This is all very odd. I had no idea the government was involved in anything like this."

"Well, it's only been official since the second world war. The Nazis conducted many cult rituals and experiments that had caught the Allies off guard. Truman had quietly started a small operation after the war to try and stop anything like that happening again. It's grown a bit since then."

Gabriel was in over his head, and he knew it.

"It's been a long day, and I think I'd like to go take a shower and sleep this off." He smiled and looked her in the eye.

"But I'd like a chance to talk some more about this stuff with you. If you'd like to..."

"I'd love to," Sam cut him off excitedly; her reaction nearly made Gabriel jump. "Here's my number. Call me anytime."

Gabriel took the paper with her number. and put it in his pocket.

"Thank you; I think I will." He smiled then turned to walk out. "How do I get out of here again?"

"I'll walk you out." Sam took Gabriel's arm and escorted him out.

Christian's mind churned with images of the day's events as the hot water showered down on his head. He had seen some weird things since he started with this agency, but his mind kept returning to the book. Surprisingly, it was the thing that unsettled him the. most from the day. He normally trusted his senses and instincts, but seeing the words change and morph in front of him, was really messing with his head. He only wished he had been able to read some of it.

"Rafeo..." he said aloud. What had he meant by his 'eyes weren't meant for that'? Christian knew that his first order of business was to try and find the old man and get some answers.

He finished up in the shower and got dressed. Christian walked back out into the main area of the facility, and found Sam.

"I'm going out to the farm to see my mom. Why don't you get some sleep?" he said, then paused. "You got his number, didn't you?" he asked coyly.

"No," she answered, then smiled, "I gave him mine."

"Yeah, I thought so," Christian answered with a grin He put his hand on her shoulder. "Get some rest. I'll call you later."

It had been longer than intended since Christian had visited his mother. He was always busy with work, and it wasn't easy sharing that part of his life with her. The things he saw and experienced was something he wanted to shield her from. He figured that was part of the reason he had never been married, or even close to it. Raising a family in his line of work just wouldn't be possible, or so he thought.

Christian always loved the farm; it was peaceful, even if it did bring back some bad childhood memories.

His upbringing had been difficult; his Father had been an alcoholic, and it hadn't been easy on him or his mother. Christian was the one who found him when he died; his father had hung himself in the barn. Christian had managed, so far, to avoid the sins of his father. He didn't drink often, but when he did, he had to admit it was to excess. He figured he was too busy to fall into that trap, but given the chance, it could happen. After many of the cases he had been on, he had wanted to drink himself into forgetting, but always managed to avoid temptation.

The farm was a good hour's drive out of town. The land wasn't worked anymore, as it was too much for his mother to handle on her own. She still maintained a small vegetable patch, and a few chickens, but only for personal use. The house stood at the top of a hill, a good half a mile off the road. It was flanked by several willow trees that stood next to a small stream that ran through the property. He always felt good coming out here. It was like a free space, a sanctuary, where he didn't have to worry about work, or Cults, or the evil that men do.

His mother looked up from the tomato plant she was working on when his car started up the driveway. He hadn't called to tell her he was coming, but he knew she was expecting him. He could see her smile as he pulled the truck to a stop next to the house. He opened the door and walked over to her. Without saying a word, he gave her a long hug.

"I hope the case wasn't too bad," she said, as he let her go. She wasn't judging him, but he always seemed to visit at the end of a case.

"I bet you don't want to talk about it," she confirmed, smiling again. Christian was warmed by her understanding; she knew why he didn't talk about his work, and he was glad she never pried.

"No," he answered honestly. They stood in the setting sunlight, and Christian took a deep breath of the country air. He could feel it soothe him as it entered his lungs. He closed his eyes briefly, and enjoyed the serenity of it all, before looking to his mother again.

"Well, come on. Let's get dinner started." She motioned Christian towards the house, and wiped the dust from her hands on the apron she was wearing. Christian stooped over to pick up the basket of fresh vegetables she had picked.

"I've got some stew and was going to make a salad."

"Sounds wonderful. Can I help?" Christian put his free arm around his mom, and they walked into the farmhouse.

They finished up dinner as the sun was hanging low in the sky. There was no rush to clean up; they were happy to sit and catch up with each other.

"You look tired." His mother always worried.

"I feel tired."

"That job of yours is no good." She never liked the fact that Christian had left the priesthood, especially not considering his chosen vocation.

"Mom, we've been over this," Christian said as he got up and started to clear the table. "There was too much corruption and politics - which are two things that definitely don't belong in religion."

"The church isn't perfect, but I believe they were better with you than without you," she argued.

"Yeah, well, I wasn't." He paused and swallowed the last mouthful of wine from his glass. "Maybe I'm too critical, but at least now, I don't feel like a hypocrite. It frustrated me to see the rules of the church change to suit the times; whatever is convenient. I don't believe that the doctrine of faith should change to make it easier for the congregation to feel better about themselves. Either you believe, you have faith, or you don't."

His mother sighed and walked to the sink. She put her hand on his arm in an attempt to calm him down. He was always so defensive when it came to talking about his decision to leave the church. His mother figured it may stem from guilt, but she never wanted to voice that opinion.

"I'm sorry. You make me proud, and I shouldn't give you a hard time. You do important work; I get that. I just wish that..." She gave him a kiss on the cheek.

Christian let her words sink in. He was not a parent and didn't really understand how she felt.

"Thanks, Mom. I always feel like I've disappointed you when I left for the army. His head bent down looking at his reflection in the sink water.

"Never, Chris. I'm proud of you, even if I don't know exactly what it is you do. I know you help those who need it, who can't help themselves. You're a wonderful son, and a good man."

Christian looked up again, looking out the window towards the setting sun, and thought for a moment. "Sometimes I have to wonder about that." he said quietly.

"About what? Whether or not I think you're a good man?" His mom sounded almost hurt by this.

"No, no." He turned and smiled at her for a moment, trying to reassure her, then turned to look back out the window.

"Whether or not I actually am a good man."

His mom really didn't know how to react to this.

"I know I never talk about what I do, Mom, and for a good reason. There are some scary things out there that I've seen. And it doesn't matter how hard I try, there's always something worse."

"Maybe someday things will be different... Some day." Her words were quiet but didn't really console Christian. In truth, they seemed hollow even to her, not knowing the horrors he had seen.

Christian looked to his mother, again, and could see the pain in her eyes. For the first time, he understood that, as a mother, she wanted to take his pain for him. To do so, he'd have to tell her all, and he understood, now, that she would listen, if for no other reason than to help him, but he knew he could not do that to her.

Let's talk about something else," he said, and forced a smile on his face.

CHAPTER 5

FATHER BALLE SAT AT HIS DESK, preparing his sermon for Sunday. The room was illuminated only by the small light on his desk. His parish has been slowly shrinking over the years, but particularly since the big hurricane. People who had lost everything had also lost their faith. In a city like New Orleans, it was difficult to keep people interested in the church. Corruption and scandals throughout the past decade had also lead people away from the congregation, even though he had never been involved in anything of the sort.

Father Balle accepted this as his own challenge to win them back. He really tried to put a mixture of humor and value into his homilies to get his message across, but it was never easy.

He was looking up a passage in the Bible when he thought he heard something in the church. There had been vandals coming around lately, spray painting the walls, and even breaking windows. He was tired of this and wanted to catch them in the act. He called the police and rushed out from the rectory. There was a single man standing in the middle of the dimly lit church, and Father Balle paused, thinking he had overreacted.

"I never want to turn anyone away, my friend, but it is late," Father Balle said as he walked towards the man. The figure turned to face him, and the priest couldn't help but react to the scar on his face. Obviously, this man had suffered some kind of horrible accident, and it looked like he was lucky to have survived. Father Balle didn't recognize the man as a member of his church, but he wasn't about to send him away.

"Father Balle," the other said with a grin. "You are one of the better priests, I understand. You truly take your vows to heart."

"Why, thank you," he answered slowly. He wasn't sure what this was all about. He did not recognize the man and was uneasy with the level of familiarity he demonstrated.

"What can I do for you?" he asked, trying not to betray his trepidation.

The other man smiled, contently. "My name is Quintus. I need to find someone, and I was hoping you could help me."

"Well, I'm not sure. Who is he?" Father Balle answered tentatively. He let his guard down and moved closer to Quintus. He felt a little guilty for having judged the man.

"I don't know his name, but I know he investigates Satanic cults, and I thought if I killed you, a good honest priest, he would come here." He slowly pulled a long-twisted blade from his cloak and looked into the priest's eyes.

Father Balle began to back away. “Now... I’ve already called the police. They should be here any second.” He panicked.

“Good. That should speed up the whole process,” Quintus answered, and lunged at the priest, driving the blade into his chest.

“I saw Rafeo the other day...” Christian’s mother said, trying to change the subject. She knew that Christian didn’t really want to tell her what was bothering him, and she wanted to try to cheer him up. After his father’s death, Rafeo had been a father-figure to Christian growing up. She figured talking about their old family friend might be a nice change,

“He said he was checking up on you.” She put a dried, clean plate into the cupboard as she spoke. “He told me you were doing well.”

Christian thought about that for a moment. “Yeah, I saw him the other day, too.” He was slow to answer, he considered for a moment not telling her. “Did you tell him where I was?” he asked after another moment.

“No. I didn’t know where you were.”

“No one did. I was on a case, my location classified.” He spoke more to himself, but it seemed to confuse his mother. A multitude of thoughts were going through his head. Maybe it wasn’t chance that Rafeo showed up when he did. Maybe someone in his agency told

Rafeo something. Maybe he was involved in that cult in Florida.

"What is it?" His mother could tell he was upset. His face was blank, but his eyes darted around as if he was reading or looking at a picture. "Rafeo is our oldest friend; why would it bother you that he checked up on you?" she continued defensively. "He followed your career through the military; he's helped me out when you weren't here."

Christian snapped out of his line of thought and looked at his mother again.

"Yeah, I know. It's just strange." Before Christian could explain, his cell phone rang. There was a text message from his office. He read it slowly, and then sighed.

"Mom, I'm sorry, but I have to go." Christian said, then walked to the door, and started putting his shoes on.

"Already?" His mother had hoped he could stay; she could tell he needed a break.

"Sorry, Mom," Christian answered, standing to give her a hug.

"Take care of yourself."

She didn't want to let go.

"I will, and I'll be back soon," he said, forcing a smile.

"You better..." she answered and tried to hide her fear.

Christian opened the door and walked out to his truck. He fired up the engine and tore out of the driveway. According to the message he had received, his unit had picked up a report of a priest in New Orleans who had been murdered under disturbing circumstances.

Christian had driven all night to arrive at the church. Sam had arrived a little earlier and managed to assume responsibility for the scene. The local forensics team had gathered their initial samples and data. They had been requested to suspend their investigation until Christian and his team had examined the scene.

"Any problems with local law enforcement?" Christian asked Sam as he walked under the yellow tape surrounding the church.

"Not really." Her answer surprised Christian, as it always seemed to be a struggle with jurisdiction and credentials.

"Oh yeah?" he asked in surprise; but before Sam could answer, Christian heard another voice he recognized.

"I took care of it for you."

Christian turned to see Agent Frost smiling back at him. Sam also had a guilty grin on her face; Christian looked back and forth between the two. He shot Sam a childish grin, then turned his back to her to talk to Gabriel.

"Ah... Gabriel. Keeping tabs on me now, are you?" he asked, not that he was upset at seeing him again, but rather that he didn't like feeling that he had to answer to anyone.

"Well, after a talk with my director, he decided that if we were going to keep bumping into each other, I might as well act as liaison between our two agencies."

Christian allowed his words to fall silent, simply staring at him. He had his doubts that this was a strictly friendly encounter.

"Mm-hmm," was all he replied with as genuine a smile as he could muster. Gabriel looked around Christian, and smiled at Sam quickly, then continued.

"I was really interested in working with you, as well. I have a lot of questions about what happened in Florida, anyway." Christian was at a loss for words. "Actually, it was sort of Sam's idea," Gabriel finished with a smile, and glanced at Sam again, hoping she would say something. She was grinning from ear to ear now. Christian knew he was outnumbered, so there was no point arguing.

"Well, I guess having an FBI special agent around could help in instances like this," Christian said slowly. "Welcome to the team." Gabriel freely took Christian's outstretched hand, and they shook on their accord.

"Let's leave what ever happened before, in the past," Gabriel said, before he let go of Christian's hand. "This is your team, your show," Gabriel admitted, giving Christian something to smile about. "Besides, some of this occult stuff freaks me out."

"I'll take care of you, Agent Frost," Christian said, with just a hint of sarcasm. "Let's get in there and see what we have." Sam grabbed her gear. Gabriel gestured for the others to go in first.

The church was quiet and dimly lit, as they usually are. The light coming through the tall stained-glass windows cast an eerie colored hue and long shadows on the scene. The body had been laid out across the altar to look like a crucifixion. Gabriel was noticeably uncomfortable; Christian figured he wasn't much of a church goer.

For some reason, even Christian didn't care for empty churches. He found, even as a seminarian, that a dark, empty church gave him an uneasy feeling, and this was the first time he had been in one that had a ritualistically murdered priest on the altar.

Sam stayed back out of the way, closer to Gabriel, while Christian moved in for a closer examination of the body.

"What kind of questions.?" Christian asked, while he started his investigation of the body. Gabriel was caught off guard, his discomfort showing.

"What? Sorry?" he asked Christian, who was studying the body.

"You said you had questions about Florida when we were outside. What questions?" Christian answered without looking up. Christian realized that he knew the priest. He had spent some time in Father Balle's parish as a deacon. Christian was uneasy with the coincidence, namely because he didn't believe in chance. Since he had left the Catholic church, he had begun to explore other faiths. In particular, he found the whole concept of fate, destiny, and karma, that were the main stays of many eastern religions, made more sense to him.

"Ah... okay," Gabriel began nervously. "The fire, for one. Our investigation shows no sign of an accelerant, or what the source of ignition was. One eyewitness account says that a wall of fire simply erupted out of the ground, while at the same time, the wind changed direction to push the fire towards the compound."

Sam moved around, quietly photographing the scene, then moving in for close-ups of the body and the wounds.

"What else?" Christian asked, still not looking up, as he moved around the body. He took a pair of tweezers out and moved the clothing around for a better view.

"What about the body that exploded? We know that they had surgically implanted the charges in the body, but at least three people checked that guy when he was hanging on the wall; he was dead. So how did he get up, and start to run around?" Gabriel was pacing, nervously; it was definitely a sight to behold, to see a seasoned FBI agent visibly shaken. Christian understood; he had worked with many law enforcement personnel over the years. The reaction was usually the same when dealing with the darker, less easily explained aspect of his specialized field.

"I got one for ya," Christian said, as he took the tweezers and pulled back a piece of clothing to have a closer look at the body. "Why did Clara go from a homicidal maniac to a scared, seemingly innocent victim, almost instantaneously?" Christian looked up now. Gabriel stood, postured like a man awaiting a revelation.

"Oh, I don't have any answers; I thought we were just spit-ballin'." He put his head back down to cover a wry smile. He pulled open the priest's shirt, and saw a symbol carved into his skin. He motioned for Sam to take a picture of it.

"For that matter, how did that guy get up after being shot?" he said quietly, almost without thinking. He was concentrating on the symbol more than his conversation, now, but for a moment, he saw Quintus in his mind, lying dead on the floor one minute, then up and running out the door the next.

"What guy?" Gabriel asked. But Christian didn't answer.

The body was marked from a blade. Pentagrams and other symbols were carved into the skin. He was no forensics specialist but many of them looked like they were made before Father Balle died. There was a small amount of blood that had drained from the cuts and dried. The knife that was used to kill him was still sticking into his chest, up to the hilt.

"Definitely not a typical stabbing," he said out loud, more to himself. "But these markings..." He trailed off as he opened the priest's shirt to uncover his chest and more symbols. He studied them closely.

"A cult?" Gabriel asked. Christian noticed Gabriel's hand was resting on his holstered gun.

"Hard to say..." Christian answered and stood up. "That word gets misused a lot. Would it surprise you to know that Catholicism was considered a cult at one point in its infancy?" He paused and glanced at Gabriel. Gabriel's blank look told Christian to continue. "Cult is a word given to small religious groups that are deemed socially unacceptable. But no matter the ultimate intension of the leader or founder of the cult, they are a religion. All religions are very similar. They extend a feeling of belonging and comfort to its members, since they all have a common meeting place, recite the same prayers, believe the same things; it's all a form of control. The leaders use this to bend the masses to their will. They claim divine inspiration to make their will the common goal of the people. Some are simply more acceptable because their "Message" is easier to believe. They may not ask for human sacrifice, for example."

Christian thought he'd give Gabriel a chance to process the information. He walked around the body, looking into the dark corners of the church, hoping to find something in the shadows to help make sense of this horrible act of violence, but none was to be found.

"So, did the killer think he would summon the devil or steal the priest's soul or something?" Gabriel's stomach flopped with anxiety; he was afraid of the answer Christian might offer.

"In all my years, either in the church or as an investigator, I have yet to see anything that would make me believe in any miracles or magic or divine intervention. So, to answer your questions. Gabriel..." He paused to look Gabriel in the eye. "I have no idea."

Gabriel and Sam were both somewhat surprised by Christian answer. They stood there and stared, and Christian realized he had, perhaps, said too much.

"But in this case..." he said, and turned back to the body, pointing out the wounds that were carved into the priest's body, in the hopes of moving on. "I'm not sure what their purpose was here. These symbols don't make sense, together. This one, here, for example..."; he pointed to the body, "is an ankh – the symbol for life. This is a demonic pentagram. Here is an upside down cross. And here..." He stopped again, and pointed at a small symbol, almost easy to miss amongst the others. "I think you recognize this one."

Gabriel stepped in to take a closer look. There, under his left nipple, a very small hourglass. Gabriel recognized it right away. He stepped back and drew his gun. "That's the same symbol that was on the bodies in Florida."

"Indeed," Christian answered, as he stepped back. They were both thinking the same thing. Was this body going to explode, and take them as well? They decided to leave until the bomb disposal unit could come in and clear the scene.

As they walked down the aisle towards the door, there was a noise from the loft at the back of the church. Both Gabriel and Christian drew their weapons and trained them in the direction of the noise. Neither one of them saw anything.

"I thought the building was clear," Christian said quietly.

"It was. You think it's the press or something?"

"Or something worse. I'm not taking any chances after the shit we've seen." They all ran for the door after a few seconds, and notified the local law enforcement officers that there might be someone inside. Christian stayed with Sam in the truck, while Gabriel led another sweep of the building.

"We found no one," Gabriel said after he came back out to Christian's truck. This murder was connected to the case in Florida, and that didn't sit well with anyone. They thought they had apprehended or killed everyone from that group. But somehow Quintus had escaped, after being fatally shot.

"What guy?" Gabriel blurted out. Now it was Christian's turn to give a blank look. "You said before... the guy got up after being shot?"

"Oh, yeah. The leader of the cult. He had been shot in the neck or head, and then a few minutes later he got up, shot at me, and ran out."

"Are you sure he was shot?" Gabriel didn't want to believe it.

"Yeah, Raf shot him through the window – good thing, too, 'cause the guy had me otherwise. But yeah," Christian shrugged, and nodded to emphasize his point, "he should have been dead."

"Wait – Raf?" Gabriel asked. "You mean Rafeo?"

Christian hid the fact he was upset that he had used Rafeo's name; he wanted to keep some of the details to himself, but hearing that Gabriel knew Rafeo, or at least knew of him, was worth the slip of the tongue.

"Yeah... Why? You know him?" Sam inquired. She and Christian were both surprised.

"As far as I know, Rafeo was just some old priest from the town where I grew up. How do you know him?" Sam asked.

"You never told me he was there... in Florida." Gabriel seemed a little upset.

"Yeah, I guess I forgot. Or didn't think it mattered." Christian conveyed honesty, quite convincingly.

"Rafeo is no priest. He's on our most wanted list. He is wanted in connection with multiple homicides," Gabriel explained. Christian didn't know what to say.

CHAPTER 6

CHRISTIAN DREAMT. A SERIES OF DISJOINTED images flashed through his unsettled slumber: a woman a princess… he knew her but couldn't recollect how. The image vanished, and quickly faded from memory when his eyes popped open in response to a sound, a ticking noise.

"Mary," he said quietly to the shadows. He had seen her many times in his dreams, but nowhere else.

He took a few seconds to establish where he was. In that time, the girl's face was all but forgotten.

Being very cautious, he scanned the room, only moving his eyes. Once he established that there was no immediate threat, he moved, and listened carefully for the noise to repeat itself.

All he could hear was the ticking of a stopwatch. For a split second his pulse raced before he remembered he had fallen asleep with the TV on. The ticking was nothing more than the opening credits of *60 Minutes*. They were doing a special report on the peace talks going on in the Middle East. For the first time in a very long time, the upcoming summit was believed to have real promise. The Israelis, PLO, everyone had grown weary of seeing their citizens dead; and what's more,

the Americans were promising a complete military withdrawal from the region. The talks were only weeks away and it was as if the treaties and agreements had already been signed.

With a sigh, he moved slowly from his slouched position on the couch, to his feet. The book he had been reading dropped to the floor. Christian looked at it for a moment, studying the cover: *The Prophecies of Nostradamus.*

"That would explain the weird dreams," he said to himself as he bent down. There was a sound again, and Christian stood up cautiously.

"Jesus!" he yelled, as he came practically face to face with the person responsible for the noise.

"Why not just come in, Gabriel? Should I get a fuckin' key cut for ya?" Christian demanded, obviously disgruntled, as he slammed the book down on the coffee table for emphasis.

Gabriel couldn't help a slight laugh. "I'm sorry Christian; just making sure I still got it; can't be sloppy as a field agent."

Christian leered at him for a few moments before he spoke. He felt awkward for some reason "What the hell do you want?" he said, more calmly. Gabriel made himself comfortable in a nearby chair.

"How 'bout a beer?"

The answer caught Christian off guard, and he couldn't help the smile. "A social visit, is it?" Christian moved to the fridge and grabbed a couple of beers.

"Yeah; I figured we're gonna be workin' together, we might as well get to know each other a little better, huh, partner?" Gabriel watched for a reaction that didn't come. Then he turned his attention to the book on the coffee table. He read the cover and turned his nose up. "You actually read this shit?" he asked. This time Christian merely shook his head and sighed.

"He's been right about literally hundreds of things, you know," Christian responded defensively. I've studied many world religions, particularly the bible, even the gospels they didn't include. I was even ordained as a priest."

"This is before you joined the Army Rangers Delta Force?" Obviously, he'd done some checking into Christian's past. The point was not lost on Christian. "Usually, that goes the other way around, doesn't it? How do you go from thou shall not kill, to shoot first and ask questions later?"

Christian could feel the sarcasm, but underneath that was an honest question. He hadn't ever discussed it with anyone before. His mother had asked, but he never wanted to tell her the truth.

"As a kid, I found my father after he committed suicide, hanging in our barn." Christian paused and made eye contact with Gabriel before going on. "Never quite knew how to feel about that. He used to beat me and my mom. I always blamed myself for that, even his death. Guess the psyche is a strange thing." He figured Gabriel already knew this, too, but figured he'd share. I joined the priesthood at the behest of Rafeo, and only went along with it to hide my own guilt. It wasn't for me, though…" He paused, as it seemed to be a little too personal. Then took a sip of his beer and looked back at Gabriel. "What do you really want, Gabe?" Christian asked whimsically, as he took a sip of his beer.

Gabriel shook his head as he finished his sip. "Mmm. Honestly, I just thought we should get to know each other. I just happened to be in the neighborhood, and stopped in."

"Broke in," Christian corrected, then smiled. Gabriel's stock just went up, if in fact that's all there was to this visit.

"Right," Gabriel said with a chuckle. After a brief silence between the two, he continued. "I applied to the bureau right out of high school and was accepted. This is all I've ever known; taking down bad guys," he explained with a hint of sarcasm "I don't often stop to consider the human factor, never mind the spiritual – just the facts."

"I know; I checked you out, as well." Again, they enjoyed a pause of seemingly less awkward silence.

"The night before my graduation, someone blew up a house party we were at." Gabriel figured he'd share as well. "Until that night, I had no idea what I wanted to do with my life."

They were beginning to realize they had enough in common.

"Did you get the boot?" Gabriel asked. "From the army?"

"I would have." Christian took a sip of beer; apparently not every detail was in his FBI file. "I went AWOL after I got word that Sam had been taken into a cult; I left to get her out, and in the process, discovered that the children of a few Senators, and other government officials were there, as well. It was with their insistence that I took the lead in this little agency. I have no official standings, but my credentials seem to hold sway."

Gabriel had to admit he hadn't known anyone to get in and out of federal crime scenes without being arrested.

The two of them sat quietly, smiling, and sipping their beers.

"To be honest, I had another reason for coming over," Gabriel admitted after quite a pause; he spoke quickly, almost nervously. Christian felt his shoulders tense in anticipation of bad news.

"Your, ah, associate, Sam, is it a problem if I was to see her, um, socially?"

Christian laughed, feeling relieved that that was all he wanted.

"No! God no! No problem!" Christian looked up and he hoped he didn't sound too defensive, like there was some reason he wouldn't want her. "She can be a handful, though," Christian continued with a smile. Gabriel couldn't hide the large smile at the thought of Sam.

"Yeah! A handful," Gabriel said, without thinking. Obviously, his mind was somewhere else "Uh, you two aren't an item then?" he stammered quickly.

"No. No. Go right ahead, I think she likes you.'

The two sat and talked for a while longer, swapping stories.

"I had no idea I was dealing with such a man of the world," Gabriel said, now feeling the effects of several beers. "But at least you don't treat everyone else like they're beneath you. When we first met, I was an asshole." He held up his hands to quell the anticipated objection from Christian. "No, no, I was," Gabriel said, but Christian hadn't tried to argue the opposite. Still Gabriel continued.

"I was just expecting the usual hassles I normally get when working multi-jurisdictional cases, but to be honest..." He paused, and his face grew dark; he swallowed, and fought back a chill. "...this case seems more your deal. I mean, what the hell is with that dead guy running around... till he exploded, anyway? And as if it wasn't hard enough to find bombs before, now they're inside of people!"

Christian sat upright in his chair, suddenly appearing very serious, and sober. "This guy's making a statement." Gabriel nodded and put his beer down. "The hour glasses threw me for a bit, but it's all a reference to time, to a count down."

"Dooms Day?" Gabriel asked. Christian was glad that Gabriel was comfortable enough with him to voice his opinion.

"Think about the ticking. He's trying to say that anyone - you, me, anyone - is like a ticking time bomb. He believes that he can make anyone do his bidding. I wouldn't be surprised if he was actively looking for ways to recruit us." He paused and took a sip from his beer. "He believes it's only a matter of time."

"And killing a priest for nothing more than to get your attention? He really wants into your head, "Gabriel continued. Christian nodded to agree.

"Yeah, this one's sitting pretty high on my weird-shit-ometer."

The two of them chuckled a little.

The conversation stopped as the late news came on the TV. They were still talking about the case from the other day. The media was still reporting the cover story Sam had made up. The two of them watched the piece but refused to talk about it yet. They were having a good night, and who wanted to think about that kind of horror. They were quiet again, before Christian mumbled.

"I can't help but feel there's more... a lot more to this picture, and it's going to get a lot worse."

Rather abruptly, Gabriel stood up. "I should get goin'," he said, feeling guilty, and looking out the window.

"Okay," Christian answered, and got up to walk his new friend to the door. He didn't feel that Gabriel believed totally in Christian's theories, but they had made some great progress tonight. Just by the door, Gabriel stopped.

"I got to tell you somethin'," he said cautiously.

Christian stepped back slightly. "What?" he asked, feeling bad again.

"I was assigned to you," Gabriel blurted out.

"I know that."

"No, not to work with you; to work on you. Keep tabs on you, for the bureau."

Christian didn't know how to react.

"...Don't worry. After tonight, I'll only give them enough to shut them up; I'll keep you in the loop, too."

Christian smiled and reached his hand out. They shook hands after a brief pause of uncertainty. Gabriel soon smiled, then turned, and walked out.

"Wait a second!" Christian yelled after him.

"Yeah?" Gabriel answered.

"Since you're keeping tabs on me, and all... I'd like to be there if, or when you catch Rafeo. I want to be in on the interview." Gabriel nodded; he figured that was obvious.

"See ya tomorrow, then. I guess you know where." Gabriel waved and got into his car.

Christian closed the door, turned out his lights, and headed for bed. It had been a good night, but he still had one question on his mind. He paused for a moment to look out his bathroom window before he turned on the light. There, across the street, was a figure in dark tattered robes; Christian did a double take to be sure the beer hadn't messed with his vision. When he realized the figure was really there, staring straight into Christian's window, he felt is pulse immediately quicken. When he looked back a third time, he saw only the edge of the cloak flutter away from the illumination of the streetlight nearby. In a fit a rage, he ran through his apartment, grabbed his gun, leaped over the second story balcony, and gave chase.

CHAPTER 7

CHRISTIAN HAD REACTED RECKLESSLY. HE HADN'T grabbed his cell phone, or anything to contact anyone. He had just taken off on foot. At least he had grabbed his weapon. The thought had occurred to him that this could be a trap, but he didn't care right now. He only wanted some answers. But to be sure, he stopped short, and fired two rounds at the dark figure he was chasing. He may have scored a hit, but the man didn't slow down. If nothing else, the gun shots would warrant a call to the police, or at least, so he hoped.

While in pursuit Christian's mind raced. He tried desperately to identify his quarry in the hopes that might help him catch his prey. It only made sense that this was someone connected to the cult from the Everglades and wow, could this guy move. It had to be Quintus, it was the only option that made sense Christian had always been quick and nimble, but this suspect was giving him a run for his money. "Not bad for a guy who should be dead," he thought to himself.

The chase led him down one alley after another. Christian had to dodge around people and other objects, making it hard to make up ground on Quintus.

Quintus ran into a building, up the stairs to the third floor. He tore down the hallway. Despite his muscles and lungs beginning to burn, Christian had made up some ground, and figured he might have him trapped at the end of the hall. Quintus stopped a few feet back from the dead end, smiled at Christian, then leaped through the window, and back to the street level. Christian had to examine the fall, fearing the chase was over. He spotted a streetlight and jumped to the pole. He managed to hold on enough to slow his descent. With a tuck and roll at the landing, he was able to resume his pursuit.

Next, they ran into a parking garage, and up the ramp. Christian hurdled parked cars just to keep his quarry in sight. They made it to the roof level. Quintus sprinted across the level to the edge and jumped over the side. When Christian got to the edge, he stopped to check things out. He looked over the side and had to dive backwards to the ground as Quintus fired three shots at him from his position on the adjacent rooftop. Christian wasn't sure if Quintus was trying to scare him, or shine him on, but he had obviously missed intentionally when he fired; he could have easily killed Christian with such a clean shot.

He slowly looked over the edge in time to see Quintus throw his gun aside. It may have jammed, or he might want Christian to think it did.

It had started to rain heavily, and quickly turned into quite the storm. Christian judged the distance to the next building, and decided he wasn't going to give up just yet. He took a short run, and jumped for the next rooftop, landing on it easily. Quintus was already there. Christian didn't hesitate to continue the chase. He didn't know the area that well, at least not from the roof tops. He still couldn't shake the feeling that this was a trap, but he thought he could end this whole thing, here and now.

Over the rooftops, Christian was catching up to Quintus. His adrenalin was pumping and there was no way he was going to miss this chance. He was within a few feet of Quintus now.

They jumped for the next rooftop. Christian reached out his hand and grabbed Quintus. As he did, he realized they weren't going to make this jump because of it. They crashed onto a fire escape. Both got to their feet right away. Christian reached for his gun, but it was knocked out of his hand before he could fire. Without a word, they began to exchange blows.

Christian had been quite accomplished at hand-to-hand combat. He had studied Taekwondo as a boy and had gotten more training in the military. He had tested his skills in many fights before, but he had to admit to himself that it had been years, and even longer still, since he'd faced an opponent like this. For the first time, he wasn't sure of a good outcome for himself.

Quintus kicked and blocked like a pro. They were also trying to get off the fire escape, and onto solid ground. They tumbled and scrapped most of the way down the ladders, until they were only one level from the street. Quintus dove at Christian, and they both rolled over the railing, and dropped to the ground.

They dropped like a stone into a puddle, with Christian landing on top of Quintus; this time they weren't as quick to get up. The blood from their wounds joined the rain drops as they splashed into the puddle. The alley they landed in was dark, illuminated only by a single flood light near the street.

Christian needed to catch his breath but was aware that Quintus was already on his feet. Christian slowly got up, and as he did, he realized that Quintus had brought help. He started to see other cultists come into the alley from the street, their shadows stretched into the darkness. Christian knew he had landed at least two serious blows to Quintus's face, drawing blood, but as he studied him now, he could see no sign of any wounds.

"So, it was a trap," he said quietly to himself as he struggled to his feet. He looked around quickly and did a head count. "Looks like five to one," he thought to himself. "I could use the workout."

Christian waited; he wanted them to make the first move, plus every second they stood there was another chance for him to catch his breath and prepare.

While he waited, he desperately scanned the surroundings for a weapon, or his gun, or even an escape. Something from the corner of his eye caught his attention; there was someone else in the alley. Standing on another fire escape was a man, shrouded in shadow. He couldn't discern a face; almost like it was only a shadow. He took a second to take a picture in his mind as to where this man was standing, so he could anticipate an attack from there.

The attack finally came. A man from behind charged, armed with a pipe. Christian side stepped as if he had seen him coming, grabbed the pipe and redirected his energy, flipping him into the puddle. The other three attacked at once, while Quintus watched. Christian held his own for a time. He managed to put two of the men down, and was working on the third, when another hit him from behind. He stumbled forward, and after that, was in a panic to defend himself.

He realized that the four attackers had him. They all rushed him at once. Christian braced for the beating he knew was coming, but another man dropped in from above, landing on the group and sending everyone falling to the ground.

Christian didn't take the time to identify his helper; he just resumed the fight. He figured maybe this was the cloaked figure he had seen earlier. As he grappled with an attacker, he turned to try to see the fire escape. The cloaked figure was still there. Obviously, whoever joined the fight was someone else.

Christian had lost track of Quintus, and his mystery helper. He was otherwise occupied with three other combatants. He managed to throw one into a pile of garbage, allowing him to focus on the other two. He had them both in a series of arm locks, keeping them from landing any serious blows. A quick jerk and a jab, and he heard the cracking sound of bone or sinew; one of them had a broken arm now, effectively taking him out of the fight.

Christian then managed to kick another in the knee, dropping him to the ground. A quick knee to the face, and he was left with only one attacker. As he turned to face the man he had thrown to the side, he saw his weapon on the ground.

He charged the last man, leaping into the air and planting both knees into his chest. They tumbled to the ground, and Christian rolled out towards his gun. He scooped up the weapon, turned, and fired. The target dropped. He could hear something else behind him, and rolled over, ready to fire on another target.

Christian paused as he lay in a puddle. Looking up through the rain drops, he was barely able to identify Rafeo standing over him. Christian recognized him a split second before firing and had held fire and lowered his weapon. Rafeo held a gun, but it was not pointed at Christian.

"Easy son," Rafeo spoke calmly. "They're gone."

Christian took a deep breath and released the hammer on his weapon. "So, you let Quintus get away," he grunted and stood up. He was surprised to see the old man and wasn't sure what to say. He wasn't sure how Rafeo had ended up here at this time. He wondered if maybe his old friend was working with Quintus. Christian could now hear sirens in the distance as he slowly got back on his feet. Fortunately for him, someone, a passerby or perhaps a local resident had called for the police.

"Hardly," Rafeo answered, as he held his hand over a bleeding wound on his right shoulder. "He got the better of me and fled the first chance he got."

They stood in the alley for a few minutes, looking at each other. "You alright?" Christian finally grunted. He relaxed and put his hands on his hips, bent over and coughed. He had a little blood in his throat that he wanted out.

"I'll be fine, but how about you?"

"I'm okay but confused as hell." Christian rubbed the back of his neck, sort of a nervous tick when he was at a loss for words.

"Yeah, I bet," Rafeo answered with a smile. "That will get worse before it gets better."

"What? The bump on my head or the confusion?"

Christian's question was only met with another smile from Rafeo.

"Well, who the hell was that other guy on the fire escape? These guys all shop at the same place? Cloaks-R-Us or something? How the hell did you end up here?" Christian was notably upset now, and not holding anything back, the questions spewing from him like an unmanned fire hose.

"That's all part of what I need to tell you, but not here." Rafeo answered holding his hands in front of himself in the hopes of calming Christian down before someone else heard him.

Before Christian could respond, an SUV came roaring into the alley, its lights and sirens going, followed by other police vehicles. It looked like Gabriel had brought the cavalry; he jumped out of the truck and drew his weapon.

"Chris, you alright?" he yelled.

"Yeah, but..."

"Rafeo! Don't move!" Gabriel ordered.

Christian looked back at Rafeo; he wanted to reassure his friend that everything would be fine, but he couldn't. Christian did notice that the bleeding had already stopped from the wound on Rafeo's shoulder.

He didn't bother to say anything as Gabriel took Rafeo into custody.

Christian climbed into the front seat of the SUV. He had questions for the old man, and wanted to be around when he was questioned by the Feds.

No one spoke in the truck all the way back to the FBI field office. Sam was there ahead of them, waiting. When they arrived, Gabriel hauled Rafeo out of the SUV. He didn't seem concerned about whether he was hurting the old man.

"Hey, take it easy..." Christian had grabbed Gabriel by the arm.

"Don't worry about him," Gabriel said, trying to maintain his composure; he looked at Christian's hand where he had gripped his arm until Christian released him.

"Why don't you go see the medic on staff and get fixed up? I have a few questions for our friend, here. We'll be in Room Two, you can find us there when you're done," Gabriel said smugly. His tone didn't leave any room for discussion, or make Christian feel any better. Rafeo stayed quiet but gave Christian a smile as Gabriel pulled him down the hall. An agent at the door stopped Christian as he went to follow the others.

"Sir, you'll have to sign in," he told Christian, as he pointed at a ledger on the desk in front of him. "You'll need an ID badge as well."

Christian stopped, reluctantly, and signed in. He clipped the ID badge to his shirt; Sam did, as well.

"You go with them; make sure they don't rough him up or anything," he said to Sam. "I'll be there when I'm done at the med station."

Sam nodded and squeezed his arm reassuringly. She could tell Christian was upset. She smiled, let go of his arm, and turned to follow Gabriel.

"Where is your med station?" Christian asked as he turned back to the agent at the desk.

Christian's head was pounding, and he felt pain all over his body. He couldn't remember the last time he had been knocked around so much. A flood of random thoughts also raced through his head. He had seen and heard so many strange things in the past few days, and they all involved Rafeo.

Was the man he thought he knew someone else? What connections did he have to this new cult? How was Rafeo able to show up at the right place, at the right time? He watched as the medic placed a bandage on a cut on his arm. Fortunately, he did not need stitches, nor did he show signs of a concussion. The bandage reminded him of something, but he wasn't sure what. He was too confused to think straight.

"That should do it," the medic said, as he finished up. "It'll probably be worse in the morning." The medic tossed a small bottle to Christian as he made his way to the door. "Those might come in handy."

Christian read the label - it was codeine. He shook the bottle, and nodded his thanks, slowly making his way to the door. As he pulled his shirt back over his head, he had a thought. Before Christian left the room, he pulled out his cell phone and called his mom. He had a suspicion and hoped his mom could help.

"Hey Mom... No, I'm fine. How about you?" He let his mom go on for a few minutes about the weather. He smiled as he listened to her, and almost forgot why he called her.

"You sound like you need something," she finally said.

"Yeah... uh... sorry. I'm a bit distracted. I was wondering if you had any old photos of Rafeo."

His mom was silent for a moment. "Why?" she asked, tentatively. "Is he ok?"

"Yeah, Mom. The FBI have him, but I think it's a case of mistaken identity. Do you have a photo?"

"Well, I think I must have something. He did baptize you; I think we took a picture or two back then."

"Perfect." Christian answered. "What's your office Fax Number?" he asked the medic.

"Mom is your fax machine working?" he asked her.

"Yes, it is."

"Can you fax me that picture, please? Here's the number..."

Christian waited impatiently for the fax to arrive. After a few minutes, the machine beeped, and the image came through. The quality wasn't that great, but it was good enough for Christian's suspicions to be confirmed. His eyes widened as the implications became clear to him. He didn't understand it, and even worse, it made more questions pop into his mind.

Christian wandered out of the medic's office and stumbled down the hall. He barely took his eyes off the picture the whole time. The medic had given him directions to the interrogation rooms, but he found himself having to ask three other people for directions along the way.

He stumbled into the observation room where Sam was waiting. He made eye contact with her, then stood, and listened to Gabriel while he questioned Rafeo. The old man was being very cool for someone being questioned for multiple homicides. After a few minutes, Christian couldn't wait any longer. He burst into the interrogation room and slid the picture across the table to Rafeo.

"Alright. Explain this," he demanded sharply.

While Rafeo studied the photo, Gabriel got up so he could see it as well. He looked at it quickly, then back to Christian. "What about it?" he asked.

"The baby in the picture... that's me. The guy holding me... is him," Christian explained, and pointed at Rafeo.

"That was taken over thirty years ago." Christian exclaimed. Gabriel didn't quite know what to do now; the man in the photo didn't look anything different from the man sitting in the chair before them.

"It's not me," Rafeo said flatly.

Christian was at the end of his rope. He rushed over to Rafeo, pulled out a pocketknife, and stabbed him in the hand. Rafeo cradled his hand close to his body and stumbled back against the wall. Gabriel jumped on Christian and subdued him. "What the hell are you doing?" he yelled, as he threw Christian up against the two-sided observation mirror.

"Let me see it." Christian yelled, as he struggled against Gabriel's hold, his conviction being emphasized as he spat the words out. Gabriel stopped to see what Christian was going on about. Slowly, Rafeo pulled his hand away from his chest; he knew Christian had figured it out. The cut on his hand had all but heeled already.

Rafeo looked at his hand, and then at the other two in the room. With a crooked smile on his face, he said. "I guess we should talk..." He then took a deep breath and wiped the smile from his face. "I would request at this time that I be transferred into Christian's custody for reasons that I will explain later," he said, as though he were in a court room and not under interrogation.

Christian and Gabriel looked at each other. "That's not really up to you," Gabriel answered first. Christian motioned to Gabriel that they should step out of the room. They both took a long look at Rafeo, and pondered what was going on, before they stepped out.

"Maybe we should." Christian started stepping into the hall. Gabriel didn't really have a rebuttal; he was still very confused. Before they could say another word, a group of men came around the corner and started down the hall towards them. Christian could see several 'Suits' and two men in uniforms, including the head of the Joint Chiefs. Christian and Gabriel shared a glance; each was thinking the same thing.

The group of men included the Director of the FBI, the Director of Homeland Security, the Head of the Joint Chiefs, and their entourage. They herded Christian and Gabriel into the observation room and closed the door.

"Sir..." Gabriel started, addressing the FBI director, but was cut off.

"Do you have any idea just how big your fuck up is?" It was the HLS director who spoke. "We've been getting bits and pieces of this group for a few months... Not only are they one of the biggest drug rings in the country, but they're big in the sex trade and domestic terrorism. We also know that they have ties to terrorist groups around the world. We figure they have something big planned, but before we could get the intel we need, you..." he pointed at Christian, yelling even louder now, "you had to go and play hero, and scatter them to the wind."

He was screaming at this point. Christian wanted to say something, but figured it wasn't worth it. "And the only thing you have to show for it is this..." he pointed through the two-way mirror at Rafeo, while he searched for a word "...guy."

"Sir..." Gabriel started, but again, was silenced by the raised hand of the FBI Director. He looked at both Gabriel and Christian before he spoke to Christian. "You must have some pretty influential friends, 'cause we've been instructed to let you go. I would strongly suggest you stay away from this man, and this case." Christian smirked, and looked away through the window at Rafeo, who sat quietly and still in the next room, as if he hadn't a care in the world.

"And you, Gabe..." the director continued. "...I need you to take some time off, without your badge, if you understand me," he said with a frown.

"Sir?" Gabriel asked in disbelief, then looked around at the others in the room. He turned to Christian with a huff, then pulled his credentials from his wallet, and handed it to the director, still looking at Christian.

"Thanks," he said under his breath as he handed his ID over. Christian figured it best to keep quiet. The HLS director smirked, then motioned to two of the suits at the back of the room. They immediately left and entered the interrogation room to take Rafeo into custody. The directors and company left the room, leaving Christian and Gabriel alone in silence. Both felt as though something important was being taken from them; they wanted nothing but a chance to solve this case.

They watched Rafeo get slammed up against the mirror, as the agents tried to cuff him. Though it was a two-way mirror and Rafeo could not see the men on the other side, he seemed to stare directly at them; he held their gaze as if he knew he was. Then, Rafeo winked at Christian.

Christian wasn't sure what he had just seen. He saw the wink but wasn't sure what to make of it. He looked to Gabriel who, by the look on his face, had seen the wink as well. Before they could react, Rafeo spun with great speed, dislocating his shoulder in the process. He had taken the agents off guard, and used the surprise to kick the first agent, sending him flying. By now, the noise had alerted the others still exiting the observation room, that something was happening.

The HLS director was momentarily stunned, then slammed his hand down on the alarm. Armed men from a nearby station flooded into the hall and ran towards the interrogation room.

In the meantime, Rafeo had subdued the other arresting agent, and had made a break for the door. Christian had a bad feeling; he had been taken completely off-guard by this. He turned to run for the exit, wanting to try to convince Rafeo to stop and cooperate, but he was too late.

The shots rang out, Christian entered the hallway in time to see Rafeo fall, shot three times through the chest. It all happened so fast.

"And now we don't even have this guy!" the Director yelled, as though finishing a previous thought, then turned on his heel and stormed away. Christian walked over and knelt next to Rafeo's body.

"Goodbye, old man." Christian reached for his bag and took out the book. He examined it closely; it seemed old and yet displayed not a single tear or mark on the binding or cover. Even harder to fathom was how familiar it felt to him. Holding it, he felt a rush, or surge of energy that he couldn't understand. Then all too quickly, the rush was gone as the book was ripped out of his hands.

"This is evidence," an agent said bluntly, as he bagged the book.

Christian stood next to the agent; he wanted to ask for the book but knew there was no point. They all watched as Rafeo's body was covered by a sheet. Gabriel gave a dissatisfied huff, then turned, and walked away. After a few seconds, Christian chased after him and stopped him further down the hall.

"Sorry," he said plainly to Gabriel. He watched as the other man's face went from angry to indifferent.

"Whatever," was all he replied, shaking his head in defeat and disappointment. After a moment to consider his options and coming up empty, he slowly turned and walked out.

CHAPTER 8

QUINTUS HAD MADE IT BACK TO the old warehouse where he had been set up before Florida. This place was still unknown to the authorities, and as far as he knew, Rafeo was unaware of it, as well. He was extremely cautious before entering, circling the entire building twice before going in.

It had been a meat packaging plant at one point, and the smell of it was still strong. This served the purpose of covering other smells coming from the building now.

He made his way through the upper level, which by all appearances, was abandoned. He reached for his key to unlock the stairwell door, and as he did, he could feel the presence of his master; he did not look forward to having to explain losing the book.

The lower levels were more like a dungeon with holding cells for cult members who had yet to be broken, living quarters for those who had, and rooms used for a variety of unpleasant means for convincing those who tried to resist, to give in to the cult.

He could hear the screams from men, women, and some children as they were subjected to torture, electrical shock, sensory deprivation, and, of course, rape and defilement.

He paused at the entrance to one such door to observe some of the women as they were brutalized. He felt nothing for them, not pity, or sorrow, or even pleasure. He was indifferent to almost everything now.

"Come to me, Quintus". The voice was more in his head then audible, but he obeyed the command, nonetheless. He left the doorway right away, and continued further into the building, to where his master waited.

They had built a large hall in the middle of the substructure of the building. It was adorned by many disturbing images, not the least of which were several bodies hung on the wall, upside down. The imagery was wasted on Quintus, but usually had quite a strong effect on others. In the middle of the dimly lit chamber sat a raised altar, and behind that, a large throne-like chair. A dark figure in a cloak sat in the chair, beckoning Quintus to approach.

Quintus crossed the chamber and stopped at the foot of the altar. He knelt to one knee and waited for a moment before speaking.

"Lord Mabus" Quintus spoke, then looked up to face his master.

"Quintus." The other answered, then stood and walked towards the altar. He paused, then moved around the side, and stopped right in front of Quintus.

"I see your trap has failed, and you were unable to kill those responsible for disrupting our other operation. Now the authorities are really on to us."

"My Lord I..." Quintus began but was cut off.

"Silence!" Mabus' voice boomed throughout the hall. "Not only that... but you have managed to lose my book." He raised a hand, and Quintus began to float above the ground. He writhed in pain, as he was raised higher from the ground.

"My Lord..." Quintus tried to speak but couldn't. His airway was blocked. He struggled in vain against the invisible grip that held him. With a wave of Mabus' hand, Quintus was thrown across the room. He slammed into the wall and fell limp to the ground. Mabus walked over to where he lay in a heap. His long tattered black robes seemed to end in shadow, his movements more floating than walking. Again, he picked Quintus off the ground with a motion of his hand. Quintus opened his eyes and glared at him through trails of his own blood running over his eyes. His body was broken yet healed as he spoke.

"You cannot kill me. That which sustains me is from a power greater than your own, and you need my help". He spat blood as he spoke into the dark face of Mabus. The truth was, Quintus had his own agenda, and needed Mabus to achieve it.

"I know I cannot kill you. But I can make your eternity very unpleasant," Mabus said in a quieter tone. "I also need you, unfortunately. I cannot directly influence the mortal realm, not yet anyway. Until I can, I guess I am at the mercy of your ineptitude." He slowly lowered Quintus to the floor, and released him, walking back towards the altar.

"I know what you are thinking, Quintus, and you cannot kill me either," Mabus said, with his back towards Quintus. Quintus slowly released the fist he had made;

he had, in fact, been thinking about attacking his master. Even though he was immortal, he knew he was no match for a god. "Now, tell me, how is our plan coming for the summit?" he asked as he took his seat again.

Quintus took a moment to straighten himself before answering. He slipped his blood-stained shirt off, and stretched, his bones cracking back into place as he did. Quintus stood in the middle of the chamber staring at the one seated on the throne, his thoughts still lingering on defiance. Perhaps he could just leave, find a better way to carry out his mission. Could he think of a way to bring down his dark master? After several heart beats, Quintus swallowed his anger and calmly approached the altar once again, deciding to stick to his present course.

"Reports from our outpost in the Middle East suggest that all is proceeding according to plan. We remain undetected, and our people are ready to strike," Quintus explained slowly.

"Good. See to it, personally, that this goes as planned. The chaos from this should be enough to ensure my victory, and will leave Earth unto you Quintus,"

"Yes, my Lord," Quintus replied. He may not like how things were going, but the temptation of the final prize was too great to resist. Quintus would help Mabus become a god, and in return he would be King of the World.

Gabriel sat on the edge of his couch in his apartment. The shades were drawn, though light still found its way through the cracks. What light managed to come in was diminishing as the sun set. Dust in the air danced in the rays of light, and he watched as the spots of light traveled across the floor.

He was spinning a knife on the table in front of him, the same knife he had taken from Christian, the same knife that had cut Rafeo's hand. He kept seeing it over and over in his mind as he spun the blade on the table. The wound had healed right before his eyes, but how? The wink from the old man was still haunting his thoughts. There was more going on here than he knew. Normally, the Joint Chiefs of Staff don't take an interest in a drug ring, even one as odd as this. He wanted answers, and wasn't sure where to get any; except for, maybe, one.

He rubbed his face in frustration, and loudly blew out a breath, making the dust particles dance in the wind he had generated.

"Fuck it!" he said out loud and jumped to his feet. He slid the knife into his pocket, then slipped his gun and holster on under his leather coat and stormed out. He had to see Rafeo's body, though he didn't understand why.

"Look, this is me as a kid, and him. He's been a family friend for years." Christian explained and pointed at the picture he had brought to the man at the desk at the coroner's office; he figured he had no more strings to pull, but needed, for some reason, to see Rafeo's body. He figured he could play on the clerk's emotions. "I don't think he has any surviving family; I just want to pay my respects."

The man looked at him, then at the photo, then quickly at his watch, and rolled his eyes. "I'm going on my supper break, so do whatever; but you and the other guy better be gone in one hour."

"Sure. You bet, and thank you," Christian said. The clerk sighed, turned, and walked away.

"Other guy?" Christian said to himself and walked through the door marked "Autopsy". He stopped short once in the room, looking at the body on the table, the light over the body being the only one on in the room, making it somewhat dark. He could see the silhouette of another man in the room, perhaps the one whom the clerk had spoken of. For a moment, Christian feared a trap, until Gabriel stepped out of the shadows. Christian began to walk towards Gabriel; he wanted to apologize, again, but didn't get the chance.

"Why did he wink?" Gabriel asked quickly, as he pointed a finger at his own eye to emphasize his question, He was obviously agitated with the whole situation. He pulled the knife out of his pocket and held it up for Christian to see. "And what the hell was up with this whole thing?" he said, shaking the knife again to make his point.

Christian smiled. "Well, I certainly hope that Hell had nothing to do with it."

Gabriel scowled back at him.

"Ok... not at the joking stage, yet..." Christian replied to his own comment, and moved closer to Gabriel, so that he could talk more quietly.

"I've never seen anything like it, I wish I could see that book he was carrying – it might have some answers."

Gabriel slammed a piece of evidence down on the table, next to the body.

"I may be in a world of hurt for this, but it was really buggin' me, too," he explained. Gabriel stepped back, and pointed at the bag, with a tilt of his head, still agitated. "This guy was into some strange shit. The only other thing he had on him were three vials... read the labels." He was shaking his finger, indicating the three containers laid out with his clothing at the end of the table.

Christian reached for the vials and paused briefly as his hand passed over the book. He picked up the first vile and read the label.

"Perfume," he said quietly and grabbed the next.

"Mouthwash? Gold dust?" he thought for a moment, then quickly read further on the first two labels to see the base components of each substance. He looked up at Gabriel; his expression of shock and surprise was echoed in Gabriel's face. Gabriel already had seen the labels, and recited the relevant and curious information before Christian could bring himself to say it. "Gold… Frankincense… and Myrrh."

They both stood quietly, staring at each other over the body, Christian was now somewhat agitated.

"What the hell?" Christian murmured, his mind was racing, trying to think of any reason for having these three particular items.

"Well, I certainly hope NOW that hell has nothing to do with it." Gabriel lightened the mood a little with his comment, allowing Christian to refocus.

"The book," he beamed proudly, as if he had made a great discovery. "Maybe there's an answer in the book." Gabriel motioned for him to go ahead and read it.

Christian picked up the book and opened it. His ears began to ring, quietly at first, then growing louder. He felt as though time itself was slowing down, and all that mattered was the book. The rest of reality around him blurred and smeared into a dark blob, while his vision became focused solely on the tome before him.

The energy from the book was palpable, intoxicating, and familiar to Christian. He recalled finding the book amongst the cultists' things back in Florida, just before Rafeo showed up. As it had done before the very ink on the page began slithering across the pages surface like a swarm of insects or worms to reform itself from, an ancient text to something slightly more recognizable. The ink suddenly all but disappeared until only two discernable words remained on the page.

"Huh?" Christian was obviously disturbed by this.

"Well, what does it say?" Gabriel asked as he walked around the table to see for himself. He investigated the book and saw the completely blank pages. He looked at Christian, confused as well, Christian closed his eyes, and tried to steady his nerves; he licked his lips, and quietly spoke the words that were written as best he could.

"Rafeo Resurectu."

There was a moment where nothing happened, until the three vials shattered, mixing the contents together on the table. The resulting slurry began to bubble, as if boiling on a hot plate; the vapor formed from the ingredients floated up the nose of Rafeo's body, and with that Rafeo took a deep breath, and sat up on the table.

He stretched, and in doing that, forced the slugs out of his chest. He turned away from Gabriel and Christian and jumped off the table. By the time he turned to face them, he also faced their drawn guns. He raised his hands to them, to calm them.

"No. I'm not going to eat your brains, before you ask," he said with a smile.

Gabriel pulled the hammer back on his gun.

"Okay, we're not at the joking stage yet," Rafeo answered under his breath. "If you permit me, I can explain, but best not to do it here. The attendant's supper break is almost over, and he did say to be gone by the time he got back."

Christian remembered his conversation from when he came in; he shook his head to try and clear his mind. He slowly lowered his weapon, and put his hand on Gabriel's arm, to persuade him to do the same. Gabriel, in turn, put his gun away, and shrugged towards Christian.

"In for a penny; in for a pound. Let's get out of here." Gabriel motioned for them to leave.

"Of course... feel free to put some clothes on." Christian didn't want the old man running around naked and noticed he had started to walk away from the table.

Rafeo smiled. He knew that the other two men in the room were in a state of shock. "I spent more than a decade with a Mayan tribe in Central America; clothing was strictly taboo with them." Rafeo went on.

"Yeah, well, just cover yo damn self; this ain't the jungle, old man." Christian just wanted to get out of there. He was notably disturbed, not having missed the fact that Mayan culture was believed to have been extinct since 900 A.D. So, if Rafeo had spent time with a Mayan tribe, well... he couldn't even consider the implications of that.

They walked out into darkness of the night, through the back door of the facility. A van moved from a parking spot towards them, and Sam rolled down the window.

"Father Rafeo… I... I thought Chris said you were dead!"

"No, my dear; just another of this boy's crazy stories," he answered, and ushered them into the van. "Now, let's go somewhere quiet. I've been dying to tell you a story," he said quite tongue in cheek. The van pulled away and drove off into the night.

CHAPTER 9

THE VAN ROLLED ON FOR MILES. The engine had been the only sound the entire time they drove. The occupants exchanged nervous glances, no one spoke, mostly because they had no idea what to say.

The headlights from the van were almost the only source of light, only supplemented by the half-moon, and light pollution from the distant city. The lighting effects, combined with the corn field they were traveling past, made for eerie scenery.

They drove out from the city, with no particular destination in mind. Without thinking about it, Sam was heading to an old abandoned farm house just outside of town. The van pulled onto a long gravel driveway off the county road. Back in high school, Sam and her friends would come out here to party, but after one of the kids burned half the abandoned house to the ground, they stopped coming here. Sam couldn't stand it any longer; she slammed on the brakes, sliding to a halt in the gravel, thirty feet from the house. There was enough light from the moon and the headlights for them to watch their own dust cloud float past them and dissipate.

"What is going on?" Sam asked. "I feel like we're on our way to a funeral."

"Rather appropriate," Christian said under his breath. Gabriel turned in his seat in the front, to face Rafeo, but before he could ask the question he wanted to ask, Rafeo opened the door of the van, and walked out toward the old house. The other three looked at each other, then got out, and stood in a group beside the van, watching Rafeo walk away. He finally stopped, and turned back to them.

"Well, we're not going to do this on the side of the road, are we?" he asked, and continued into the old house; the others followed. They made a quick check of the house to ensure it really was abandoned. They found some old wood from the partially-collapsed roof, and built a fire in the fire place.

Rafeo turned from the fire and reached into his inside jacket pocket. Before he could pull his hand out of his coat, he heard the tell-tale sound of a hammer being drawn back on a pistol. He froze, and looked up to see both Christian and Gabriel had him in their sights.

"What are you doing?" Sam implored from the two men holding their weapons and moved closer to Rafeo, as if to come between him and the others.

"Agent Frost... Christian," Rafeo said slowly, looking each person in the eye, trying to calm them.

"I can assure you...it's me," he said, trying to appease them. He slowly continued to pull a small package from his pocket, and held it out for all to see. He pulled a small cigar out, and put it between his lips. With no reaction from the others, he decided to light it, as well. He slowly puffed the smoke out, and smiled warmly.

The smoke slowly settled towards Christian, and he took a deep breath. The smell was familiar to him; he remembered it from his childhood. Rafeo had been almost the only father figure he had, or at least that he cared to remember. Christian slowly smiled faintly back at the older man.

"Those…" Christian spoke slowly, and pointed at the cigar. "Those things'll kill ya,"

The room fell silent as Christian lowered his gun. Gabriel did as well. He was more distracted by what Christian had just said and started to laugh. It took a few seconds, but the whole room erupted in laughter, all but Sam, of course. She looked more confused than ever.

Eventually, they were overcome with an awkward silence again. Everyone wanted to speak, but could not find the words, until Gabriel couldn't hold it in any longer.

"Are you Jesus Christ, or a vampire, or something? I... I... I mean you were dead... I saw you... then you weren't... then there's the whole gold, frankincense and myrrh, rising from the dead thing... I mean, what the fuck?"

"Rising from the dead? You said you weren't dead," Sam interrupted.

"Yeah, and what was with that book? The words just appeared..." Christian yelled over the top. The three of them were yelling all at once. Rafeo turned from the fire to face them, and slowly raised his hand to silence them.

"Okay," he started and the other three fell silent. Rafeo took a large drag from his cigar and blew the smoke out slowly, letting it hang in the air. "My name is Rafeo Lancia, I am one thousand six hundred and fifty-seven years old. I was born in the year four hundred and two Anno Domini. I am a Magi, one of three who set out to meet the mortal Guardian, after his birth was foretold in the stars. Our task was to deliver his book," he stated, holding aloft the old tome for emphasis. "And carried with me the elements needed to restore life, if necessary. But I never made my destination in time."

He waited a moment, for the others to process the information, before continuing. He had only managed to confuse them further, though no one spoke. Based on what Gabriel and Christian had just witnessed back at the coroner's office, they were willing to take him at his word, though they needed much more to make sense of it all. Rather than ask questions, they kept quiet, wanting Rafeo to continue. Sam, on the other hand, was more confused.

"What do you mean? You're a priest from a small town in the southwest. You baptized Chris and me. I've known you most of my life." She was nearly frantic, pointing a shaky finger at Rafeo.

Christian stepped closer to her and put a hand on her shoulder. After what seemed like an eternity, Sam finally snapped her head to the side, to make eye contact with Christian.

"Chris?" She was nearly pleading with him, and her eyes had begun to well up with tears.

"I believe him," he answered, and waited for Sam to lower her arm. "Let's let him speak." He tried to smile, though it seemed forced, even to him.

Sam then shuffled over to a stack of old newspapers and slumped down on them, holding her head in her hands. "I always thought you had aged remarkably well," she spoke to the floor.

Rafeo sighed. He'd had to tell this story a few times over the centuries. It was never easy. "I was born and raised in a small dessert village in what is now Jordan. We lived in houses we had carved into the rocks there. We were the Magi, a small, learned, and quite secret society, which had been chosen by the Guardian to be the keepers of his knowledge while he was in an earthly form."

"Earthly form? What do you mean? Is this Guardian you keep referring to some kind of god?" Christian asked quietly.

"He has been called many things, many times, by many peoples, but, yes, at one time, he may have been from Nazareth."

Rafeo exhaled another puff of smoke and looked around the room. Christian walked up to Rafeo and grabbed the pack of cigars out his pocket, without saying a word. The old man did not resist, but rather, took out his lighter. He sparked it to life, and Christian slowly lit his own cigar.

"So, who is He?" Christian asked through pursed lips.

"He, or they, may not be the creators of the universe, but certainly that of man. He is the oldest and wisest of a race of immortal, celestial beings, known as the Quies, from the Latin meaning *Those Who Are*."

Gabriel slowly squatted next to the fire. He put another piece of wood into the flames, rubbed his hands together to warm them, and stared at Rafeo through the glow of the fire while he continued his story.

"They are incredibly intelligent, and nearly omnipotent, though they lacked that which they admired most of their creation, emotions and free will. The Quies are bound to their tasks and if they are derelict in their duties, it could destroy the universe. So you see, despite their power and knowledge, they are more a slave to their purpose whereas humans can dictate what their purpose is." Rafeo didn't want to overwhelm the others, so he would pause to allow them to absorb what he had said, and gave them a chance to form questions. After confirming everyone was still paying attention, he continued. "However, in their beginnings, the Quies abandoned their feelings long before our solar system had begun to form, in order to evolve into a higher form of existence, these immortal beings."

Again, Rafeo paused and puffed on his cigar. "The way it was written, the Quies only had one punishment for any crime, and as a result, had very little crime to worry about. On one occasion, a friend of the Guardian was framed and condemned to death. The Guardian took advantage of his position and demanded the sentence be reduced in this case. As a compromise, they decided to grant his friend a mortal existence, and if he could reform, then he would be allowed his immortality to be returned, and if not, he would simply cease to exist. The Guardian became the warden to the largest prison in the universe." This time, when Rafeo paused, he looked around the room. Gabriel was staring at his badge.

"Doing the same damned job, day after day, putting your life on the line for the scum of humanity, no wife, shitty pay, and at the end they tell you to piss off. I always said it sounds more like a life sentence than a life." Gabriel was emotional. He had taken his suspension harder than he had let on.

Rafeo continued. "The Guardian's friend obviously was able to prove he was a better person after his time on earth, and was granted a second chance. Upon his return, he was very different. He would go on and on about how it 'felt' to be mortal, a concept that was very intriguing to the other Quies, and the Guardian. Over the course of time, more crimes were committed, and the same treatment was demanded by the others. The book even tells of Quies purposely committing crimes so they could be sent to Earth. Soon, the prison became more crowded. The Quies, when here, soon discovered the pleasures of the flesh, adding to the population. When the courts discovered the population of humans had grown and was now a breed of life unto their own, they demanded the Guardian end his little project."

Sam fidgeted in her seat; she was the most visibly shaken by the story. Gabriel was looking at the floor, but Christian simply stared so intently at Rafeo that the old man was becoming concerned.

"The Guardian begged the courts to allow the humans to survive. He could not bring himself to terminate them. For his compassion, he was bound to earth, and to the human race, in order to convince his judges to let them..." Rafeo paused, and chuckled at the reality, before he continued. "Us, really... that the judges let us survive. The Guardian won our existence that day. In an effort to understand those he oversaw, he would assume human form, and live among them, sometimes as an unknown farmer, and other times as a spiritual leader, to try to guide his people on the right path. After a few times to Earth, he became almost addicted to the human experience. Human emotion, it is written in one account, is *the most potent, most incredible experience*."

Christian was nodding while Rafeo spoke. He was making the connections faster than the other two. He had studied religions and history and could identify with Rafeo's explanation. Gabriel and Sam remained in their near state of shock, and were not as quick to accept the news.

"There was an unexpected side effect to these visits, however," Rafeo continued. "The Guardian soon learned that faith, human prayer, and devotion were sources of energy and power for him. The more people who would pray to him, or followed his teachings, the stronger he could be. For a time, he would allow others of his kind to visit Earth and establish followers of their own."

"That would explain Polytheism; the Greeks, Romans, Egyptians all believed in more than one god." Christian was putting the pieces together, just ahead of the others. He spoke aloud as the 'Eureka!' moment swept over him. Rafeo nodded his approval and continued.

"Then problems arose. Other Quies tried to use the power they gained for evil. Through the humans, the Quies even learned of murder, which had not existed amongst their kind, ever before. The Guardian would not allow it, and he put an end to it." There was a note of finality to his last statement. Rafeo again took stock of the people listening. He knew this was not easy for anyone to hear, and he was usually forbidden to tell the story, but Rafeo needed their help.

"In order to immerse himself completely in the environment, and enjoy the experience as a human, the Guardian had to shed all of his knowledge and power. He designed a vessel to contain his entire consciousness; a book, in fact. This book would appear on earth, and when he found it, and read it, he could return to his true form. The Guardian's first trip to earth, millions of years ago, was spent almost entirely searching for the book. He had discovered, though, that he was vulnerable, both to humans, and others of his own kind, in that time."

"Uh... excuse me." Gabriel began, raising his hand as if he was in school again. "Millions of years ago? There were no humans here millions of years ago," he snorted, not trying to find fault with the story, but Rafeo recognized questions as comprehension.

Rafeo recognized the need for deeper comprehension and gestured restlessly, waving his arms to allow himself to finish. He knew there would be objection to this point of "yes of course, that's what they taught you in school ya? Indeed, there were, but I'll explain later." He waited for an uneasy moment, drawing a deep breath, before continuing. He could see the information was getting to them. Every preconceived notion of religion, and their own origin, was being redefined. Rafeo knew how they felt; he had seen it before.

"The Magi were a race of people living in an isolated village. They were scholars, mostly, but overall, a very noble people. They were chosen for their purity to be the keepers of this book. They would receive it as a sign that He had taken human form. They would study the stars, and find his location, then set out to find him to deliver the book, so that when the time was right, the Guardian could read from the book, regain his power and knowledge, and return home. There were always three chosen for the task. One for their knowledge to keep them on the right track, one for their skill with a blade for the group's protection, and one for their piety to keep the group morally focused. For their service and to protect them on the often-perilous journey, the three Magi selected for the task would be given temporary immortality."

There was a long silence in the room, only the crackling of the fire and the sound of the crickets cut the stillness.

"Immortal?" Gabriel blurted out. "So, you would have...."

"Yes, I would have healed from the gun shots on my own, eventually, even without the spell. That just moved up the timetable, and, thank you, now I have to get more gold, myrrh and frankincense." Rafeo threw another piece of wood on the fire.

"So, nothing can kill you?" Gabriel perked up at this.

"Almost nothing," he answered quietly. His gaze went distant, as though remembering something. "Only the will of the true Guardian, or a weapon touched by his blood can end our lives." Rafeo pulled a flask from his pocket, and tossed it at Christian.

"You look like you could use a drink," Rafeo said, as Christian caught the flask. He stood frozen, still staring back at the old man. Gabriel didn't hesitate to grab the flask from Christian's hands, popped the top, and took a long, deep drink. When he swallowed, his eyes went wide, and he began to cough.

"You learn a thing or two about fermentation after sixteen hundred years," Rafeo chuckled with a warm smile as Gabriel continued to cough. Sam glanced between Rafeo and Gabriel, then grabbed the flask, and took a sip of her own.

Christian fidgeted before he spoke. "Yeah... so what happened?" he stammered. "This all started... how long ago, and you're still around?".

Rafeo smiled, then continued. "The book had a will of its own. It would call to men from great distances, wanting to be read. Any mortal who read from the book would be given great power, but no knowledge of how to control it." Rafeo paused, with a look of remorse in his eyes. He walked to Gabriel, and took the flask from him. "Entire civilizations have been wiped from the map by the power of the book in the wrong hands; people who never would have seen it, nor should have, had I not failed." He took a drink from the flask, then passed it back to Gabriel.

"This book shouldn't even be here any longer, and neither should I." Rafeo spit into the fire, causing a small eruption of flame from the alcohol in his mouth.

Christian took a drag from his cigar. He could feel the old man's self-loathing, and wished he could convince him otherwise. He blew the smoke out, and as he did, his thoughts quickly changed as he went over in his mind what Rafeo had said earlier.

"That guy... the cult leader... Quintus. He was reading from it. We have to stop him. I mean, you just told us very bad things happen when someone reads from that book and. . ." Christian was obviously agitated. The prospect of seeing the entire population of a state wiped out because of this was not appealing to him, to say the least.

"That was no man; he is a Magi..." Rafeo's face softened slightly, and he hesitated, as though the words were hard to say. "...and my brother!" There was a flutter of restlessness all around the room after that statement. Rafeo looked as though he was in pain for speaking of Quintus; he winced and paused before continuing. It seemed he had little good news to tell in all of this. "The book had called to him, and corrupted him. Part of our training and devotion to the task was to be able to read from sections of the book and control the book's power. Quintus decided he wanted to kill the mortal Guardian, perform the rite of ascension, and essentially, steal the Guardian's power."

"Is that even possible?" Christian's mind was racing now. His eyes grew wide as Rafeo nodded, confirming his fear.

"He attacked us on the way to what is now England, where we were to meet the Guardian. Quintus had acquired one of the nails used to hang Christ on the cross."

"Yo... Hold up!" Christian interrupted. "...Christ?" He was disturbed by the reference.

"Indeed!" Rafeo answered calmly. "As I said, he's been called many things, many times, by many people; I believe he even promised to return. You didn't think he meant to the same place, did you?" Rafeo called out their ignorance; it wasn't their fault, though. This information had been covered up so well over the years. People and organizations had profited from the Guardian so much that the world had easily overlooked the simplicity of the truth.

"The Guardian would travel to all parts of the world, to all cultures, to experience and share. Humans were the ones who came up with the audacious idea of labeling his teachings into Religion." He spat the word, as if it was bitter.

"But thereafter, there were that many more humans praying to him and bolstering his energy." Rafeo looked around, and figured the geopolitical and religious tangent was best kept for another time, and went back to the matter at hand.

"Quintus forged a weapon from these nails. The Lance of Longinus would have been easier to use, I guess, but it had been lost when the other Magi, fearing what it could do, threw it into the Mediterranean Sea." Rafeo realized he had started another tangent. He cleared his throat, and continued.

"Quintus stabbed Balthazar, the third of our trio, and threw him into a deep crevasse, but my brother managed to take the weapon into the crevasse with him, leaving Quintus with no means of killing me. Quintus and I fought for hours to a stalemate, until he ended up stapling me to a tree with a sword. It took hours to free myself, and several days to recover. But fate, it seems, is not all against me."

Rafeo paused as though remembering the events.

"I arrived in England, where the Guardian was living, to find a fierce battle between two clans raging at the sacred site where the ascension would happen, During the battle, the Guardian's young mortal body was slain. All I had to do was find the book, perform the resurrection and the right of ascension, and all would be restored. But I was too late; Quintus had already performed the right of ascension before I caught up to him, However, the leaders of the two clans, locked in mortal combat, stumbled into the beam of divine light before Quintus could get there, and ascended in his place." He nodded and smiled.

"That's the good news?" Gabriel piped up, feeling emboldened by the drink. "Two humans are running around with stolen power of God... instead of one. That's the good news?" Gabriel asked, before taking another drink from the flask.

"Indeed. It will take them a millennium or two to learn the powers they possess, particularly without the aid of the book." Rafeo was proud of the fact that at least he still had the book in his possession.

"All I need to do is find the true Guardian, deliver the book to him, and he can restore things to the way they need be." Rafeo answered, making it sound simple.

"Oh, is that all? It's only been sixteen hundred years, so you're just biding your time?" Gabriel was already feeling the effects of Rafeo's brew.

"What do you mean, find the Guardian? I thought he was killed back then in 437 AD," Christian finally said.

"His mortal body was, but his soul had nowhere to go. It is trapped, here, on earth. He is reincarnated every hundred years or so," Rafeo shrugged.

"At first, it was easy to determine where he was by reading the stars, but transportation was not the quickest. I'd often be too late, and he, or she, would have died before I could even get to him. Now that I can fly around the world in a day… it is becoming more difficult to find him. In truth, I am all but guessing anymore."

The room fell silent again. Gabriel and Christian looked to each other quickly. They each had the same question in their head, and each could tell this of the other, but it was Gabriel who got the words out first.

"And do you know where your best guess is now?" He gestured out of frustration, not liking being kept in suspense.

"Safe," is all Rafeo said, making his best poker face. For now, they would have to except that as the only answer they would get.

The sun had just broken over the horizon when Gabriel opened one eye, slowly. Instantly, he was greeted by a headache. That brew of Rafeo's was potent indeed. He realized he was stiff from having slept on the floor.

"...In fact, it is this book that has inspired the use of sacred scriptures in most of the world religions. Yes, they are to chronicle the actions of Christ or Moses, but the concept is modeled after this." Rafeo shook the book in his hand to make his point.

"What about Muhammad? He wasn't born until 570 AD," Christian asked.

"Ah... a devout profit..." Their voices seemed to trail off, or the pounding in his head drowned it out. Gabriel realized Rafeo and Christian had been talking all night. He also came to realize the lump next to him was moving. He rolled over to see Sam stirring awake next to him.

"Mmm..." she grunted, and rubbed her head.

"That stuff has a hell of a kick, huh?" Gabriel tried to smile as he noticed that Sam, despite the hangover and the fact they had slept on the floor of an abandoned farmhouse, was still quite attractive.

"Yup," was all Sam could muster in response. They both slowly sat up. Rafeo noticed they were awake. He brought them over a mug of hot coffee.

"Where did this come from?" Sam asked, as she took a sip, and passed the cup to Gabriel.

"Oh, I never have this…" Rafeo raised the flask. "…without having some of this for the next day." He finished, showing them a small empty bag of coffee.

Gabriel took a drink, and winced as he swallowed. He handed the cup back to Sam, cleared his throat, and looked around.

"So, what does this have to do with us? What do we do now? I mean, you're a fugitive; I'm on suspension and probably for a while. And you two…" Gabriel pointed at Sam and Christian. "I don't know. You're a couple of quacks." Gabriel looked at Christian, then Sam, whose face portrayed a look of betrayal.

"No offense," he added quickly, with a turned-up hand.

"Actually, I'm a dead man," Rafeo answered, pointing at his chest.

"And we're not the ones on suspension," Christian answered with the same tone and adding a shrug as though to make his point sound innocent.

They all sat and stared at each other for a minute before Gabriel waved his hand, as if to dismiss their comments, and spoke again.

"Okay! If God, or the Guardian, or whatever you call him is out of the picture, should we be ready for the Devil to take over, or somethin'?"

"Actually, there is no Devil," Rafeo answered. The others perked up at this point. The statement obviously surprised them, and at this point, none of them expected anything to surprise them anymore.

"The Devil was a construct of man, made as an excuse for the devil that dwells within. It is man's own choice to do right or wrong – his own test to face." Rafeo paused for a moment. "It wasn't until more recently – the onset of Christianity, for example – that the concept of a "Devil" came about. There have been gods of death, the underworld but not the image of a rival to God himself, that is recent. Mabus is the driving force behind this. In life, he was an animal, now that he has partial godly powers, well." Rafeo scoffed, sneering as though the very words had left a bad taste in his mouth. He looked up, noticing Christian absorbing the information

"But something has changed.", he said, nodding slowly. He saw a look from the others, begging for an explanation. "Do you remember the other clan leader who I mentioned earlier; the one that ascended?"

The other's nodded, remembering the story from the night before.

"The one was a Druid, a very pious leader; the other was a murderous savage. Since that day, I've noticed the population becoming more and more polarized, and evil is winning out." He paused and looked up sharply at the three of them in the room.

"Polarized?" Christian asked

"You are all, in some fashion, in law enforcement, right? But ask yourself… have you ever cheated on your taxes? Ever used excessive force when dealing with anyone? Have you ever turned a blind eye to a homeless person, or an elderly person in need of help?" Rafeo looked around the room to each of them in turn. "Have you ever made excuses for yourself to get over the feeling of guilt for doing these things?" He spoke the last question slowly to emphasize his point. Rafeo looked around to see their reactions before continuing. Not one of them was looking him in the eye.

"There was a time when this didn't happen; when people were honest and pure; when they would work together as a society, towards common goals, but now...? Well, even those who are the best among us are not without sin."

The room fell silent for some time, as they all thought about what was said. Sam slowly stood up and took a step forward. "I may not be perfect, but I promise you right now, I will do whatever I can to help you." Her voice cracked at the end. Christian and Gabriel stood up, as well, and nodded to each other.

"Count us in too," Christian said as Rafeo stood up and smiled warmly at them.

"So, what do we do first?" Sam asked.

"Well... The first thing we need to do is find the missing pages from this book," Rafeo said. He was greeted by confused looks from the others.

He didn't wait for the question to be said aloud and continued his explanation. "During the Second World War, the Nazis dabbled in the occult, hoping for supernatural help, or divine providence. Quintus was a man behind the scenes guiding them in this pursuit.

Quintus was clearly in the service of Mabus, either willingly or under duress, I no longer care. Quintus guided **Heinrich Himmler** and the S.S. through many rituals. He would tell them that these rituals were intended to make the Third Reich last a thousand years, but in truth they were only meant to strengthen Mabus."

"Churchill said, and he was right, that all evil needs is for good men to do nothing. But regardless of how you justify it, killing is an evil act. The conflict fueled Mabus immensely, I believe tipping the scales in his favor." Everyone in the room felt the chill settle in on them and shared an uneasy look at each other before Rafeo continued.

"Think of the world as it is now." He fell silent for a moment while the others searched their memories and came to the same conclusion. "Mankind is capable of such greatness, compassion and love, but lately..." Rafeo started counting on his fingers. "Look at world poverty - one percent of the world live in excess while the rest suffer in squalor, drugs, famine, crime and war going almost unchecked." He trailed off, trying to stay on track. "But I digress." Rafeo cleared his throat.

"During the Second World War, the Nazis Occult lunacy came to a crescendo at a place called Hauska Castle. It's a rather long story but I ended up stumbling across the mortal Guardian, he had been unwittingly helping the Nazis as a specialist in ancient history or something like that. He had seen Quintus use the power of the book to do some fairly horrific things. I had not counted him as an ally until one night he stole the book and fled into the night.

"I followed him, for no other reason than to get the book back. The Nazis caught up with him before I could. We were both captured and taken to Auschwitz. The young man – I forget his name now – wrestled the book away from one of the guards and started ripping pages out of it. That is when I knew who he was. I rushed to his aid but they shot us both.

"I woke up the next day to learn they had burnt his body along with the book. Of course, the book survived, I believe it was taken by Quintus after being pulled from the pyre. The Guardian was again lost to me.

"Foremost, we need to find the missing pages from the book and return it to the Guardian. And just in case, we need to find out what Quintus and his master are up to, and stop them." Rafeo was all business in his tone."

"Sam and I can use whatever connections we have left to find out about Quintus, and track him down," Gabriel said, hiding any evidence of his hangover.

"Right." Rafeo turned to Christian. "And you, my boy... it looks like we're off to Poland."

CHAPTER 10

GETTING THROUGH SECURITY AT THE AIRPORT was easy. Christian's ID came in handy for him. As for Rafeo, he was dead after all, and had also learned the value of multiple personae when you live forever. He had come prepared, with a completely different passport and birth certificate, and they passed muster without question.

The same could not be said for a man just behind them in line. Christian could recognize the man as a Muslim cleric, and security was giving him the full treatment. Christian made eye contact with the man, who only smiled politely in return. He seemed to accept the treatment as standard operating procedure, even when they knocked his copy of the Qur'an out of his hands. Christian told Rafeo to continue on to the plane, and he'd join him there.

He made sure Rafeo boarded without incident, then turned towards the cleric. He stooped down to pick up the man's book, and handed it to him. The book was intercepted by a member of security.

"Step back, sir, or you will be detained," the man grunted towards Christian. In turn, Christian took out his ID and flashed it around.

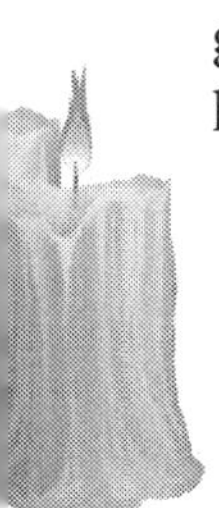

"We're on the same flight, maybe I can keep him in cuffs for ya the whole time... or how 'bout a cage?" Christian spoke up; the sarcasm was not wasted on security.

But before anyone else could speak, the cleric interrupted in a very calm voice. "It is okay, son; these men have done nothing but what is required in this age of senseless violence. I will be fine, please." He nodded towards the boarding gate, as if asking Christian to leave.

Christian hesitated, then looked into the cleric's eyes. They felt warm and honest. After another moment, Christian nodded, turned, and made his way to the plane.

The security guards were slightly taken aback, but tried not show it. They finished their search, though more gently than before. Finding nothing suspect, they sent the man on his way.

Christian's ears popped as the plane climbed away from the runway. He had always hated this part of flying. After swallowing hard a few times, his hearing finally cleared enough.

Rafeo smiled. He enjoyed flying, particularly having been alive long enough to remember a time when the suggestion of flight was considered heresy. He turned to Christian, and could almost read the questions in the man's face.

"You have questions," Rafeo stated the obvious.

"Well... yeah." Christian wasn't sure exactly where to begin. Rafeo just stared back at him, waiting. "The other night, you said that there were humans, millions of years ago, and why haven't the other Quies come to find the Guardian, or done something... anything, to help?" He was speaking so quickly that Rafeo held his hand up to calm him, before he answered.

"The rest of the Quies do not have anywhere near the level of power that the Guardian does. I think there may be some who have come to help, but in mortal form, there isn't much that they can do, I'm afraid. And there are some who have tried to take advantage of the Guardian's absence," Rafeo sighed.

"The Devil?" Christian asked quietly. In turn, Rafeo's eyes grew large, and the man's facial expression changed completely.

"The Devil." Rafeo looked at his hands, as though the answers would appear on his fingers, then looked back up at Christian.

"The Devil goes by a different name these days, I'm afraid.", Rafeo began quietly; he didn't want anyone sitting around them to hear what he had to say. "Do you recall from our talk last night that I mentioned the leaders of two opposing clans that were taken, by mistake, into the light of ascension?"

Christian thought back, and nodded as he went over the key points in his mind, from the night before.

"Well, Constantine was the Druid leader of the Britons at the time. He was pure of heart and mind, quite pious, really. He is said to have received the Guardian's kindness and empathy. He has the power to grow life, and influence the noble spirit within man. His power is in inspiring man to the right thing, simply because it is the right thing to do." Christian nodded.

"And what of Mabus, was it?" Christian had absorbed as much as he could, in the short period of time, but didn't want to confuse any of the facts.

"Yes, Mabus." Rafeo fidgeted in his seat slightly, as though he really didn't even want to have this conversation. "And Mabus' powers grow from the evil that men do?"

"Evil begets evil, doesn't it?" Christian asked, after a while.

"Mankind is at a tipping point. The good that man does is so easily overshadowed by his evil." Rafeo had been around long enough to see the decline of mankind; he was something of an authority on the subject, if for only the moment of time he has had to observe.

"And not just mankind; the Quies themselves are being exposed to evil in ways they have not considered for an age. Some of them are trying to establish themselves, here on earth, exploiting their gifts to become rulers of men, and others, still, are trying to take over their immortal existence. At first, they even believed evil was contagious." Rafeo scoffed, as he finished his rant.

"All because of..." Christian didn't finish his statement. He realized just before he said it that the thought had occurred to Rafeo before and haunted him for sixteen hundred years.

"All because of my failure." Rafeo finished the thought for him, his head sinking into his chest as he spoke. The two sat in silence for a moment, Rafeo took a sip from his water bottle to help him clear the lump in his throat. He was glad to have help on this mission. It had been a very long time since he had trusted anyone enough to reveal this reality.

"Over time, mankind had learned of the book of power. Its purpose is to be read, it has a desire to be read, and has actually called out to those it feels it can influence. I have had to ward off attacks from men and gods, alike. Anyone of those attempts to read from the book could have ended all life on this planet, or even worse than that. So, the Guardian isn't really here to protect mankind."

Rafeo leaned in and made close eye contact with Christian.

"He is here to protect the rest of existence from mankind. That was his vow, his bond, when he refused to destroy us; that he would accept responsibility for us."

Rafeo sat back into his seat. The look on Christian's face betrayed the fact that he truly understood what was at stake, here, now. His train of thought was broken when an attractive stewardess leaned over in front of them.

"Excuse me. Christian Perditus?" she asked. Even she could tell she had interrupted something fairly intense. "Sorry," she said with a polite smile.

"Yes, that's me.", Christian finally answered.

"We have a call for you," she explained as she straightened up and gestured towards the phones. Christian nodded, then hesitated, to look at Rafeo. The old man smiled back, the way he had as long as Christian had known him. It was the same smile he had seen at his father's funeral. Christian knew that it wasn't Rafeo's intension to disturb his life like this, and the smile was a gesture of comfort. Christian nodded, then stood to follow the stewardess.

"Hello," he said awkwardly, realizing he'd never taken an in-flight phone call before.

"How's the peanuts?" It was Gabriel's voice on the line. Christian was happy to hear from a friendly voice and welcomed the reprieve from his conversation with Rafeo.

"Actually they've…they've given me a bit of a headache, Gabe. What's up?" Christian sounded tired, but Gabriel didn't bring it up.

"Well, we've run into a bit of luck on the case, literally. This crazy guy ran into the front of my truck while Sam and I were, uh, going for dinner." He nervously cleared his throat, awaiting some kind of comment from Christian.

"Oh yeah?" was all Christian replied. Gabriel wasn't sure how to take his response, and quickly carried on the conversation.

"Yeah. He was going on about some warehouse when we got out of the truck to check on him. He also has pentagrams carved into his skin, just like the ones in Florida."

"You've gotta ask him where he came from." Christian was a little more in tune with the conversation, having shaken out some of his other thoughts, and focusing on the matter at hand.

"That may be difficult," Gabriel explained. "The guy is in bad shape, and being hit by a car didn't help. Based on his condition, we know he couldn't have been on foot for long. I called it in... Oh, yeah... I'm back on the case again, for this... we're canvassing the area for a warehouse. Sam's staying with the guy in the hospital, in case he wakes up."

This was a lucky break and was now the only way to pick up the trail. After Florida, this group all but disappeared, but Christian and Gabriel agreed that they were only consolidating their forces for something else. Now they had a chance to find out what that something was.

"That's great, Gabe. We should be landing in Krakow in about 6 hours. I'll call you when we've cleared customs." Both fell silent for a moment, before Gabriel spoke again.

"This is like nothing I've ever done before... I mean, doesn't it seem strange? I'm not even religious."

"You don't know the half of it," Christian muttered under his breath. "Look, let's just stay focused on the case. Regardless of whatever else is going on, we have a bad guy to catch." Christian tried to reassure Gabriel, as well as himself.

"10-4. Hopefully, I'll have some news for you when you call." Gabriel sounded better already.

Christian hung up the phone slowly, his hand lingering on the hand set. "Good luck," he whispered. As he turned to go back to his seat, he noticed the cleric he had tried to help at the airport. The man was still wearing his warm and polite smile.

"Good news, I hope?" the cleric questioned. Christian didn't understand it, but he felt like talking to this man.

"I guess," Christian answered with a sigh.

"Sounds like a crisis of faith."

Christian was surprised that the man would say that, given what they were involved in, and the fact that this man knew nothing about him.

"What makes you say that?" Christian asked.

"Most things are," he replied with a shrug.

"No offense, sir, but I'm not Muslim, so..." Christian trailed off, but was caught off-guard by the clerics response.

"Well, no one's perfect, but I was talking about faith, not religion." His smile seemed to broaden, even in his eyes.

"Most people have problems because they lack faith... in themselves, in their friends, in what they are doing. You need to have faith." The words made so much sense to Christian. He had been taken aback by all that had transpired of late, and in doing so, had lost faith in himself, and others. Christian smiled back at the cleric.

"And you, sir? How do you affirm your faith when you need to?" he asked after a still moment. The cleric didn't miss a beat; he took a long, deep breath, and looked Christian in the eye.

"Oh, I go outside when the sun is highest, lay down on the ground, and stare at the stars in the sky." He winked as he finished.

Christian was confused by the man's response.

"But… you can't see the stars when the sun is up," Christian finally answered. The cleric smiled very wide and pointed at Christian.

"Ah... but you know they are there, all the same."

Christian thought for a moment, then slowly started to nod. "You're right," he whispered and smiled at the cleric.

"Shukran Jazeelan." Christian thanked him in his own language, the sign of respect was not wasted on the cleric.

"Ma'a salama," Christian said his farewell with a nod and a smile. He walked back to his seat. He had to admit he felt better.

Faith. He found himself needing it more, just to believe what Rafeo had told him. This was unraveling everything in his life, all he had ever studied about any religion, almost all he had ever known. If this was all true, every person on earth had been deceived. He wanted to believe but was conflicted. Although seeing someone return from the dead did make for a compelling reason to go along with it.

"How do you... how could you know this?" he finally asked, quietly, after a very long pause.

Rafeo nodded, as if remembering a distant pain.

"After two centuries of searching for the Guardian, I grew weary. I began to question what was happening to me, not to mention longing for death… for an end."

"A crisis of faith," Christian interrupted, noticing the relevance of his other conversation.

"Indeed," Rafeo agreed, and continued. "I decided I wasn't going to bother to look any more until I had some answers of my own. I returned home, only to find my village completely destroyed - the vast library, everything, It was almost completely abandoned. Quintus had seen this as a point of support for me, and he made it a priority to destroy. However, he had been originally chosen for his strength, not his wisdom. He had missed the Chamber of Knowledge, the place where the book of the Guardian would materialize. It was a highly guarded secret, and a place where the elders hid our most sacred writings. I spent a hundred years reading on the events that have shaped the human world."

Rafeo yawned and stretched. It had been a long and tiring day, and they would need to be rested when they reached Auschwitz. The old man reclined his seat and closed his eyes.

Christian reclined his seat and looked out the window; he found himself looking up, to the stars.

CHAPTER 11

IN ANOTHER LIFE, HE COULD REMEMBER his name; he could remember he had been in the army; now it was all a haze. Everything, and everyone, moved around him as though he was watching himself under water. The man sat nervously shaking in the back of the command-and-control vehicle. He had shown Gabriel where they had held him. Gabriel checked the monitor in front of him, and turned to the man.

"Luke," he said with a smile. "Cool Hand Luke... do you remember? That's what your buddies from your old unit used to call you, 'cause you were always calm around the explosives. Do you remember?" Gabriel had moved closer and squatted next to the man. He was beginning to doubt the information Luke had given him. The man had been strung out on some pretty strong drugs for some time; probably since he'd gone MIA in theatre in Afghanistan, nearly a years ago.

Sam sat next to Stenner. She held his hand, trying to help keep him calm and also show her support for Gabriel. She could feel the young man tense up after hearing his name.

His real name was Corporal Lucious Stenner. After running frantically into traffic, and nearly

being rundown by Gabriel's truck, the FBI had done a background check on him. Gabriel made the connection to their case through the man's nonsensical ramblings. He had led them to a large building in a rundown industrial park on the east side of town. The building had been a meat processing plant, until the board of health shut it down.

Gabriel had been allowed to participate as an advisor for the raid they were about to conduct. He was still under suspension; had he not been able to prove that he had found Corporal Stenner purely by accident, he would be facing criminal charges.

Stenner looked blankly back at Gabriel, and scratched at the intravenous line taped to his hand. He was uninjured by his run in with Gabriel's truck, but had been put on a variety of fluids and other medical drugs to help accelerate his detoxification from the illicit drugs he'd been on.

Gabriel couldn't help but feel for the man. Apart from the drugs, this man had been tortured, his body was a road map of pain, misery and scars. According to his record, he had volunteered to serve his country after losing an uncle in the 9/11 attacks. He had suffered more than anyone should have to.

"Is this the place?" Gabriel asked, as he pointed to the monitor. Stenner eventually turned his gaze to where Gabriel was pointing. He began to shake, tears rolled down his cheeks, and he wet himself.

"Oh, for fuck's sake, Gabe... This wasteoid ain't gonna do us a bit of good." The agent in charge, who was also in the van, had done little to hide his contempt for

Stenner, or Gabriel, for that matter. In his eyes, Gabriel was just pulling a stunt to try and get his suspension lifted.

"This 'wasteoid'..." Gabriel spat, then tried to console Stenner, before turning to face the other agent. "...has paid a hefty price for his country. I think, if nothing else, you could extend him some professional courtesy, if not a measure of sympathy."

Gabriel turned back to Stenner and smiled. The Corporal could not hold his gaze, and buried his head in his chest. Gabriel stood up to address the other agent again.

"Seeing as how this soldier, who had been trained for and faced combat, has just wet himself… I'd say we're on the right track," Gabriel said with a smug smile.

"Ok, but this is your call,", the agent warned. He picked up his radio and keyed the mic. "All teams move in... go-go-go."

Like a precision machine, the three entry teams positioned near the three doors to the plant moved in. They had all breached their doorways and gained access within seconds of each other. Gabriel listened nervously to the radio. The chatter was minimal, but he wanted to hear that they had found something important. He could hear each team lead report as they cleared the building a section at a time... that is, until team one proceeded to the sub-levels.

Team one was a typical four man fire team. One shotgun, two MP-5s, and the Sergeant carried his H&K 416 to pack a little extra punch, if called for. Sergeant Tom Pennman was the lead, and was confident in his team. They were operating like clockwork, as they usually did, despite the fact the dark, damp, and filthy building wreaked of rotting meat.

Pennman opened the door to reveal the stairs. A quick check with his tac light showed there were no immediate threats. His teammate on the shotgun, a rookie named John Rawlins, took point, while he followed up right behind.

At the bottom of the stairs, they could see a large, open space, and what appeared to be multiple bodies.

"I think we've got something here," a voice on the radio reported, breaking the silence in the van. "Oh, gawd, what a smell! Wait… what the hell?" The radio went quiet for a few seconds. Gabriel couldn't help step closer to the radio, as though it would help him hear better, even though there was nothing to hear

"Command." The voice finally broke the silence again. "The good news is, this is the place, but the bad news is, I think we're too late; all I can see is bodies, quite a few of them, unfortunately."

Gabriel was disappointed, but still hopeful they'd find some information that might help them understand this case better.

"Kinda creepy... the way they're hung on the wall like that."

Gabriel's head snapped up-right. That last sentence tweaked a memory. He fumbled for the talk button on the radio.

Pennman had moved around the room. He'd counted twelve bodies so far, three on the floor and nine pinned to the walls. They were checking for survivors when Gabriel's voice came back over the radio.

"Team one lead... repeat your last." Gabriel spoke clearly.

"The bodies, some are hung on the wall, upside down."

Gabriel's eyes grew large, as the hairs on the back of his neck stood on end. This sounded all too familiar to him. "Fall back... I repeat, fall back. Get out of there." Pennman heard the words, but was frozen for a split second in shock. The body he had just checked for a non-existent pulse, opened its eyes and looked at him.

"Everybody back to the stairs!" Pennman yelled, as he fired two rounds into the corpse that was staring at him. Other bodies around the room had begun to pull themselves from where they were mounted, and moved towards them.

The sub-machine guns they carried had little effect on these walking dead, as the room erupted in gunfire. The shotgun was only effective enough to put them down for a few moments, if only long enough for the team to withdraw. The young man with the shotgun emptied his weapon, and frantically reloaded, as he covered his team's escape.

In the command-and-control van, Gabriel heard the gunfire over the radio. He grabbed a shotgun from a weapons lockbox, and racked the first round. He burst out of the back door of the van and raced across the street. When he reached the building, he ran towards the door, noticing only then that Sam was right behind him, gun in hand. They had almost made it to the door when the ground shook and the windows of the building blew out, the building rocked by multiple explosions.

Gabriel and Sam were stunned momentarily; they looked at each other in fear, which quickly turned to resolve. They shook off the shock, and continued to race for the door.

Smoke poured out of the building. The door flew open just before they got to it. They both took up firing positions, ready for the worst, but were soon relieved to see uniformed SWAT members come through the door into the daylight.

Sam moved closer to help the disoriented officers away from the building to a safe rendezvous point. Gabriel stood fast with his weapon pointed at the door, in case there were any more cult members trying to get out.

Sergeant Pennman stumbled out of the door, blood dripping from his ears and nose.

"That's it!" he yelled and slumped into Gabriel's arms, Gabriel helped prop him up and walk towards the rendezvous point. From behind, they heard a blood curdling scream like some kind of rabid creature. Both Gabriel and Pennman swung around, and fired frantically at the walking corpse coming at them. Both fired until their weapons were empty, and the body dropped to the ground and lay motionless.

"Rawlins… he kept firing and reloading... he bought us enough time to get back to the stairs and out. He was at the bottom of the stairs when the bombs went off." Pennman was yelling; his hearing was obviously affected from the blasts.

"We'll find him." Gabriel tried to comfort the man, but the sergeant stood up, turned to the other teams, and grabbed a shotgun from a younger looking man. He racked back the slide and held his hand out to the man who emptied his pockets of shells and handed them to Pennman. Pennman loaded the shotgun and walked back over to Gabriel.

"Yes. We will." He headed back towards the building. Gabriel was impressed with the Sergeant's sense of duty to his own men.

By this time, the SWAT truck had met them at the rendezvous point, and the rest of the men slowly made it to their feet, exchanged their weapons for shotguns, and filed into the warehouse as well.

They made their way back down to the sublevel. Pennman found Rawlins' body, while the others spread out to clear the room. Gabriel put his hand on Pennman's shoulder. Pennman reached down and closed the young man's eyes. He motioned to two of the team members; they unfolded a body bag they had brought with them and loaded the body into it.

Gabriel and Pennman were back up and moving forwards. Towards the back of the room, they found what could only be described as a throne. It seemed that whoever had sat there did so in order to admire those who had been hung on the wall. A disturbing thought.

"Over here!" one of the team members called out as he opened a door off to the side from the throne.

Gabriel walked over and looked through the doorway. They found a light switch and turned it on.

"Jackpot," Gabriel said quietly under his breath as he looked around the room. The walls were smothered with maps, some crude blueprints and plans.

"If nothing else..." Gabriel turned to Pennman "...no one died in vain today." He smiled.

Penman stared him down for a moment, then nodded slowly.

CHAPTER 12

After some eight hours, they finally landed at T1 Krakow International Airport in Poland. Renting a car, Rafeo had decided on their route, taking motorway 790, and avoiding the larger A4 or E40 routes. It may take a little longer, but thinner traffic would make spotting a tail easier. The pages they were after were only safe because the enemy didn't know where they were. The last thing they wanted was to lead the enemy to them.

Rafeo handled all of the arrangements, speaking the language fluently. Christian was surprised at first, until he remembered that Rafeo had been alive long enough to know the first people to speak the language.

They had got through customs quickly and easily, and were soon on their way. The drive was going to take about an hour, and Christian was content to sit quietly and stare out the window. He was trying to come to grips with all that had happened lately. Rafeo could sense the emotional state of his friend, and didn't want to let it go. After they had watched several mile markers whisk past them, Rafeo couldn't contain his concern.

"Are you alright?" he asked knowingly.

Christian was slow to respond. He had become mesmerized by the scenery. With a sigh, he turned to

face the older man. “It’s just that every question I ask seems to breed a hundred more… and I can barely grasp what you’ve told me already.”

Rafeo nodded. “My indoctrination to all of this lasted seventeen years, and then I was allowed to begin my studying. From childhood, I had been prepared for my task and to receive this knowledge, and you’ve had all of what... a few days, to come to terms with the fact that everything you’ve been brought up to believe isn’t the complete truth? I certainly understand how you feel.”

Christian wasn’t sure if he did. There was one other searing question burning away at him, though he dared not ask. They drove on in silence for several miles more. Christian was trying to think of the right way to voice his concern when the silence was broken by a cell phone.

Christian dug it from his pocket and smiled when he saw the call display. He flipped the phone open and put it to his ear.

“Hey Gabe... I hope the raid was successful.” Christian stretched in his seat. He was surprised when he heard Sam’s voice.

“Well, it was full of surprises, but a gold mine of intel.” Her voice seemed very relaxed.

Christian sat forward in his seat slightly. “Is Gabriel okay? Are you okay?” He figured if Sam was calling on Gabriel’s phone, maybe something was wrong.

“No... yeah... we’re fine,” Sam stammered to explain, realizing the cause for Christian’s concern. “Just thought I’d use the FBI’s dime to call you. We did lose a few of the ERU team. The warehouse was full of more exploding dead guys. I'm a bit freaked out still, but..." Sam's voice trailed off as though she was waiting for Christian to speak.

Christian keyed the phone over to speaker, and held it out so Rafeo could join the conversation.

"It's Sam," he explained as he did so.

"Hello, my dear," Rafeo announced his joining the conversation.

"Hi Raf..."

"How many men did you lose?" Christian asked, even though he didn't know the men, he still cared.

"Three," Sam answered quietly.

The car rolled on in silence again, as they all came to terms with the news.

"Was it worth it?" Christian finally asked.

"Well... we found a number of IED prototypes, some pretty complicated things. Weren't sure how they managed this level of complexity until we started identifying the victims. All of the people found here were listed as MIA from either Iraq or Afghanistan, and get this… they were all demolitions experts... all military special forces. So, we know whatever they're up to, it will involve more bombs or explosives." She hesitated for a moment.

"Sounds like a little more than snuff-heads and socially inept men trying to get laid." Sam may have been adding a jab at Gabriel for his earlier statement, but Christian wasn't sure.

"Definitely not the status quo," Christian thought to himself.

"Great..." he said quietly, and let Sam continue. They then heard Gabriel's voice join in on speaker phone.

"We've also identified the charred remains of a map of Cairo; it's a bit of a leap, but I'd be willing to bet they're going after the peace conference next month."

"That would make sense. Mabus wants to breed more hatred and evil in the world; it will help bolster his power. If enough of the human's embrace his ways, he may be able to overpower his counterpart and assume the Guardian's true position, even without the book," Rafeo explained. This didn't do anything to cheer up any of the others. The silence grew again.

"I'll text you some coordinates, Christian, and I will be going there, once we finish here. Can you meet us? We may be able to do something about all this, once we restore the Book to its original state."

There was a brief silence from the other end, before Gabriel spoke up.

"We'll be a few days cleaning up here, then I'm supposed to head over to Cairo with a team to help bolster security. We won't be far from these coordinates, I'm sure we can meet you there a couple of days after we arrive, and get things set up."

"We?" Christian asked. "Are you able to bring Sam with you?"

"I think that can be arranged."

"Alright, well... good luck to us all, and we'll see you in about a week," Christian said and flipped his phone shut.

"Yes, good luck," Sam answered, even though she knew Christian had hung up. She rolled over, and put the phone down on the night table. She paused for a moment in thought. She felt Gabriel's warm breath on her naked hip, then his lips as he kissed the small of her back. He ran his tongue up and down her back, giving her chills. Then Gabriel playfully bit down on her fleshy buttocks.

Sam let out a small yelp, and flipped around to come face to face with Gabriel. He was smiling playfully, and tried to nip at her midsection and breasts. Sam put her hands out to stop him, and took a moment to marvel at his form. She winked at him, then let her arms down, giving Gabriel access to her body. What began as some more playful biting soon turned to serious licking and kissing each other.

Gabriel positioned himself over Sam and entered her gently. They hadn't planned this or discussed it, and Gabriel almost expected her to object. Instead, she smiled, and wrapped her legs around his back.

"I think we have a tail," Christian said as he straightened up in his seat. They were nearing Auschwitz, and

Christian had been watching the vehicles behind them for some time.

"I know," Rafeo answered calmly, then reached into his pocket, and pulled out a piece of paper. It was a map of Auschwitz.

"We will slow down, and you can jump out after the curve up ahead. You should be able to get into the camp, here." He pointed at the lower left corner of the map.

"This is right by Block 11, and you need to get to here... Crematoria 1." Rafeo pointed to the top right corner of the map.

Christian looked back at Rafeo; he was unconvinced of the plan.

"They are expecting me," Rafeo explained. "I'll distract them as long as I can, and with any luck, will buy you enough time.", Rafeo smiled. Christian's change of expression relayed the fact that his confidence was growing.

"Now, the man at the car rental was a friend; look in the back, and see if you can find it."

Christian hesitated, then leaned his seat back, and got into the back seat. He lowered the fold-down seats, gaining access to the trunk.

"Find what?" he asked, as he groped around in the dark; then his hand came to rest on a gun case.

"Oh!" he said, as he pulled it out of the trunk and popped it open. He tucked a Sig Sauer 9mm into his pants, loaded the Steyr Aug Assault rifle, then rolled into the front seat again.

"Not my favorite plan, but this helps," he said, motioning towards the rifle as he spoke.

"Get ready..." Rafeo whispered as he pulled the hand brake slightly to slow the car down without showing the brake lights; they started into the turn.

"Now!" he yelled, and Christian popped open the door, and jumped away. He rolled into the ditch, then got to his feet, and put as much distance between himself and the road as he could before the following cars drove past.

Christian found his way into the camp. This place gave off a vibe that spoke the work 'evil'; this was made worse by the darkness of night and the thunderstorm that was rolling in on them. He made his way from building to building; so far, he had met no resistance.

There was a scream in the distance that caught Christian's attention.

"Raf…" he said to himself and ran into the nearest building and up to the top floor.

Rafeo had parked near the main gate, and walked calmly to the entrance. He paused to read the inscription over the gate.

Arbeit Macht Frei "Work makes you free," Rafeo translated out loud. "Maybe someday," he said quietly, then sat down, cross-legged in meditation, and waited.

He didn't need to wait long; within minutes, the other cars pulled in, and several men emptied out of them, including Quintus.

"So, you've decided to surrender, I see," Quintus said loudly.

"I didn't die here all those years ago, and I don't think I will be tonight, either," Rafeo answered without looking up.

"We shall see." Quintus motioned to his men. They moved out to surround Rafeo, still sitting calmly on the ground as the rain began to fall.

"Damn it, old man; don't just sit there." Christian was watching through his scope. He knew he had a job to do, and didn't want to give away his position by opening fire. Without any movement from Rafeo, Christian feared he may have no choice, and targeted the first man.

Before he could fire, he watched in amazement as Rafeo sprung backwards from a seated position to standing. This had caught his attackers off guard, as well, hesitating, even as Rafeo taunted them with a wave of his hand to attack.

A flash of light caught his attention, and he altered his view. He saw Quintus, and then he seemed to disappear. Within seconds, a sound right next to him caught his attention. Before he could bring his rifle around, Quintus kicked him, catching him in the midsection, splintering his rifle into pieces in the process. Christian fell backwards, and looked up at Quintus, who stood over him.

"Not that it would have done you much good." Quintus said, pointing to the broken weapon, in pieces on the ground. He then lunged at Christian, unleashing a flurry of punches and kicks.

Christian tried to block the attacks, and did manage, more from luck then design, to stave off any serious injuries. A split second later, Quintus landed a hard kick to his midsection, lifting him off the ground and sending him flying. Christian landed in a heap and Quintus strutted towards him very confidently. The smile on his face faded quickly as Christian rolled over and produced the Sig Sauer and fired on Quintus at point blank range.

Rafeo moved like grease lightning. His attacks were a blur. Though not intended to be fatal, it took more and more time for his opponents to get up again. His movements were what you would expect from a man who had studied martial arts for a millennium. He was surprised that three of the six men still had the will to fight; Quintus had found some rather committed devotees. With another flurry of punches and kicks,

Rafeo lowered the number of men he faced, from three to two, then he heard the shot in the distance.

"The Germans sure did come up with some terrible designs," Christian said, as he ran his hand over the bars in front of Quintus. Quintus struggled, not quite sure why he wasn't able to attack.

"These cells are barely wide enough to fit even one man, and they'd often stick two or more in there. Could you imagine?" Christian had found an interrogation cell, basically a closet barely a foot deep. They would put a man in the cell, pinning him between the wall and the bars in front, not allowing the prisoner to sit or lay down or move at all, really. Truly a disgusting apparatus, but he had to admit that it was being of use to him tonight; he sarcastically admired the Nazis in that moment.

Quintus began to yell, but Christian simply shot him in the neck.

"I can do this all night," he said, as the room fell silent. He watched the bullet hole heal right before his eyes.

"I know it won't kill you, but that's gotta hurt..." Christian winced at the thought, and rubbed his own throat. They stood silently and starred at each other. Quintus was scathingly furious for ending up trapped in this cell. He wasn't in the mood to speak to this mortal, and glared at his captor.

"You can stare at me like that all night; in fact, that's all you'll be able to do." Christian chuckled, making light of Mabus' situation, which only infuriated the prisoner more. Christian took in a deep breath and held it, before letting it out slowly, all the while staring right back at Quintus.

"So, you're the bad guy," Christian finally said quietly.

"I'm not the one shooting a defenseless prisoner," Quintus answered. He could see in Christian's face that what he said had an effect. They say that all evil needs to succeed is for good men to do nothing, but I say it's more expeditious… and more fun to have the good men commit the evil." Quintus smiled and tilted his head slightly; he was trying to play it off like the cage he was stuck in wasn't bothering him.

"Well, if I am one of the bad guys, you might not want to piss me off," Christian answered. He didn't want Quintus to know he was getting to him.

"You may want to come to a decision on that. Good guy, bad guy. Pick one."

Christian thought for a moment. He still had an objective, and this conversation wasn't getting him anywhere. He also wanted to get over to help Rafeo. Christian eyed Quintus closely, then shrugged.

"Fuck you," he answered flippantly, then raised his gun and shot him four times in the chest. Before Quintus could wake up again, Christian ran out.

Outside, he darted between buildings, making his way towards the crematoria. He could hear Quintus screaming from the cell where he had left him; he had recovered already, and wanted his men to come and free him.

Christian rounded another corner, and came face to face with Rafeo.

"Are you okay?" they both asked of each other simultaneously. With a shrug and a grin, they realized the answer to their own question and headed towards the crematoria again.

"I didn't actually see where the Guardian threw the pages, so as awful as it may be, we may need to sift around in the stoves for a while," Rafeo explained. They entered the building and saw the ovens ahead of them; they each opened one of the doors and began to reach inside. "...but when Quintus' men get up, they will let him out, and we'll have a real problem." As focused as he was on the mission, he had a hard time reaching into the crematorium. The evil of the Nazis still lingered here as though they had been in use yesterday.

"Got 'em!" Christian said quietly. Rafeo stopped at mid-thought, and slowly closed the door to the oven he was about to search. He had to admit that he was surprised, but relieved, at how fast Christian had found what they had come for.

"Well, that's good... nice to have some luck on our side.", he said slowly, then motioned for them to leave. They ran outside and sprinted back to the main gate and their car. They sped off into the night, leaving Quintus to wait for his men to regain consciousness before he would be free to pursue them, and by then, Rafeo knew they would be long gone.

CHAPTER 13

THEY DROVE FOR HOURS, STOPPING ONLY for gas and food. Each took turns driving and sleeping. They had heard reports of a suspected terrorist attack on Auschwitz, leaving two men dead. The news reports on the radio went on to say that the authorities had no leads, nor any understanding of the true nature of the event.

All the same, they pushed their car as hard as they dared, usually exceeding any posted speed limit by an acceptable margin.

When it was Christian's turn to sleep, he had dreams of Mary. He was trying to get to her before something happened, all the while something was chasing him. He didn't sleep much, but didn't really feel like talking, so he would keep his eyes closed, pretending, until it was his turn to drive.

After nearly sixteen hours, they arrived in a small Greek port town of Salonika, or Thessaloniki, as it was now known. It was interesting how, in a matter of sixteen hours, they had traveled through five other countries before arriving in Greece, losing sight of the Alps, and now to be in a completely different temperate

zone. Back home, they would have only been able to drive from one side to the other of their own country.

The scenery had changed dramatically from the cold gothic architecture of Austria to the red clay roofs of the villas in Croatia, and then on to the classic period buildings of Greece, not to mention ancient ruins dotting the landscape along the way.

Christian had always enjoyed history and culture. He had always wanted to visit this part of the world, meet its people, maybe even share a meal with someone from the area, but under these circumstances, he knew this was anything but a vacation.

Again, Rafeo spoke the language as though he was a native. He arranged passage to Jaffa Port in Israel, aboard a small private yacht. They sailed close to the coast, and along the way, they saw many splendid ruins left by ancient Greeks.

Thessaloniki is one of the busiest ports in the Mediterranean; they had to weave their way through a lot of traffic on the water, until they reached the open Aegean Sea. Christian and Rafeo stayed below deck for the first part of the voyage to avoid being seen unknowingly by any agent of Quintus. They sailed for Crete, and spent the night in a small private dock near Chersonisos, sleeping on board, again to lower their exposure.

The next morning, they were underway at first light, heading for Cyprus. As they passed near the north eastern point of Crete, Rafeo came upon Christian leaning on the railing, looking across the water to an island they were about to leave behind.

"You seem disturbed..." Rafeo finally said. He had felt some friction from Christian for some time now.

Christian smiled slightly. He wasn't exactly mad at Rafeo, only more unhappy with the situation. He paused, and pointed at a temple.

"It's beautiful," he said, with a hushed amazement. He smiled and turned to face the old man. "Hell, you've probably seen it when it was much newer."

They both paused, and smiled at his comment. It took a few seconds before the smile slipped from Christian's lips.

"I have a hard time thinking that this is all a result of a prison, or a mistake; Mankind is capable of so much wonder.", Christian explained, indicating the temple, to illustrate his point.

"Indeed..." Rafeo nodded, and looked down at his feet for a moment, before looking up at Christian; he leaned in to talk quietly to the younger man. "...but we are not a mistake; an unforeseen event, maybe..."

Christian's face betrayed his confusion. He had heard so much in the past few days, and was trying, desperately, to make sense of it all for himself.

"The Guardian didn't make the decision easily, to allow us to exist, but only after seeing our true worth. We are capable of so much, even more then what we know..." Rafeo spoke from the heart.

"You must have faith that you are here for a reason, that what you are doing is worthwhile." Rafeo explained.

"There's that word again." Christian thought to himself. "Faith...", he said aloud, with a hushed scoff and a wry smile. He turned slowly to face Rafeo. The other's face had no sign of the sarcastic amusement currently showing on Christian's face. Christian could feel his smirk slink away.

"Yes, faith," Rafeo answered forcefully. "I may know some things as facts, but that just makes my faith more important; there is nothing more important to any man." Rafeo was passionate on the subject; his faith had been the only thing to keep him focused, and he had floundered for nearly a millennium and a half.

"Yet it cannot be questioned or altered by anyone else. It is my own, and only for me to figure out." Rafeo allowed Christian to absorb that before continuing. He had switched from speaking in general terms to personal experience; the change had not been missed by Christian.

"The same is true for every other person alive."

Rafeo turned to lean on the side rail of the ship and looked out towards the shore. His face hardened even further, as though he was experiencing pain, and he turned again towards Christian.

"But, because it is so important, some will try to influence the faith of others, and that is where man falls into trouble."

He paused and admired the beauty of the sun rising out of the sea and bathing the ruins they were passing in a variety of colors.

"It also doesn't matter what you believe; it could be simple things, such as faith in the fact that the sun will rise." Rafeo paused briefly, indicating the cosmic light show unfolding before them while Christian pondered that point for a split second, and had to nod in agreement.

"If your faith tells you that any man is capable of beauty and kindness and able to rid himself of evil..." he trailed off, and shrugged. "Who am I to tell you that you are wrong? How could anyone?"

The ship sailed on for minutes before Rafeo spoke again. This time, he watched Christian for comprehension.

"It matters not wherein it lies, just that you have faith." The sound of his voice had barely faded before Christian smiled, as though comforted by a revelation Rafeo had helped him to see.

The seas were calm, and they were able to make port early that evening.

The next day of travel was uneventful. Christian was happy to arrive in Joffa Port. They thanked the crew of the ship and got directly into a 4x4 truck Rafeo had arranged, and drove across into Jordan.

Christian had never been in this part of the world before. He was amazed by the cultures, the food, the architecture, and enjoyed the differences. Rafeo spoke whatever language he needed at every stop. He knew the customs and guided Christian through every encounter so as not to offend anyone.

"So, where are we going?" Christian finally asked.

"To a safe place," Rafeo answered with a smile. They crested a hill and the terrain gave way to a spectacular sight – buildings carved right into the living rock. The unmistakable pink hue of the surrounding rocky terrain erupted out of the dessert. A once great civilization had flourished here, carving their lives out of their environment, literally. The pink sand stone mountains had been chiseled into buildings of beauty and splendor but the truly astonishing thing was less obvious to the untrained eye. The creators of this place had carved an oasis out of the desert –creating a series of channels and cisterns to collect and store rainwater.

"Petra," Christian said quietly. He recognized this place from the movies. "This is a World Heritage Site. You have a refuge in the middle of a UNESCO World Heritage site?" Christian was confused and in awe. He had always wanted to come here, albeit not under these circumstances.

"Hide in plain sight." Rafeo answered with a grin.

They parked the vehicle and grabbed their bags. They then joined a tour group going into the Treasury. As they moved through the structure, Rafeo held them back, and suddenly, they stepped through a wall. They were in another corridor.

"What the hell was that?" Christian asked with a hushed urgency.

"An optical allusion," Rafeo answered calmly as they continued down the hall.

"Aren't you afraid some archeologist might stumble onto your little trick?"

Rafeo shrugged. "They came close during the filming of Indiana Jones, but, really, this place can only be found by someone who knows it's here." They had reached the end of the hall at this point, and Rafeo stopped walking. He waited for Christian's reaction, and he was not disappointed.

The hallway opened up into a huge cavern. It was like a tiny ecosystem unto itself. There were insects and small animals, grass, plants, and even trees as far as the eye could see. A waterfall at the far end fed a small stream that ran through its entirety. Somehow, Christian could feel what felt like sunlight, although they were inside a cave, and even a gentle breeze lapped at their faces and carried the scent of wildflowers and honey.

The pathway ahead of them led down a small slope towards a small group of simple houses. Christian stood at its edge, staring, mouth agape. The breeze picked up, as if to greet them, and Christian closed his eyes and breathed deeply. He slowly turned to Rafeo, unable to do little more then gesture his disbelief as words escaped him.

"Welcome to the Garden of Eden.", Rafeo said with a smile; he didn't even attempt to hide his pride. Christian seemed almost hurt when he heard the name

"Wait... what?" He looked around in amazement. "The Garden of Eden?" he questioned, as though he knew the answer but still couldn't believe it.

"Sometimes the Quies simply wanted a place to come and be human and not have to worry about interfering with man," Rafeo explained.

"Yeah, a vacation from being God – makes sense." Christian let his sarcasm shine, and emphasized what he said with a bewildered shrug.

"When it was first used as a prison, this is where the fallen Quies were sent. The hope was to rehabilitate them, and all they had to do was follow simple rules; anything else they desired was provided for them. Some of them used those provisions and discovered ways they could hurt the Guardian, and the others..." Rafeo let his voice taper off, not really wanting to tell the rest. Christian raised his eyebrows repeatedly, letting Rafeo know that he had no intension of letting him off the hook.

"They once managed to summon one of the Quies to human form, at which point the 'prisoner' killed the Quies' mortal body and tried to ascend with the power of her Book."

"What? Like an escape plan?" Christian asked, as he regained his composure slightly. They began to walk towards a group of houses that sat in the middle of the cave just down the trail from where they were.

"Quite," Rafeo said with a nod. "After that, the fallen were forced out into the world and made to fend for themselves."

As they walked, Christian could not keep his eyes fixed on any one thing for very long as the overload of information become disorienting.

"The transformation process was altered, as well; no longer would they be able to retain so much knowledge from their life as a Quies. Much of the understanding of magic and power is lost to humans now – probably a good thing."

"Probably," Christian whispered. He wasn't completely sure what he had agreed to but didn't really care at the moment.

They walked on in silence until they were almost to the small village.

"Who lives here now?" Christian asked as he noticed a few people moving about the village attending to various tasks. There were some rolling dough and preparing bread; others tending a small vegetable garden; and yet another smithing metal at a forge. It was like they stepped back in time. The people noticed Rafeo, and stopped what they were doing to come and greet them.

"These are the hopefuls," Rafeo said, with a smile. "Those who I believe may be the Guardian, and other friends who have dedicated their lives to protecting and providing for the hopefuls."

It seemed like a truly utopian existence. Christian looked around, excited by the friendly faces. He hoped he would get a chance to speak to as many people as possible, simply to immerse himself deeper into the lore of the Guardian.

"We have lived like this for hundreds of years," Rafeo said proudly. The people gathered around Rafeo like children greeting their father after a business trip. Christian was suddenly troubled by the imagery and by what Quintus had said to him in Auschwitz. These people looked to Rafeo like a father figure or even more, similar to a cult. He shook the thought away as Rafeo introduced him to those gathered around them.

"Hello," he said as genuinely, still troubled by his sudden doubt in Rafeo, fleeting though it was.

A woman towards the back of the small crowd caught Christian's eye. She smiled, nodded and turned to return to her previous task. She was striking – dark complexion, with long flowing brown hair tied back under a handkerchief, her piercing blue eyes were brilliant, noticeable even at a distance. He felt as though he knew her somehow.

"Mary," he whispered and followed her with his eyes. This was the same woman that had haunted his dreams for years. She walked away from the gathering to return to her previous duties. The rest of the world seemed to fade into the background for Christian as he watched her. She turned to look back and smiled; his heart raced.

"Come, my boy." When Rafeo spoke, it surprised Christian and snapped him back to the present. He did have to shake his head to chase away his trance-like state. Rafeo noticed his reaction and waited, studying Christian quickly before smiling and continuing.

"You must be tired from your journey. I will show you to your quarters. You can wash up and rest before dinner."

Christian nodded and went with Rafeo. He did want to clean up before meeting the girl of his dreams.

They entered the first house. Rafeo motioned Christian to the room on the far side of the building.

"Make yourself comfortable, we may be here for a while. I must consult the library to see if I can learn how to restore this book." He indicated the Book of Power, and its missing pages. "I will send for you before supper."

Christian nodded, turned, and entered the room. He slowly closed the door and dropped his bag onto the bed. There was a wash basin on the dresser; he stripped his shirt off and immediately began to wash the desert dust from his face and body. As he did, he stared into the mirror. A multitude of questions raced through his mind, especially about the girl. Who was she?

He braced himself on the dresser, and stared into his own eyes as if the answers were there. He took stock as he stared at himself and the many scars that adorned his body. He could see the bullet wounds from where he had been shot in the church and many others, each baring a memory more painful than the physical wound. His arms began to shake. He wanted to scream, but held it in. He tried not to let his past dictate his future, but when tired or stressed, it all seemed to come out and kick him when he was down.

A knock at the door startled him back from his thoughts. For a moment, he had to consider how long had he been standing there. Was it dinner time, already? He awkwardly shuffled to the door.

"Yeah... I'm…I'm coming. Sorry, Raf, I was just thinking" He swung the door open, only to come face to face with the girl. She looked down, slightly, so as not to make eye contact with him.

"Mary?" he inquired. She looked up at him, slowly betraying a moment of surprise at him knowing her name.

"Yes, that is my name," she responded, with a quiet smile, and looked down again shyly. "I suppose Rafeo told you my name?"

Christian had to think for a moment – maybe the old man had said something.

"Yeah, I guess," he said eventually, not wanting to blurt out the entire story and scare her off completely.

"If you require a clean shirt, I can see if someone here has something in your size," Mary said awkwardly, still looking towards the floor.

It still took Christian a few seconds to realize he had answered the door shirtless.

"Ah... shit. Sorry!" he apologized and rushed to the bed and pulled his T-shirt over his head. "I was just... well, I was just washing up." He finished the sentence with a little more assuredness.

"Of course," Mary answered, looking up at him with a smile.

"We have prepared a welcome meal in the courtyard. If you care to accompany me?" she offered with a smile, then turned on her heel and walked towards the main door of the hut, then out towards the center of the village.

The table was massive, able to accommodate at least thirty people. It was set for twenty-four this time. The dishes were simple wooden plates with typical utensils. There were candles, and what could only be described as a feast; roasted meat and what looked like a spit-roasted pig, potatoes and fresh vegetables, and homemade bread.

Christian stood awkwardly to the side and watched as others placed dishes and carafes full of wine around the table. Others took their seats, some ripped into the fresh bread and ate, while they waited for the rest of those still to come.

Christian felt as though he had stepped back in time. He was overcome with the serenity of the scene before him. He could not remember the last time he had shared a meal with anyone, let alone a group of this size. He had always preferred his solitude, and realized he was becoming slightly uncomfortable feeling like he did not belong.

"Come, boy. Sit, and eat with us.", Rafeo said with a slap on Christian's shoulder as he walked up from behind.

"Yes, of course.", Christian answered, feeling shy for the first time in many years. He took a seat near the end of the table where Rafeo was seated. He had to admit he was extremely happy when Mary sat across from him.

All of the seats around the table were quickly filled and the group fell silent. Rafeo stood and held up his glass.

"My friends...let us eat," he said simply, then took a large gulp of his wine before sitting down again. Christian joined the others in the toast. When the liquid from the glass reached his tongue, he could not believe the flavor. He had never considered himself a wine connoisseur, but this was the most incredible wine he had ever tasted.

"Guess we learn a thing or two about wine making over a few millennia, huh, boy?", Rafeo winked, having obviously noticed Christian's reaction. "Mind yourself though, it packs a hell of a punch!" Rafeo laughed.

The food was passed around. With every bite, Christian was stunned by the sensation that accompanied the food. He had previously eaten everything being served, but never to this level of enjoyment. Christian smiled, and took another deep drink of his wine. He placed the glass on the table, and looked around before turning to Rafeo.

"So, who are all these people?" he asked.

"Most are what is left of the Magi. They live here and help protect and provide for the hopefuls," Rafeo explained. He seemed proud, much like the patriarch of a large family.

"Hopefuls?" Christian noticed his head was a little cloudy already, from the wine.

Rafeo finished chewing and swallowed before answering. "Mm-hmm. Years ago, when the Guardian was first lost to us, the heavens would foretell his reincarnation. All we'd have to do is study the stars, interpret their message, and race against Quintus to get to his human form first, in the hope of restoring the Guardian. Lately, however, the interpretations are far vaguer." Rafeo took another bite of food from his plate. He looked around the table while he chewed and swallowed.

"Now to be safe, I bring anyone who is born under a sign to this place. Mary and many others..." He gestured around the table, and Christian followed with his eyes. "...are potentially the Guardian, trapped in a human body. We won't be able to know until the book is restored."

Christian stared across the table now at Mary, the implications of Rafeo's explanation now sinking in.

"This woman was possibly… God?" he thought to himself. He reached down and took up his glass, emptying its contents down his throat.

"That's gotta do something to your mind..." Christian blurted out. If the statement bothered Mary, she didn't show it. She simply swallowed a piece of meat she had been chewing, looked up at Christian and smiled.

"I am only a hopeful," she explained. "I try not to think about it, actually."

"Probably best," Christian answered in amazement at her seemingly casual answer.

The dinner ended. As Christian rose from his seat, he fell over backwards, not realizing the full effects of the wine until that moment. He let out a slight laugh at his situation.

"Did I not warn you?" Rafeo grinned, leaning over the table to look down at Christian, lying on the ground.

Christian could only shrug and grin in response.

"Come on, boy. Up with you." Rafeo helped Christian to his feet, then gestured for Mary to help him.

"I must get back to the library," he explained. "Can you see this one to his quarters?"

Mary smiled shyly again, then stepped in closer to Christian. He put his arm over her shoulders for support. They took one step, then he stopped, and looked into her eyes.

"Get some rest, boy. You'll need a clear head in the morning – I've got a mission for you."

Christian wasn't sure what was meant by that, and right now he didn't really care. The old man chuckled, then turned towards the library.

"Guess you're stuck with me… sorry," he said with a fleeting grin.

"Oh, I think I can handle it," Mary answered, then moved towards the building that Christian was housed in. The walk seemed long to Christian and neither one spoke until they reached his door.

There was a slight, gentle breeze, and a faint sound of music.

"Do you hear that?" he asked, as he held a finger up in front of him, as though it would help him hear. "... sounds like wind chimes."

Mary paused, and listened for a moment.

"'Tis the wind… and nothing more," she answered. Christian stared at her again. Her answer had surprised him. He studied her face now, noticing her deep blue eyes, the redness of her lips, and the way the wind blew a few stray strands of hair into her face.

"I trust you can..." Mary started but was cut off as Christian leaned in and kissed her. After a moment, Christian could feel her kiss him, too. Their tongues met gently, as their lips pressed lightly together. The moment lasted mere seconds before Mary pulled back slowly. Christian sighed and opened his eyes in time to see her hand racing towards his face.

"How dare you!" she demanded.

"Wow! Whoa!" he pleaded. "Wait! This isn't what you think! I know I'm drunk, but... here it is." He braced himself against the door and took a deep breath. Before he could continue, the door opened against his weight, and he fell to the floor.

He was surprised to see Mary come to his aid and help him to his feet. She quickly stepped away from him, though. He could see a look of pain or anger in her eyes, and he held up his hand to keep her from speaking.

"This may sound crazy, but I... I love you," Christian slurred.

Mary shook her head. "No," she said plainly.

"Yup," he answered with a grin.

"You cannot."

"Well, it's a long and sort of strange story, but hear me out," he insisted.

"No... I mean, you cannot; it is forbidden for me."

Christian was taken aback by this and scowled for a moment. "What? Forbidden? By who?"

"It is forbidden for a hopeful to become romantically entwined," she explained.

Christian tilted his head, and stared at her in disbelief. He straightened up and shook his head.

"Before you make a decision you might regret, ask yourself if this is that what you believe, or is it what someone told you to believe?"

"Typical man. You don't like the answer, so you blame everything else." Mary's voice was raised, and she was far from the quiet shy girl she had been up to this point. "Well, here's something else for you – I'm not even attracted to you." She paused, and stared at him. "So, what about that?" She paused and waited for his reply.

"I'm sorry," he said quietly, and sat down on the bed. She looked at him for what felt like an eternity. Then she waved her hand in the air. "Whatever," she answered and walked out, closing the door behind her.

Christian sat on the bed for a few moments longer, trying to absorb what had just happened. His heart was pounding and his mind racing. His dreams had always been different, and it had never occurred to him that she would not feel the same.

He became agitated and stood up. He looked around the room, trying to think of what to do. From a lack of options, he wandered over to the door and stepped outside. It was dark outside, as though the passing from day to night had an effect within the cavern. He closed his eyes and felt the gentle breeze lap against his face. He could hear the wind chimes; the pleasant melody was so calming, he felt as though he could be lost within the sound.

"'Tis the wind and nothing more...". He repeated the words quietly to himself and the silence. He stood there with his eyes closed for a few minutes longer, wishing that when he opened them, Mary would be there.

He opened his eyes and found himself still alone. The wind had died, and with it, the sound of the chimes. He took a deep breath, turned and walked back into his room. He slowly pulled his shirt off over his head and dropped it on the floor. Feeling almost surreal, he carefully lowered himself onto his bed and lay there awake, thinking he would never find slumber that night.

CHAPTER 14

THE NEXT MORNING ARRIVED GENTLY FOR Christian. He awoke to the sound of a song bird singing near his window. He was amazed by the way the sun seemed to rise, even within the cavern. He felt better rested than he could remember in recent days.

He lay in his bed, staring at the ceiling. His mind began to wander through all of the events of the past few days. It didn't take long for the wandering to become racing. Rafeo's resurrection, the knowledge of the Quies... even knowing of the Garden of Eden and the hopefuls.

"The hopefuls..." he repeated slowly, then cringed. "Mary… What did I do?" His thoughts were now fixed solely on the previous night. He wasn't sure if he felt embarrassed or just rejected. His dreams, his feelings, they had all felt so real, still did, although he could not justify it. He rolled out of the covers and sat on the edge of the bed with his head in his hands. He felt so different, here; last night had felt like high school all over again; the excitement of talking to a woman, all of it... and right now, he cared not to think of how many years ago high school actually was.

"Oh, this should be a fun morning...", he grunted and rubbed his face in a vain attempt to chase away his awkward feeling. He stood and walked to the wash basin, and splashed some water in his face. It felt good, but did little to change how he felt.

"Let's hope this mission Raf has for me will be a good distraction.", he said aloud again as he looked in the mirror. He then stopped, and could not help but grin.

"Let's hope you, at least, stop talking to yourself." He raised one eyebrow, then turned away from the mirror to get dressed.

He walked out of his room into the morning air, nervous that he would come face to face with Mary. Instead, there stood Rafeo. He wore an odd grin on his face; odd in the fact that the man did not grin very often. Christian could not help but think the old man was aware of what had happened last night.

"Morning, boy," Rafeo said loudly, and motioned Christian over towards him. "I trust you slept well." There was no sarcastic tone, Christian was relieved, and actually did think back to his night's sleep.

"Indeed, I did." Christian started feeling his guilt dissipate.

"Good." Rafeo's grin returned slightly.

"You said you had a mission for me?", Christian hoped to avoid any further questions from Rafeo.

"Indeed. Though it is now two-fold."

Christian furled his brow, silently inviting Rafeo to continue.

"First, I will need you to pick up a few old friends at the airport in town."

"Who?" Christian asked.

"Gabriel and Sam will be joining us. They have some information we might need."

"Good. We could use an extra gun-hand." Christian was very relieved to hear they were coming, though he wasn't sure why his thoughts automatically went to strategic defenses. He paused, noticing Rafeo was looking at him with probably the same question in his mind, and shook his head.

"It'll be good to see some friends, ...and second?"

Rafeo turned slightly and pointed to an awaiting vehicle.

"Shopping." Rafeo grinned again, wider than the last. Christian could see a few people waiting within the large SUV.

"Huh..." Christian stammered, having been taken completely off guard.

"The hopefuls usually travel to town for market every other day.", Rafeo explained walking towards the vehicle. "They need the interaction… they are not prisoners here."

The words seemed to help disprove the warning Christian had received from Quintus back in Auschwitz. He smiled in relief.

"I want you to keep an eye on them; protect them. I feel the enemy may be closer than we can tell."

"Makes sense." His heart sank slightly as they had reached the vehicle and he could see inside. Mary sat in the passenger seat, waiting and smiling at Christian.

He panicked slightly, before another thought occurred to him. He held up his hand nervously, to gesture to those in the car that he would need a moment.

"Uh... do you have an armory here?", he asked Rafeo. The old man chuckled, and faster than Christian expected, he drew two pistols from around his back.

"I figured you might need these; one for Gabriel, as well.", he handed the weapons to Christian. Then, with his free hand, he drew a third and held it, as though pointing at Christian. The young man gave Rafeo a glance; he never quite knew how to take Rafeo. ...did he really trust him? Perhaps it was an unspoken warning to stay away from Mary, or just Rafeo horsing around.

"One for Sam, as well," he spun the gun around to hand Christian the handle.

Christian took the weapon with a wry smile and tucked it away. His attention returned to the occupants of the SUV, and his nervous grin returned.

"Well, I guess we're all set.", he said with a shrug of defeat, and walked to the driver's door.

"GPS?" he asked Rafeo, hoping to stall some more.

"Of course… I may be old, but not old fashioned," Rafeo answered, again with a grin.

"Of course...", Christian said under his breath. Then, with a sigh, he opened the door, and got into the vehicle, ready to face the music.

He slid into the leather seat without making eye contact with anyone and fumbled for the ignition key.

"Good morning, Chris," Mary said warmly, and placed a hand on his forearm. He paused for a moment and looked at her hand, then turned to face her. The look on her face was not at all what he expected; she wore an honest and affectionate smile. Despite how he felt, he couldn't help but return the smile, his heart slowing as he took a deep breath. His eyes darted back to her hand which was still on his arm, then back to her eyes.

"Hi..." he sounded like a love-struck school boy, before remembering there were others in the vehicle. His eyes then focused on the rear-view mirror where he three other sets of eyes met his own – two women and one man sat, waiting to depart.

"Morning all," Christian spoke quickly, as Mary moved her hand from his arm. He hoped that none of the other's had picked up on his nervous exchange with Mary. They all greeted him in turn, and he started the vehicle.

The road out of the cavern emerged from a crevasse in the hillside; a matter of a few feet away he could no longer identify the spot in the rear-view mirror. He keyed the airport into the GPS and continued on his way. Another vehicle emerged behind him.

"At least I ain't the only babysitter today," he thought to himself.

They pulled up to the airport and found parking. Christian stepped out of the vehicle and took a long, cautious look around. He motioned to the others in the second vehicle to take up defensive positions while he retrieved Gabriel and Sam. He had to stop himself and remove his weapon, tucking it into the inside door flap of the truck before carrying on into the airport. His credentials would probably not be sufficient here to explain him carrying a gun into an airport.

He stood at the arrivals gate and waited. In no time he could see Sam and Gabriel walking down the ramp towards customs. He was surprised to see them walking hand in hand. He was unsure how to feel about this, knowing all that Sam had gone through at the hands of the cult he had rescued her from. Sam smiled in a way he had not seen in a very long time, and he couldn't help but feel better... a little.

They had made it through customs in no time. Gabriel's credentials held a bit more sway than Christian's.

"Chris!" He heard Sam's voice and waved to greet them both. He noticed they were still holding hands.

"Hey!" He approached with a renewed spring in his step and gave Sam a hug and Gabriel a firm hand shake.

"I can't tell you how glad I am you're here," Christian greeted them with a warm smile.

"Wait till you hear what we have to tell you; the good feeling might not last." Gabriel answered, and took Sam's hand again.

"This is new." Christian pointed at their joined hands. It appeared as though Gabriel went to pull his hand away but Sam caught him.

"And?" she asked defensively, knowing she could shut down the criticism before it came. She wished to spare Gabriel the awkward big brother line of questioning.

Christian walked a few paces further before he shrugged. "Just making an observation… not a judgment." Christian led them towards the exit. He didn't see the smile and relief that Sam and Gabriel exchanged, but he knew it had happened.

They had made their way out of the terminal. Before reaching the vehicle, Christian stopped. He wanted to talk business without anyone else over hearing.

"You look like shit, by the way." Christian pointed at the scruff growing on Gabriel's face.

"You're one to talk." Gabriel rubbed his face out of reflex. He had to admit to himself that he did wish he had shaved on the plane. "And thanks for that, by the way."

"Sure," Christian answered sarcastically.

"Yeah! It's been a hell of a week. Not sure of the last time I had a good night's sleep." Gabriel threw a quick glance and a smile at Sam. She tried to stifle her reaction, unsuccessfully.

"I know the feeling. Maybe not for all the same reasons." Christian looked between the two and smiled. There was a short pause in the conversation; everyone knew what was meant by the comment, and each of them enjoyed it on a different level.

"We found all kinds of intel on these guys, though," Gabriel answered quickly.

"These bastards are everywhere," Sam interrupted. She was accustomed to briefing Christian. She looked at Gabriel, who didn't seem to have a problem with her taking over the conversation.

"They seem to be planning a terrorist attack on the peace conference here in three weeks. Worst of all, we've learned that they have enlisted the help of several US military specialists – we found their fingerprints all over the place." She paused for a moment, crossed her arms, and somberly added, "Their specialty training was in explosives and IEDs."

They fell silent for a minute as Christian absorbed the information.

"Gabriel will be leading a special security team; they arrive one week before the conference. We're here to check things out," Sam explained.

That may come in handy," Christian answered.

"They're up to all kinds of no good." Gabriel spat the words, reminding Christian how much he hated to lose.

They started to walk towards the vehicles again, and Christian pointed as he spoke.

"I'm escorting a group of potential Quies," he said flatly. He hadn't noticed that Gabriel and Sam had stopped walking right away. Finally, he did, and stopped and turned to face them again.

"What?" he could see the looks of surprise on their faces.

"Quies?" Sam asked "Do you mean… the Guardian?"

"Yeah. They refer to them as the Hopefuls, though I couldn't imagine hoping for a burden like that."

They fell silent again. Gabriel walked closer to the SUV and curiously tried to look inside before turning back to Christian.

"So, one of them could be…?" he trailed off.

"Apparently..."

"And what the hell are you doing driving around with them? They must be targets?" Sam asked frantically.

"We're going shopping," Christian answered with a small grin.

"That reminds me… you guys strapped?"

"No," Gabriel answered quickly, suddenly feeling naked without his sidearm.

Christian opened the door of the truck and took out the sidearms he'd brought from Rafeo, and gave one to each.

"Shopping?" Sam tucked the holstered gun into the back of her pants.

"Yeah," Christian answered, sarcastically again. They fell silent and looked around.

"We need to sit down and fully compare notes afterwards. Where are you staying?" Gabriel asked.

"Oh, you'll like it. It's like a paradise." Christian smiled and raised his eyebrows.

CHAPTER 15

MARY DIRECTED THEM THROUGH THE CITY towards the old town-center to the location of the centuries old open-air market. Christian had never done any sort of protection work, although he had received training in the military, and was aware of the complexities. He was anxious, knowing the sheer scope of the task at hand – a large open and public area, filled with people, any of whom could be the enemy.

His anxiety was made worse by the fact that their vehicle, a black SUV, stood out like a sore thumb. The fact that there were two of them weaving through the streets of Amman seemed to shout that they were transporting VIPs. He had also noticed a heightened sense of alertness from Gabriel.

His eyes darted down every side street or back alley they crossed, expecting an attack that fortunately never came. He couldn't help but notice the number of buildings displaying bullet holes, like scar tissue on the living city.

Christian tried desperately not to allow his nervousness to be picked up by Mary and the other hopefuls. It wasn't easy, and he was sure things would get worse once they left the relative safety of the vehicles.

They pulled over and stopped where Mary indicated a decent place to park.

"We're only a couple of blocks from the market here," she explained. Christian put the vehicle into park. He watched to make sure the second vehicle had room to park close to them, then shut the ignition off. He quickly made eye contact with Gabriel through the rearview mirror.

"Let's shop," Gabriel said sarcastically, indicating his own discomfort with the situation.

Mary had heard his tone and quickly turned to Christian. She appeared nervous until Christian quickly put a smile on his lips.

"Sounds like fun," he said, nearly convincing even himself.

They got out of the vehicle. Christian tried very discreetly to adjust the position of the gun he had slipped into the back of his pants waistline.

They were joined by the others from the second vehicle. Gabriel and Christian quickly organized the other security personnel who they sent ahead into the market. They placed their earpieces that Gabriel had supplied, into their ears and separated.

In the meantime, Sam introduced herself to the other hopefuls she had not yet met. She was good at disguising her true emotions, and looked more like just 'one of the girls', ready to shop. She blended in quite well, as the majority of the hopefuls were, in fact, women.

As they approached the entrance to the market, Christian's nervousness was replaced by astonishment; he had never experienced a sight such as this. A large collection of what were little more than tents stretched out all around them, each one housing a different merchant's wares. There was fresh produce, dates, nuts, clothing, handmade rugs. pottery, and silver crafts. He knew he couldn't afford to be a tourist, but he was amazed at the beauty of the place.

It also struck him that this market lasted for countless generations, with the same families passing on their culture and skills from one generation to the next. Although a stranger to these lands, Christian felt a connection to the history of this place.

"You don't need to be nervous you know," Mary said with a smile. She took Christian's arm, the act of which was enough to make him nervous for another reason. He turned and tried his best to smile. He wondered if she was aware of her double entendre.

"We've been here many times without security and have never had a problem."

"Sorry," Christian answered with a sheepish grin, and couldn't stop himself from quickly looking down at her arm as they slowly walked arm in arm.

"It's in my nature, I guess." He finished his thought and looked back into her eyes. Mary smiled at him, leading him to believe that she was referring to more than the matters of security.

"I will be your guide." She carried a smile and led him towards the first group of tents. Christian looked back at Gabriel and Sam. Gabriel had made an effort to look around, as though he hadn't noticed their exchange, but Sam wore a devilish smile. Apparently, she had noticed Christian's reaction to Mary and she wasn't shy about letting him know.

The first few vendors offered a variety of fresh fruits and vegetables. Mary slipped her arm from Christian's so she could handle some of the produce and make a selection; Christian took the opportunity to look around carefully.

Mary placed her purchases in a bag she carried on her other arm and quickly took Christian's arm again.

"Did you want me to…?" Christian gestured towards her bag, indicating he would carry it for her.

"No, I'm fine," she answered quickly, then turned to face him. "Thank you, though."

Christian's mind was racing, and his heart was pounding. He could not quantify to himself the attraction he felt for her. He wanted to grab her, and kiss her, but he recalled their conversation from the night before. He felt as though she was leading him on, but he knew he could not react.

She led them down the alley towards the next vendor.

"So, why do you think you are here?" she asked, as they walked slowly, arm in arm. Christian did not answer right away. The first response that came to mind he dared not say. He wanted desperately to tell her, again, how he felt, but even more desperate was his desire for her to feel the same. He knew that was not the case, however. He cleared his throat to buy himself some time, while he considered his answer.

"Well…to make sure you're safe," he answered finally.

Mary cocked her head slightly, and her eyes narrowed.

"I didn't mean here, as in the market. I meant here as in involved with Rafeo, and us. Why are you involved in this whole struggle of the hopefuls, Mabus, Constantine, the battle of Good versus Evil?"

Christian had to admit to himself that he had been so occupied since the very beginning with trying to understand the situation and had simply gotten caught up with the whole thing, that he had never considered his purpose. Was it chance, destiny, or something else that had involved him here?

"Maybe, I'm here for a second chance," he answered finally.

"Second chance?"

"I've always done the right thing for the wrong reason, or the wrong thing for the right reason." He allowed her time to guess what he meant. They walked on, their heads on a swivel, taking in the many sights and sounds, though Mary stayed very engaged in the conversation. "I joined the priesthood because I thought that's what everyone else wanted me to do. I left that because I became angry with God." He paused again to see her reaction, he feared she may think less of him for it. No reaction came. "I joined the military because I thought that's what I wanted to do. Then was thrown out of that because I..." he trailed off not wanting to go into the details.

"I got involved with investigating cults because I figured I had to. Altogether, it's all taken a toll on my life. I felt lost, if I'm honest. But since running into Rafeo that day, and getting involved with all of this, it's just felt like the right thing to do; this time, I feel like I need to be here."

Mary nodded and stopped in front another vendor's display. This time, it was at a bladesmith's shop. She looked over the weapons spread out on a table and picked up one of them – a long knife with a seemingly simple handle of formed metal, wrapped in leather. She removed it from the scabbard, revealing a blade, slightly curved and stamped with Arabic symbols. The blade was well made and very sharp. Without saying a word, Mary purchased the knife and gave it to Christian.

"Perhaps all of what came before happened in order to prepare you for this," she said with a confident look in her eye as she handed the knife to him.

Christian was taken aback, and it took a few seconds to take the knife she offered. Even when it was in his hand, he could still only stare into her eyes. What she said had made sense.

"Everyone deserves a second chance," she concluded.

Christian blinked, then looked over the knife he was holding.

"I guess that is true," he said quietly, then looked back into her eyes. "Why did you buy this for me?"

"You never know if you'll need it," she said flatly. "Don't worry, in this country, it is acceptable to wear a knife on your belt in public."

It took Christian a few seconds, again, to pull his mind away from their other conversation.

"Yeah," he answered finally, and affixed the knife to his belt.

They walked on again. Christian looked around, as though remembering for the first time in a while, that he had a duty to perform, as well. He noticed that Sam and Gabriel had fallen back slightly. Sam was examining some silk wares at a shop a little way back.

"And you?" Christian asked, as he turned his attention back to Mary.

"Do you believe that you are here as a hopeful?" He implied a question he didn't know how to ask.

"I believe in the Quies, and the story of the Guardian. Whether or not I am she… I don't know."

"I'm not sure I'd want that burden," Christian said with a shrug. She had years to come to terms with all of this, Christian thought to himself.

Before they could say another word, Christian's earpiece began to sing.

"Three o'clock... danger close." It was Gabriel's voice.

Without hesitation, Christian spun to his right, and grabbed the person standing there. He swung the would-be attacker's hands behind his back, and slammed him down, head first onto a table. He had to pause to see who he had detained. By this time, Gabriel and Sam had caught up to them. Christian was shocked to realize he had grabbed a boy, no older then 13 years old. Christian's eyes darted between the boy and a very surprised Mary. He quickly began to feel guilty, until he noticed the boy holding Mary's purse.

"He's only a pick pocket." Mary reached out for Christian's hands, and gently persuaded him to release the child. "It's okay," she pleaded, noticing Christian was incredibly focused on detaining the boy. When he felt her touch, he relaxed and quickly let the boy up.

"Some of these kids are homeless and have no family.", Mary explained, as she looked the boy over to ensure he was uninjured.

Christian felt incredibly guilty. He took out an American one-hundred-dollar bill and handed it to the boy.

"Sorry kid," he said with a shrug, and handed the boy the money.

The boy grabbed it, and without a word, spun on his heels and ran off.

"What the hell?" Gabriel asked, having arrived in time to see the boy run off.

"It's okay," Christian said, gesturing with his hands. "Just a pick pocket."

Gabriel looked around. He couldn't help but notice a lot of people looking at them. "This was fun, but I think we've worn out our welcome."

Christian nodded as Gabriel spoke instructions to be heard by everyone with an earpiece. "I think the field trip is over. Let's all get back to the vehicles."

Christian watched for the other teams to move, then nodded at Gabriel and walked Mary towards the market exit.

They approached the vehicles. Christian, Gabriel and Sam were busy scanning doorways and roof tops for any sign of trouble. Christian, still looking around, opened the door for Mary, after seeing the other hopefuls into the SUV. She stopped before getting in and kissed Christian on the cheek. His eyes snapped quickly from their scanning motion, and focused on Mary. He took in the beauty of her eyes and the fullness of her lips; he even smelled the fragrance of her hair.

"Thank you," she said, with a big smile. Christian could not muster a response, having been taken off-guard, yet again. The puzzled look on his face prompted Mary to continue. "For being my guardian."

Mary got into the vehicle. Christian closed the door, then found himself standing next to the SUV, quite unable to even move for a moment. His mind was swirling over this kiss and the indication that she was not attracted to him – or so she said. Was there a meaning to her choice of word 'Guardian'? Did she simply mean 'protector', or had she used that word on purpose?

He slowly turned and walked around the front of the vehicle. He tried to hide his confusion, avoiding eye contact with Mary. Instead, he noticed Sam looking back at him from the other vehicle. The smile on her face betrayed the fact that she had seen their exchange. He wanted to scream, and would have, if he believed it would actually help.

Christian climbed into the driver's seat. He started the truck without saying a word. Eventually, he looked across at Mary. She sat quietly smiling, looking out the window. She turned to face him and he awkwardly returned the smile. Glancing into the rearview mirror, he noticed the others in the back looking at him. Christian shook off his line of thought and forced himself to focus on his duty. He radioed to the other vehicle that they were set, and urged them to lead the way.

CHAPTER 16

THEY ARRIVED BACK AT EDEN THAT evening. Christian wished he could see Gabriel and Sam's first reaction to the garden as they pulled in, but they were in the other vehicle. He parked the vehicle and shut it off, then smiled and nodded as the others exited and thanked him for the ride.

Christian wanted to talk to Mary but decided against it, opting instead to offer Sam and Gabriel an introduction to the Garden of Eden. He walked around the back of the SUV towards the other vehicle to find Sam and Gabriel, mouths open, staring dumbfounded into the cave. He walked up beside them and gave them a few more seconds to adsorb the wonder of this place. He wondered if his reaction had been similar.

"How…" Sam stuttered. "How is this possible?" Her voice hushed. Christian smiled, and shortly, the other two turned to face him with a look begging for an explanation.

"Sam, Gabriel – welcome to the Garden of Eden." Christian allowed that information to sink in, as they stood quietly for a moment. Sam's head turned back and forth in disbelief between Christian, and the cave.

"The Garden of…?" Christian nodded in return, not needing Sam to finish her question.

"Oh, my God."

Christian smiled. "Exactly. Come, by the looks of things, they have dinner ready.", Christian said, gesturing for his two friends to follow. "If you think it looks good, wait till you try the food. There's something about this place that seems to heighten all the senses." He led the way down to the tables in the middle of the village.

"All the senses?" Gabriel asked quietly, finally having found his voice.

Sam couldn't hide a grin at the thought of Gabriel's suggestion. Christian turned back to look at them.

"I wouldn't know about that… but I'm sure you can tell me about it." He raised an eyebrow, and continued on towards the village.

Dinner conversation was rather uneventful – mostly a recap of the day's events about the shopping and the little bit of excitement from the pick pocket. Christian found himself sitting back and enjoying the conversation more than he expected. He also took joy in the experiences of his friends. Having gone through the sensory overload that seemed to come from something as simple as eating a meal only recently, he felt as though he could anticipate their reaction to certain events.

Christian also felt himself taking more ownership of his situation. Maybe it was because of his talk with Mary, but he felt as though he was more than a spectator, or someone simply in the wrong place at the wrong time now. He felt helpless but to stare at her. The way the gentle breeze caught her long, naturally curly brown hair, and gently brushed it over her face. The way she would always gently move it away from her eyes without any sign of being bothered by it. The curve of her cheek bones, and her piercing blue eyes. He also admired the nape of her neck. He was still in disbelief about the kiss and her motifs.

"This steak is amazing." Gabriel's voice brought Christian's attention back to his friends, but his eyes had not left Mary quickly enough. Though Gabriel didn't say anything, Christian knew he had been caught staring at her.

"Oh, I know" Christian answered, trying to appear innocent, though he knew he had been unsuccessful. Gabriel didn't comment, but the look in his eyes gave it away.

"Try the wine," Christian continued quickly, after clearing his throat. Gabriel raised an eyebrow, and lifted his glass. Sam joined in, and the two touched glasses and took a deep drink from their vessels. Neither of the two was able to stifle their reaction.

"It's incredible," Sam said, as she lowered her glass and looked between Gabriel and Christian. Before anyone could say anything, Rafeo spoke from the head of the table.

"So, we know our attention is being divided," he said calmly, and looked at those closest to him, those being Gabriel, Sam and Christian. "We know they are going after the peace conference. They are also, and have always been, after the hopefuls. They also know that I am desperately trying to restore the book with the recovered pages. I fear the seed of Evil is growing."

The table fell silent, momentarily, then the hopefuls began to clear away the dinner dishes, leaving the four to finish their discussion.

"What is the seed of Evil?" Christian asked, though he was privately watching every move Mary made. "Quintus made mention of it back in Auschwitz. I didn't know what it meant, and hadn't thought about it until now."

Rafeo looked around the table. "Join me in my study," he stated, then stood and walked away. The other three looked amongst themselves and slowly rose from their seats.

Sam and Gabriel lead the way, heading towards what was more like a cave that had naturally formed in the side of a rocky hill near the middle of the Garden.

En route, Christian noticed Mary standing near the edge of the stream that flowed past the small village. He could not help himself from walking to her. She turned slowly to face him; her face barely lit from the light of the distant fires of the village. They stood, staring at each other, for what felt like an eternity. Without saying a word, Christian leaned in, and kissed her softly on the lips. She returned the kiss for a moment, then put her hand on his chest, and pushed him away.

"I believe Rafeo is waiting for you," she said and turned, but not before a single tear rolled down her cheek. She walked back towards the village, leaving Christian alone, and once again confused. When he turned back towards the study, he saw Rafeo standing in the entrance watching him.

"I shall call you Quick," he said loudly, as Christian approached.

"Quick?"

"Indeed. You do move fast, Rafeo explained, looking disturbed from the display he had witnessed.

Christian stopped and looked him in the eye. He smirked, but held his gaze.

"Oh, that." Chrisitan looked back over his shoulder to the village and Mary, before looking back at Rafeo. "I'm not about to explain myself to you, or anyone," Christian said flatly, then walked past Rafeo and into the study.

Inside the cave was a chamber lit only by candles and oil lamps. The walls were covered in scraps of paper each containing words and phrases, some in English, but many others in a variety of languages. Sam and Gabriel stood in the center of the room, looking around in amazement.

Christian walked closer to the walls in order to read what words he could.

One shall fall. One shall stand.
One shall embody the curse of Man.

Two who have loved shall reunite.
One will bear the burden of Heaven's might.

One will bring hope in the darkest hour.
One will provide a guiding power.

May their faith hold them steadfast,
When fate comes to pass.

Christian looked around; the low flickering light from the candles danced on the walls, adding moving shadows to an already creepy appearance in the cave. The scene had a familiar feeling to it, like other rooms he had been in before; rooms in which he was conducting an investigation.

Christian was reading when Rafeo finally entered the room. The old man carried no look to indicate he was still upset with Christian.

"What the hell is all this?" Sam blurted out.

Rafeo held his arms out, pointing at the works on the walls. "These are the messages the Book has… whispered to me." He lowered his arms and walked closer to a specific point. The other three walked closer to see what it was he was standing next to.

"You see, the book wants to be read, and it calls out to man to try to entice anyone to read it. Some have, over the centuries, but this power and knowledge is only meant for One. Usually, any mortal that reads aloud from the book brings great pain and destruction down on himself and anyone around. It has not been easy, but I have avoided the temptation, though I have kept logs of all I have heard."

The others looked around the room at the sheer number of verses and words scribbled on paper on display.

"This is the one." Rafeo pointed at the paper in front of him and read it aloud.

When the righteous spills the blood
of the innocent man,
The seed will bloom of evil. Mankind to be damned.

The room fell silent for a number of collective heartbeats before Gabriel spoke.

"What does it mean?" he asked. All eyes fell on Rafeo. The old man still stared at the page in front of him, then slowly turned to look at each of them... Christian last.

"I have no idea, really," he answered slowly, the others letting out a group sigh. "This is the only reference to such a thing. I am not sure if it is a figurative thing, or something literal. I believe it to be more of a warning. Each of us has a choice; to do what is right or not."

"It has been said that *all evil needs to succeed is for good men to do nothing*," Gabriel said in the silence after Rafeo spoke, the reference was not wasted on Rafeo.

"So even a choice to do nothing is still a choice." Sam was nervously rubbing Gabriel's arm affectionately. There was clearly no doubt amongst them that this struggle they were involved in was a test of character and Gabriel and Sam's intentions were obvious. They had taken ownership of their roles, here, as well. This gave Christian a feeling of hope.

"There are also those who believe that once you start down the path of evil, it will grow within you… like a seed." Rafeo finished his earlier thought. "If that is what this refers to, or, if it is something literal… I do not know."

They stood in silence for a time, each feeling that they were in great company, each one knowing that a silent oath, to do whatever was needed to see this through, had been sworn between them. A smile and a look were shared between them all; perhaps the words could not be found, but each one knew.

"So, what's our plan?" Sam asked finally.

CHAPTER 17

THE NEXT MORNING, THE REST OF the inhabitants of the garden went about their usual tasks. They noticed Gabriel, Sam and Christian getting one of the SUVs ready to leave but didn't pay much attention.

Christian was the last to join them at the truck. He had allowed himself to feel a little excited, as though they were going on a college road trip. As he jogged up to the vehicle from his cabin, he could see that Sam had already assumed the 'shotgun' position, and without a thought of objection, reached for the rear door handle. He ducked getting in and spoke without looking around.

"Anyone wanna coffee for the road? I think they..." He stopped short, amid sentence, as he came face to face with Mary, who was sitting in the spot right next to him. She looked at him and smiled as though nothing had happened.

Christian instantly felt awkward. His eyes darted around, while his mind raced for something to say. He made eye contact with Gabriel in the rear-view mirror, long enough to give the driver an SOS with his eyes.

"Mary decided to join us," was all Gabriel offered in response, though he couldn't hide a sardonic grin.

"Yes, I see," Christian answered sharply.

"And I'd love a coffee," Sam turned to face Christian, just so he could see the mischievous smile she wore.

"Me, too," Gabriel added.

"Coffee... Yeah, okay," Christian stammered, and tried to back out of the truck quickly but Mary grabbed his arm. He stopped and looked up at her. He took a moment to admire the color of her crystal blue eyes; they were so expressive and deep. He enjoyed the way the corners of her mouth curled when she smiled, and her high cheekbones. He watched, waiting for what she was going to say, and could feel a grin growing on his face as he stared at her.

"One for me, as well?" she asked and slowly slid a stray strand of hair behind her ear.

"Of course," Christian said calmly, then had to shake his head slightly. "Yeah... three coffees coming up... well, four, actually... one for me, too, of course." His awkwardness was undeniable. He sprinted away from the truck.

Christian fumbled around the kitchen pouring coffees and finding the cream and sugar.

"Thought you could use a hand." Gabriel's voice startled him, as he was already shaken, having unexpectedly come face to face with Mary. He set one of the mugs down hard on the counter and turned to face Gabriel, who was enjoying seeing Christian flustered.

"This isn't fuckin' funny!" Christian snapped, pointing at Gabriel to stress his point. "Nor a good tactical decision"

Gabriel walked closer to Christian and poured himself a coffee.

"Relax. What could happen? We'll be with my whole team." Gabriel addressed the tactics question first. "And no, it's not funny," He could see Christian's shoulders relax slightly with the apology.

"But it is kinda funny, watching you have a melt down every time she's around."

"God!" Christian yelled, and slammed the sugar pot that he was holding onto the counter. "I know... what the hell is wrong with me?" He turned to face Gabriel. Gabriel's facial expression changed as he hadn't realized how tormented Christian was.

"Sorry, man; I was just buggin'."

"I know; I know...". Christian said, while waving his hand, as though brushing the comments away. They quietly finished getting the coffees together and returned to the SUV without another word.

They drove to the edge of the city of Amman. Gabriel stopped at the side of what appeared to be an abandoned old factory of some kind. The neighborhood around them was anything but abandoned, however. Across the street, and as far as he could see, a number of busy shops and businesses seemed to flourish.

"This is it," Gabriel announced, stepping out of the SUV. The others followed, mostly looking around at the hustle and bustle of the people passing by.

Gabriel led them through a side entrance and sealed the door behind them. They walked through a short but narrow corridor which opened into a huge open area. The corridor was poorly lit, giving it an uneasy feeling as they walked through. The room beyond was dark, and impossible to see into.

In the middle of the hangar were a number of computer consoles, and a Blackhawk helicopter. Off to the side, a group of men were gathered around a table, under the only single light in the hangar. The empty space around them seemed immense, as they could not see the edges of the hangar through the darkness.

Christian could hear voices and laughter. There were a number of off-color stories being thrown around; as they approached the table; he could soon see that people were busy preloading ammunition into a variety of magazines.

There were assault rifles, pistols, sniper rifles, and an assortment of grenades and other explosives, as well. One of the men at the table straightened up as Gabriel and the others stepped from the shadows of the outlying areas and into the light around the other men. The others soon stopped what they were doing and all turned to face their visitors.

"Kinda casual?" Gabriel was a bit disappointed.

"What if we were a group of insurgents?", he questioned, with a raised eyebrow.

The room fell very silent, until one man, now near the front of the group, stepped forward, and spoke up.

"Then your brains would already be air-conditioned.", he answered calmly, and nodded to the left and right with his chin.

Four men appeared out of almost nowhere, two having rappelled down ropes from the ceiling, weapons trained on each of them.

"Mm-hm", Gabriel nodded his approval.

"Very good, Mister Pennman." Gabriel stepped forward and shook Eric's hand. The four men in the peripherals lowered their weapons and slipped back into the shadows.

Christian walked closer to the group and cocked his head to look at Eric more closely.

"Eric?", he asked. He had a hard time recognizing him, his face being obscured by poor lighting and the peak of his hat.

"Eric Pennman. Son of a bitch!", Christian said louder, having recognized him now.

"Christian, you old dog.", Eric answered, and grabbed him in a bear hug.

"Don't tell me you're messed up in all this. Gabe must be really desperate to call in a civilian hack like you." Eric laughed as he said it.

"Fuck you!", Christian laughed as well.

"'Least I'm employed. You must have told a whopper to cover up your past."

"Oh... don't start! The boss is right here...", Eric slapped Christian on the shoulder.

"You'll blow this for me." They laughed even louder.

"I assume you know each other?" Gabriel spoke up, and stepped close to the other two men; he eyed them up and down, revealing his surprise at their familiarity.

"You could say that.", Christian answered, with his hand still on Eric's shoulder.

"We served together for a while, until he ran off to work with the U.N."

They laughed, thinking back to old times.

"Didn't I tell you that'd get you into trouble?", Christian asked with a grin as he turned away slightly from Gabriel, so as to wag his finger sarcastically at Pennman.

"You did, and those words rang in my ears when they introduced me to Stumpy, my demolitions expert."

"Stumpy?", Gabriel asked, unable to join the others in a grin.

"Yeah. Eric, here, was assigned as an escort and observer as part of a two-man team working in Cambodia. Stumpy was to find and deactivate land mines laid out by the Khmer Rouge, and although he was a hell of a sniper, Eric was to observe and report, not engage."

Gabriel nodded as if impressed, but felt his smile slip away as the other's did as well.

"So, I'm in the field with a rifle with no ammunition, as per the rules of engagement." Eric took over the story. He paused for a moment, as if the memory pained him, but he covered it up. He searched for the words for a moment, then continued, forcing the grin back on his face.

"To make a long story short, Stumpy's head took me out at the knee after he tripped a land mine by mistake. I picked up his body and tried to hump it back over a mile to our exit strategy... a motorcycle taxi parked by the rice paddy we were wading in.", he explained, then turned somber again.

"The Khmer Rouge came out of the woodwork." Eric paused; he had told this story a few times, but it never got any easier. He tried to work some humor into it, but only to try and trick himself into not feeling the pain.

"How'd you get away?" Gabriel was anxious.

"Well." Eric continued, "you could buy thirty 7.62 rounds off the kids in the streets for five bucks. So, against orders, I loaded up and… defended myself..." He trailed off again, caught up in the memory, then shook his head slightly.

"I woke up in the hospital two days later, to the sound of this little weasel of a U.N. Captain yelling at me, something about rules of engagement."

None of them had noticed Sam and Mary walk closer to join the conversation.

"I got out of bed and punched that little bastard out.", Eric finished with a laugh.

"And I'd say he deserved it.", Gabriel added.

"I wish the Judge Advocate General had agreed with you.", Eric had completely lost his smile. "I got a dishonorable discharge for my efforts."

"How sad." Mary's voice was soft, but heard by all. They all turned to her, having only now realized she was standing there.

"And who might you be?", Eric asked, taking her hand, not noticing Christian back away slightly, still not knowing how to act around her.

"My name is Mary.", she reached out and shook Eric's hand in turn.

"She's also the real reason we're all here.", Gabriel cut in motioning for the team to assemble for a briefing. Before he continued, he motioned Eric a little closer, and spoke quietly.

"Thanks for sharing all that, however… I already knew.", he said, with a slight grin.

"I pulled your file a while ago.", he shrugged. "... thought you got a bum rap, so I pulled some strings to get you on my team. Figured you should have a second chance."

Eric cocked his head to the side slightly, in surprise. "Thank you.", he said quietly.

Gabriel nodded, and smiled slightly in return.

Christian gave Gabriel a nod to proceed; they had discussed it and agreed that they would be completely honest with the team.

Christian watched as Gabriel laid it all out for them; the hopefuls, the Book, and what they figured Quintus was up to. As far as he could see, they were buying in a lot more then he had expected. As he finished up, the team quietly dispersed and finished prepping their equipment. The chatter in the room was a lot quieter than it had been before. Eric made his way over to Christian.

"So, what do you think?" Christian asked.

"Well, I do appreciate your candor. I have to admit, it isn't very often we're told the truth of what we're actually doing." Eric smiled at his old friend.

"Truth is, though, I'm a soldier. I get paid to point this gun at the bad guys and make them go away.

Whether I believe or not, I still do my duty. But I can see you believe. And that works for me."

Eric looked around for a moment.

"Speaking of beliefs: I believe we're missing someone."

Christian's eyes darted to every corner of the hangar. He couldn't see Mary anywhere. He began to panic and ran over to Gabriel.

"Where the hell is she?" He had interrupted a conversation Gabriel was having with one of the other team members. Now they both began to search

"Eric, get them ready and get that bird in the air; we have a situation," Gabriel ordered. The team sprang into action, Eric yelling out instructions as Gabriel and Christian sprinted to the door. Before they made it outside, Christian's phone rang.

"Hello?" He yelled over the noise in the background.

"I thought I should let you know..." It was Sam. "... Mary and I are in the market, shopping."

Christian sighed his relief and informed Gabriel.

"Stand down from alert, but let's get that bird in the air, anyway. The chopper can fly a few patterns and keep an eye on us." They continued out the door and across the street to the market.

This time, as they walked through the market, Christian kept his distance from Mary. He watched her as she

walked and talked with Sam. His mind raced as he went over what had happened the night before, over and over again. Each time, he felt the pain of her rejection as though it was fresh.

She would occasionally turn back and smile at him, but he would look away as though he was distracted by someone or a noise.

"Why don't you go talk to her?" Gabriel finally asked.

"What?" Christian answered, trying to seem as though nothing was bothering him. "No. That would be unprofessional."

They walked along in silence for a moment, before Gabriel spoke again.

"You're allowed, you know." When Christian tried to feign confusion over his statement, Gabriel continued. "You're both adults; it's not against the rules"

Christian shook his head. "No. It'd be better if I just did my job."

"Your head is in the game, then?" he asked quietly.

"Of course!" Christian's reply seemed defensive.

"So, you did notice the guy with the marked face in the black robes on the roof top ghostin' us?"

Christian slowly put his hand under his shirt, resting it on the handle of his gun.

"Of course," he answered calmly.

"But truth be told, I'm more concerned with his spotter... about ten feet back, following us, talking on his phone for the past ten minutes. He's close enough to take."

They walked along quietly for another few seconds.

"Sorry I doubted you," Gabriel answered calmly. "What do you wanna do?" he asked as he discretely keyed his radio to communicate with the chopper.

Christian looked around slightly, then found himself staring at Mary. In the meantime, Gabriel muttered some barely audible orders to the men in the chopper and turned back to Christian. He noticed his gaze, and caught a slight nervous vibe from him.

"You're using her as bait?" Christian carefully turned his gaze away from Mary and looked Gabriel in the eye. "You gotta have faith... I just know I have to do this."

"Faith?" Gabriel shook his head slightly. "Don't you start, too, man."

Before anyone could say another word, Christian saw movement close to Sam.

"On your left," Christian spoke into his radio.

The market shook from a small explosion, then the air lit up with gunfire.

CHAPTER 18

SAM HAD NOTICED THE ATTACKER SECONDS before she heard Christian's voice through her earpiece. He had moved from her left, blending in with the many people shopping in the market. Sam pushed Mary aside, catching her completely off guard. Mary fell to the ground, and turned back in surprise to see what had happened. She was just in time to see Sam get tackled.

Sam deflected her assailant's knife attack and spun with his momentum to the ground. Sam maintained her focus through the fall and regained her feet before her attack, and did so with her gun in her hand. She did not hesitate to fire and ended the man where he lay. Sam had but a moment to look around; she could see that Mary was alright, for the moment. However, others were coming.

Christian had watched Sam's ordeal in horror. Whatever he had been feeling, or how confused he was about Mary, now his only thought was to protect her. He drew his weapon and engaged a number of men that seemed to be coming from everywhere. Gabriel had already taken out two of the enemy, and Christian soon matched his score.

"You go! The chopper is inbound... get her to it. I'll cover," Gabriel yelled to Christian over the fray. He fired and hit two more men before continuing.

"Southwest corner! The team is coming in from the west side."

Christian nodded, then turned back to the fight. He killed two more before he had a chance to look for Mary and Sam in all of this. To his shock, he found Mary, standing, frozen in fear in the middle of everything. He had to kill another man who had managed to get almost within striking distance. He then felt Gabriel's hand on his shoulder and snapped his head around to see what he wanted.

"Go!" was all Gabriel yelled.

Christian realized he had been somewhat frozen in place, but thanks to Gabriel, he came out of it, broke from cover, and bolted towards Mary.

Bullets flew everywhere; although Christian could not see the projectiles, their telltale "snap-hiss" sound was all around him as he sprinted towards Mary. Impacts from the bullets spawned multiple miniature explosions everywhere, but Christian managed to avoid being hit.

The enemy's indiscriminate fire was killing many civilians in the process. It was a blood bath: fruit and produce exploded, wooden crates splintered, dust was flying, and people were dying all around him as he darted from bits of cover in his mad dash towards Mary.

Luckily, they didn't seem to be targeting Mary directly as she still stood motionless out in the open.

Sam was pinned down, but frantically yelling at Mary to move.

They were greatly out-gunned. A building at the far end of the square seemed to light up with muzzle flashes from the enemies' weapons. The three of them were no match for this onslaught, and it would take the response team too much time to clear the building.

Christian frantically looked around for an alternate route to Mary, as he was quite pinned down. He resumed firing, and killed several more attackers in the meantime.

After what seemed like an eternity, they caught a break. Before landing, the helicopter turned its weapons on the building. The older structure was no match for the chopper's rockets and heavy caliber machine gun – it virtually disintegrated, eliminating a large threat, and freeing Christian to continue towards Mary.

A second wave of knife-wielding attackers poured into the market towards Sam, Christian and Mary. Sam maintained a steady rate of fire, keeping Mary safe.

Christian was tackled from around a blind corner, dropping his weapon. Without hesitation, he switched to unarmed combat, quickly disarming his assailant, and turning his weapon back on him. He looked up to see a man wielding a knife standing over Mary, ready to strike. Christian saw Sam frantically reloading her gun, and his own was five feet away on the ground; neither would be fast enough to save her.

Christian felt his stomach sink, and tears well up in his eyes. He felt as though he was going to have to watch her die right in front of him. He dared not blink, setting his resolve, and trying frantically to think of something.

There was a loud crack, and the man's head exploded, dropping him like a stone. Christian looked up, and with a grin, saw the chopper hovering just above the landing zone. While team members rappelled to the ground to join the fight on the ground, Christian heard a voice on his earpiece.

"You drop something?" It was Penman.

"Holy shit..." Christian swallowed his emotions and picked up his gun. He paused, and looked up to the chopper for a split second.

"I owe you one.", he shouted.

"Later...", Eric racked the next round into the chamber of his sniper rifle. "Right now, you're busy. Get her over here."

Christian nodded and ran to Mary. She still stood frozen in place, now staring at herself, covered in the man's blood, tears streaming down her face. Her sheltered life in Eden had never exposed her to the ugly side of man's existence. This had been too much for her.

Christian realized she was in shock, and would have given everything to just hold her and tell her it had all been a bad dream, that everything was alright, but he couldn't. Instead, he threw her over his shoulder and bolted towards the chopper, which was slowly descending to its landing area.

The rate of the enemy's fire slowed as Christian paused behind a half wall to check his route out and catch his breath. He was shaken, although having been in situations like this before, it had been many years.

He could see some of the team members entering the market in twos from the west; they were methodical in their lines of fire.

Christian was relieved to see they were allowing Sam to reposition and meet up with Gabriel. Then it occurred to him that maybe the decline in enemy gunfire wasn't all a good thing. Over the fray, he heard a distinct sound.

"RPG!" Christian heard someone yell. Now he broke cover without hesitation. The explosive round impacted right where he had been seconds before. The blast was enough to knock him over while running; he tumbled to the ground, unintentionally tossing Mary as well.

As if the blast had been enough to wake her up, when Christian looked up, she was staring at him.

"Can you hear me?" he yelled, and she nodded frantically.

"Do you see the helicopter?" He pointed, and again she nodded. "Can you move?" He realized he had sustained some injury from the blast, but not bad. Mary made it to her feet, and moved towards Christian; he waved her off and pointed to the chopper.

"I'm right behind you," he said calmly, before he could hear another inbound RPG.

"Run!" he yelled, as he scrambled to his feet and moved as quickly as he could. Luckily, Mary was in a sprint already. The RPG was nowhere as accurate this time, missing them by a good measure.

The chopper was on the deck now. Eric and others were out of the aircraft, taking up covering fire positions around it. The pilot sat calmly waiting for his intended passengers, who were sprinting towards the helicopter.

The blades of the aircraft were kicking up a wall of dust and dirt, nearly concealing it from sight. Mary reached the door just ahead of Christian, and scrambled inside. He tumbled into the passenger compartment, coming face to face with Mary. For an instant, he was relieved, and even smiled at her to reassure her.

Christian looked back towards the fight to see another man fire an RPG. This one was on target for the helicopter.

The chopper exploded violently. The men who had been covering the bird had been knocked around pretty bad in the blast, Eric included.

The enemy seemed to withdraw after that, thinking that they had achieved their goal, but it had never been Christian's intentions to fly out of the area. He figured a large helicopter was too big a target.

Once inside the aircraft, Christian and Mary had jumped out the open door on the other side. In the dust and debris kicked up by the rotors and the cover of the explosion afterwards, no one noticed them slip down a back alley at the south end of the market and run off into the city.

They were concealed by the rushing crowds of people desperately trying to flee the violence. They ran for blocks until they stopped to catch their breath in a dark doorway.

"Well?" Christian panted, as he looked Mary over quickly for signs of injury. "Everyone thinks we're dead."

Mary looked at him in shock, then noticed him bleeding through his shirt. She reached out as if to soothe his wounds, but he caught her hand.

"It's not that bad," he reassured her, shaking his head. Christian then peeked out of the doorway; the street was pretty clear.

"Come on," he said, taking her hand and smiling. "We're getting out of this mess, hopefully for good."

"Where will we go?" Mary was shaking now.

"I know a little place," Christian answered with a new look of determination, and lead her by the hand down the street.

CHAPTER 19

GABRIEL HAD SEEN THE TEAM SWEEPING in on foot from the west end of the market. The gunfire seemed to intensify around him from both directions. He had lost track of almost everyone in the fray.

The first person he saw was Sam. She had been pinned down, but the advancing team had secured her. He searched around frantically to find Christian, and he did, just in time for what he figured was his friend's last moment.

A sword-wielding assailant was right on top of Christian, and on his blind side. Before he could raise his weapon, the attacker's head disappeared, thanks to a sniper's round fired from the chopper that had arrived just in time.

Gabriel was too far away, and almost out of ammunition, to be of any help to his friend. Instead, he made a dash for Pennman's lines, sliding into cover right next to Sam, as though he was sliding in to third base.

"Hi, Honey," he said with a smile. Brought you some presents, baby." Pennman popped up from behind a small table he had been using for cover. He was a few feet away but had gone completely unnoticed by Gabriel and

Sam. They both jumped in surprise when Eric spoke. They all got a small chuckle out of it.

Two of Pennman's men had been carrying extra rifles. They handed Sam and Gabriel an M-96 assault rifle and some ammunition. The men then unslung their M-14s from their backs and returned to the fight.

"Where's Christian?" yelled Pennman over the noise

"And where is Mary?" Rafeo added.

Gabriel and Sam were surprised to see the old man, but not as surprised as Pennman. The soldier raised his hand as if to protest Rafeo being there, but Gabriel shook him off, then turned to answer Rafeo.

"They're in trouble," Gabriel answered, nodding towards the pair in peril. As they all looked across the market, they saw the pair break from cover, just narrowly escaping the blast from an RPG. The entire team followed the smoke trail back to its source and opened fire.

"Quintus," Rafeo muttered, and broke from the group, without a care of being shot. He was focused on his old nemesis... the man with the RPG, and paid little attention to the objections from the fire team around him to take cover again.

Rafeo took fire and Eric watched in horror as the blood sprayed from the wounds. His horror turned to surprise as Rafeo simply carried on, having paid no attention to his injuries. It took Eric a moment to re-gain his composure.

The concentrated fire from Gabriel and Pennman did cause Quintus' next shot to fly off target, sparing Christian and Mary – another close call. Little did any of them realize that Quintus had actually been shot six times in the initial exchange, but showed no evidence of suffering any permanent wounds.

The helicopter had just destroyed an entire building housing many of the enemy. It was making its way to the ground and Christian and Mary were making a mad dash for the transport.

The momentum of the battle had certainly changed to their favor. The men on the ground had rousted most of the enemy, and were also keeping the one with the RPG launcher pinned down, or so they thought.

Rafeo had found a ladder and was frantically climbing towards Quintus. Gabriel didn't understand it, but this lunatic seemed to forget that there were dozens of well-armed and trained soldiers around him. Quintus stood at the top of the ladder, taunting Rafeo, beckoning him closer. Gabriel watched from his rifle's scope. He looked away for an instant, long enough to see Christian and Mary make it to the chopper.

He looked back to Rafeo, who was nearly to the top of the ladder, when the other man kicked it away, sending Rafeo to tumble more than twenty feet back to the ground.

"Oh, enough of this," Gabriel said sternly, and fired, hitting Quintus in the head, and dropping him to the ground. As he fell, his hand squeezed the trigger of the RPG launcher, sending another round loose, and straight for the chopper. Gabriel and the others all went limp from shock. They watched in horror as the helicopter exploded, almost stopping time itself.

They stood in shocked silence as they tried to process what had happened. After all of this, their primary subject, and a good friend, were dead along with the two pilots. As they stood motionless, they heard a sinister laugh.

All turned, now even more confused, to see Quintus. Alive, in spite of a shot to the head; he stood, waved his hand in in the air in victory, and slid into the shadows. As he did, the enemy gunfire picked up again in the market.

"Didn't that seem a little... oh, I don't know... freaky, to you?" Eric screamed at Gabriel, who was still shaken from seeing the chopper explode with his friend in it.

"What do you mean?" Gabriel asked in a flat tone. Eric returned a short burst of fire at the enemy before answering.

"That guy… I saw you shoot him in the head. I saw his head splatter on that wall and he just got up and walked away. That doesn't seem out of place to you?"

Gabriel cracked a half smile, but didn't look directly at Eric. "Brother, you have no idea."

Eric Pennman, though confused, wanted to try to get out of there with as little loss as possible. He fired another volley at the enemy, who was scattering to the wind.

Gabriel had to do a double take, having spied a pair of issue-boots and a pair of sandals running from the wreckage of the chopper. He knew Christian had survived, and didn't want to trust anyone with the information for now. Eric noticed Gabriel exchange an odd look with Rafeo, who finally joined them, seeming to have suffered no ill effects from his fall. Eric allowed Gabriel to lead Rafeo and Sam out of the market, and took over, ordering their withdrawal.

In the sudden hush of the now empty market Eric had to take a moment to look around. Smoke rose from several craters throughout the market where the vendor's small kiosks once stood. The attack had been lightning-fast and effective. The hit and run attack had left a wave of pain, suffering and horror in its wake as was their intention.

The chaos in the streets was like nothing Christian had ever seen before. People were flooding out from businesses and homes, and running every which way. Some ran towards the trouble, either looking to render assistance, or for fear that a loved one was involved, perhaps. They feared for their lives; they feared for their homes. By the looks on their faces, some were angry that they were in this situation, and perhaps, that they were in this situation again.

In contrast, Christian also noticed there were some people who were just carrying on with their day. It had never occurred to him that it would be possible to get used to this type of situation. But there they were: an older woman folding her laundry off the line, two older men were drinking their morning tea and playing a game of cards. Christian was certain that none of them had been directly involved, which might explain someone's complacency in this situation. Rather, he figured that they simply had no reason to be concerned. Perhaps they were resigned to the notion that when your time is up, it's up. Or maybe their misery would welcome the end.

They stopped in an alley to catch their breath. Christian was surprised at the blank look Mary wore on her face – the experience had been too much for her. Again, Christian took a moment to look her up and down, to check for injuries. There was a water hose left unattended in the excitement. He took a quick drink, then brought the water to Mary's lips. She did not move, nor even try to drink, but continued to stare blankly into nothingness. Christian even tried to spray her a little with a bit of water to try to cool her down and wake her up again, with no reaction. Frustrated, he grabbed her hand, and led on through the streets.

In an attempt to blend more into the crowd, Christian had decided to conceal his weapon in his pants. It was a decision he was uneasy with, as he wasn't entirely sure that no one was following them. Every street or alley they came to, he turned down in an attempt to see if anyone was following them. They ran for hours; the whole time, he felt as though he was dragging Mary behind him. She was obviously in shock, but they could not afford to stop yet.

It was nearly dark before they finally reached a little inn in an old section of town near the outskirts. Christian ushered Mary into a small shed that sat in the alley behind the inn.

"I need to go register before someone calls the police. Are you going to be okay here for a few minutes?" he asked her. Mary did not respond; instead, she stood still, panting slightly.

Christian realized he hadn't really been paying that much attention to her and had barely looked at her this entire time.

"Mary?" he asked again, doing a double take and stepping right in front of her, trying to get her attention with no luck.

He was at a loss. Christian knew that he had to get them off the street, and to do that, he had to register and get the room key, but he wasn't sure if he should leave her. In an instant, he decided to move. He closed the door to the shed and ran off to the office.

He knew he could trust the owner, which is why he had led them here. Christian had worked with Chasim once before. Chasim had, at one time, lived in the US. He had come from money and lived the life of a playboy until his daughter had gotten caught up in cult activities. Christian had helped liberate her and Chasim decided to return to his country and keep a low profile. Christian had kept in touch a little, but enough to know where to go if he needed help from a friend.

He checked quickly through the window and spotted his friend. Almost empty, Christian waited a moment until one couple finished collecting their keys and headed to their room. As soon as the office was clear, Christian flipped his collar up and rushed over to the counter.

Chasim had his back to the door, but still heard Christian approach.

"Can I help you?" Chasim asked in English and Arabic.

"I need a room," Christian said quickly. Chasim hesitated, recognizing the voice and turned slowly. He met eyes with his friend and smiled with his whole face.

"Run – my friend!" Chasim shouted, throwing his hands in the air and walking around the counter to hug his friend. 'Run' had been a nickname that stuck after the first time they met. Even with all the stress of the moment, Christian couldn't help but reminisce. He could feel his lips curl into a slight smile as he thought back to that day. It was Christian's first official case. Chasim had been a very rich and powerful player in the Middle East oil scene when his daughter had been taken by a cult. He had been tracking the cult's movements when Chasim took it upon himself to join Christian in the field.

Christian had positioned himself to snatch the girl from the cult, when Chasim had given away their position. He had somehow found Christian, and in very broken English, started asking him questions about what he was doing there, and lastly what his name was, to which Christian yelled "RUN!", as the cult members were bringing weapons to bare on their position.

The language barrier had led Chasim to think that Christian's name was, indeed, 'Run', until much later, after they got to know each other as the case was winding down. Christian had managed to liberate Chasim's daughter, but the cult, which was really more an off shoot of Al-Qaeda, still targeted the family because of Chasim's position. Christian had helped the family disappear and set them up with this inn as a cover.

"No questions my friend." Christian finished his thoughts and pulled out from the hug from his friend.

Chasim looked around, then back at Christian suspiciously.

"All this excitement in the street… this is for you?" Chasim asked.

Christian's eyes dodged around from guilt before he nodded.

"I wish I could say this was just a friendly visit. It's been too long, my old friend...", Christian explained, trying to smile, but then his focus returned and his eyes darkened again.

"...but I need your help."

Chasim felt his smile fall away as he came to understand the seriousness of the situation. His gaze was drawn out the door, behind his friend.

"And the pretty girl, too?" Chasim asked, motioning out the door.

Christian spun around to see Mary standing in the street. People were yelling at her to get indoors, but she was unresponsive.

"Fuck!" Christian spat, and went to run out after her.

"Get her and bring her around back; I'll meet you at room six… Go!"

Chasim ran behind the counter, grabbed the room key, and his gun. He followed on Christian's heels. Once outside, he began to yell at a nearby crowd and fired into the air. It was obvious to Christian that this was only a distraction.

He took advantage of the situation, grabbing Mary and ducking into the back alley towards the room. She looked at him as if she didn't know who he was. She stumbled along behind him as he dragged her down the alley.

Christian fumbled with the room key for what felt like an eternity, finally opening the door and pushing Mary inside. She came to a stop in the middle of the room and remained there, motionless, while Christian searched the room frantically to ensure they were alone.

"Okay... we just gotta stay here and figure out our next move. We're safe for now, and..."

Christian froze as he came out of the bathroom after frantically searching for anyone lying in wait. He met Mary's gaze mid-sentence and stopped as he saw the poor girl standing, all but motionless, where she had stopped after entering the room.

She was shivering and staring blankly into the rear wall of the room. A single tear rolled down her cheek.

Nervously, Christian quickly checked where she was staring to ensure there was no threat there, then lowered his weapon and slowly reached out to touch her. His hand slowly slid from her shoulder to her elbow, attempting to reassure her and break her from the seeming trance she had entered. They stood in silence for a moment. Christian's mind raced to try to imagine what she was feeling.

This poor girl had lived her whole life in the safety and shelter of the garden, only to have the world violently ripped away from her in the chaos of the market today. He was at a loss for words, but his touch seemed to melt what little resistance she had to her experiences of the day. She broke down completely, collapsing into his arms.

Christian was torn for a moment over the powerful feelings he had for her. She felt so warm in his arms, but he realized that this was not the time, and reminded himself that she had made it clear that it would never happen. Right now, he just wanted to help her.

"So much death..." she finally whispered through her tears. "I have never seen so much death. sand I feel that it is all because of me."

Christian was taken aback. He pulled away to look her in the eye.

"This was not your fault," he said as sternly but as warmly as he could. For the first time, her eyes seemed to gain focus as she looked at him, as if for the first time that day.

"I know that; I didn't kill anyone today. I said it was because of me… there is a difference."

Christian took a moment to absorb her feelings. Here she was, not only having lived a completely sheltered life, but she was also, potentially, the Guardian… God, for lack of a better word. Whether it was true or not, she believed it. Christian was not sure what to do or say that could help her and the despair was harsh on him.

"Those were good men who died at the hands of those mad men", Mary continued, seemingly clearer now and crossing the room away from Christian to sit on the bed.

"They all felt this duty to protect me… and for what? Did any of them even know…?" She trailed off for a moment.

Christian began to form a response to reassure her, but didn't get the chance to voice it as she continued.

"I don't even know anything. All I know is that I'm some girl who's lived my entire life without even living. I could not bear the thought of anyone sacrificing themselves for me, ever again."

She stood, and walked back over to Christian. She looked him deeply in the eyes and gently placed her hand on his chest. She brailed a small cut, probably received after the helicopter exploded.

"Least of all, you..."

Christian's eyes widened slightly in surprise. She had made it quite clear that she had no feelings for him, but now this seemed to have changed.

Mary crossed to the bathroom and returned with a damp cloth. Without a word, she opened his shirt to expose the wound and placed the cloth on it to clean it. He winced slightly but wasn't sure if it was from the sting of the cloth on his wound or the touch of her hand on his skin.

She dabbed lightly, removing the dried blood. Mary smiled at him, then reached up to his neck and pulled him in to kiss him. After a few seconds, Christian pulled away.

"Whoa..." he said quietly, then turned away, as if afraid to look at her as he spoke. "I don't even know where to start to tell you what's wrong with this. After all the times you told me this will never happen... not to mention everything we went through today. How do I know you're not going to be mad if I let this continue?"

He turned back to face her to see her reaction and was met by her naked form standing in front of him. Christian froze in place. He couldn't help but stare, taking in her beauty. The dim light in the room caressed her figure, casting the softest shadow under her breasts. Her skin seemed radiant, despite the low light. He noticed her faint freckles for the first time; they seemed to accentuate her eyes and carried down the nape of her neck. Her radiant skin shimmered like dark cream and beckoned for his touch.

Mary picked up on his reaction and stepped even closer to him, her nipples gently resting against his tight diaphragm.

"I've thought about all you have told me. It frightened me, because…" She paused and pulled his shirt off completely, taking in his rugged form. "...because I couldn't understand how it was possible that you felt the way you did, that you knew me as you did, despite never having met me. It scared me because I felt it too."

She looked up at him, a warm but faint smile on her lips.

Christian stared into her mesmerizing blue eyes, amazed and confused. He reached up and wiped a tear from her cheek. Her skin felt like the finest silk – warm and inviting.

"But I thought it was forbidden..." he finally whispered.

"If I am the Guardian, then who is to forbid me anything? And if I'm not… well, then, those are not my beliefs," she said with a warming smile, referencing what he had challenged her with days ago.

Christian smiled, remembering the conversation.

"Good point," he answered quietly, then pulled her in slowly, his hand now gently cupping the back of her head. He kissed her gently at first, then with more and more passion. He scooped her up into his arms, only realizing then how slender her frame truly was. He carried her to the bed, lying her down, their lips never parting.

They kissed for hours, stopping only to stare into each other's eyes. Finally, Mary could stand it no longer and tugged at Christian's belt. Awkwardly, he managed to remove the rest of his clothes, and joined her, naked on the bed again.

She smiled with a mix of nervousness and love in her eyes. She nodded, inviting him.

Christian positioned himself carefully over her and gently and slowly entered her, staring into her eyes all the while. She winced slightly at the loss of her virginity, but smiled back at Christian, beckoning him to continue. She closed her eyes in elation and arched her back in a moment of rapture. Christian smiled as he enjoyed her experience more than his own. She opened her eyes to see the look on his face and smiled wide. After another moment, he kissed her deeply as they shared their bodies.

CHAPTER 20

CHRISTIAN'S EYES OPENED. IMMEDIATELY HE SMILED as he scanned the woman lying next to him. Even in the dark he could discern her amazing features. His smile faded as he slowly gave in to the thought that there was a reason why he was awake.

Silently he slithered out of bed on to the floor. Mary's breathing changed for a moment while she slowly turned in her sleep, then returned to a steady rhythm. He reached for his clothes, but only took the time to grab his weapon, then slunk to the wall nearest the entrance. His eyes were completely adjusted to the dark. In the shadows he could see the figure of a man crouching in the hallway near the door. He steadied himself while watching the figure turn from the door and carefully head down the short corridor towards him.

As the man approached, Christian waited until he was right next to him in the darkness. He pulled back the hammer on the pistol – the tell-tale sound was all that was needed for the man to know he had been discovered. He froze and slowly stood from his crouched position, resigned to the fact that he had been caught.

Christian reached over and turned on the dim hallway light so he could see the would-be assailant. He was quite shocked to see Pennman standing in front of him with his hands raised to shoulder height.

"Eric?" He could not mask the surprise and relief in his voice.

"What the fuck, man? I almost shot you." Christian lowered his gun as Eric lowered his arms.

"I've got to admit you're pretty good to get this far," Christian said quietly with a shrug. His main concern for the moment was not to wake Mary.

"You've got a lot of friends outside," Eric said with a shrug and an uncomfortable grin. After a few seconds, his eyes flashed around the room nervously.

"Maybe you could put some clothes on..." he said sarcastically and looked away, so not to seem to stare at Christian.

"Uh... yeah..." Christian conceded, then quickly moved to get dressed.

Mary stirred slightly and opened her eyes. With a smile, she murmured, "I hope you're not thinking of running out on me."

Christian tried to smile and shook his head.

"No… never. But I do think you should get dressed... something's up."

Mary sat up in bed and pulled the sheets over herself, having noticed someone standing in the hallway.

"It's okay. It's Eric Pennman.", Christian tried to reassure her. He could see the growing concern in her eyes.

"He's with us, but if he's here, something must be wrong."

Christian kissed her, then finished doing his pants up, and left the bedside.

"They're still out there, right?" Christian asked Eric.

"Yeah, but they may not be for long. They're not the only ones out there. I spotted another group near the front of the building." Eric pointed out through the patio doors.

"The back alley was clear a few minutes ago. I suggest you both sneak out that way... I'll slow them down."

"Why don't we all go out the back door?" Mary suggested, now fully dressed, she joined them in the hall.

"I'll be right behind you," Eric said with a grin. He portrayed a look that he understood her concern, as if having been there for their earlier conversation.

"I'll be a sizeable speed bump for those bastards. I've left a few presents for them out there, but no worries, ma'am. I'll be right behind you," he said with a wink. He slunk closer to the window and cocked his rifle; he brought it to his shoulder to sight through the scope.

"No sign of the leadership out there, but they're on the move. Don't mind the fireworks; just run and get her back to the Garden." Eric pulled something out of the pocket on his tactical vest.

"Gabriel will meet you half a click west of here, by the tea shop.", Eric said with a nod.

Mary motioned an objection, but Eric stepped forward and spoke first.

"I'm not gonna pretend to fully understand what's goin' on here, but I am a soldier. It is my honor to do what I do." He patted his weapon to demonstrate his point, then looked to Christian.

"Just get her out," he said plainly, and returned to his post by the window.

"Thank you..." Mary answered. She took a step towards Pennman, but Christian grabbed her arm to stop her. Eric nodded, and Christian did the same; they both understood duty, and what it meant to each other.

"Go," was all Eric said. He then pushed a button on the controller he had in his hand. The building rocked from the blast of a claymore, followed by a burst of fire from his rifle.

In the chaos, Christian opened the back door. He checked quickly left and right and caught a glimpse of movement. He reached out to grab a man who was lying in wait just outside the door. He pulled him in close and kicked him back in one motion. Mary's scream was overpowered by the shot from Christian's gun.

Christian reached out for Mary's hand, and they bolted into the alleyway. Another man jumped out from behind a dumpster but fell to the bullet from a gun not in Christian's hand. He looked around in time to see Chasim wave him on.

Christian returned the gesture and took one more step. There was a loud snap, and he felt an impact against his chest. He had just enough time to look at Mary once more before the darkness and cold took him.

Mary watched Christian fall; her senses were overwhelmed. She could hear voices telling her to run but she couldn't. Her worst fear had come true – the man she loved had fallen, dead.

Within seconds, the enemy was upon her. They carried her to a waiting van and threw her in. She landed roughly, but it was far from over. The men followed her into the van and struck her face with the end of one of their rifles. Another single tear lay on her cheek as she felt her consciousness slip away.

Christian awoke with a start, but the pain from his movement quickly overtook him and he slumped back onto his bed. His ears rang, and his chest felt as though it was on fire. He was incredibly disoriented and could not figure out what he felt, for his last memory was being shot in the chest and Mary being taken.

"You're okay, son." A familiar voice from behind him put him at ease. He tried to speak but could only manage a whispered grumble.

"I have gone through this so many times, I forget the resurrection process can be very painful," Rafeo said with a slight chuckle as he walked around Christian's bed so he could see him better. The old man greeted him with a smile; although Christian could barely see, he knew it was there. He could also tell that there was more concern than he was letting on.

"Rest..." the old man said, and as if it were a command, Christian fell back into unconsciousness.

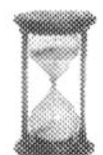

Sometime later, he awoke again, the pain having lessened, and he could see a little better. Christian looked around the room. Judging by the stone walls, candlelight, and sparse décor, he knew he was back in the Garden. Looking around a little more, he could see Pennman on another table, going through the same pains of reanimation.

"Eric... you okay?" This time his voice worked much better. Pennman lurched from the table and looked around frantically.

"If this is hell, I don't deserve this," he spoke in as big a voice as he could manage.

Christian sat up and chuckled a little. "It's not hell; it's much worse," he said, knowing full well this may really mess with Eric's head.

"You're in the Middle East..." he said plainly, then struggled to his feet and limped his way over to Eric.

"Can't be!" Eric exclaimed. "I started off good but didn't expect them to be using Fifty Cals."

Christian could see a hole in the front of his uniform, and a larger one in the rear.

"I died… I don't know how I know that, but I do."

Christian nodded, confirming what Eric thought.

"And?" Christian asked menacingly.

"AND!" Eric was upset. He swallowed and drew a deep breath, letting it out slowly.

"And how the fuck am I in the Middle East? If what you say is true, then I have one hell of a wardrobe malfunction.", Eric yelled, and ran his arm through the bullet holes to illustrate his point.

Christian got serious; he could tell he was really disturbing his friend.

"I, too, suffer the same affliction." He pointed to the blood-stained hole in his shirt.

"This is gonna be hard to understand, but let's just say that the gods favor you this day."

Eric didn't know what to do.

Christian didn't really know how to explain it and was relieved to see Rafeo walk into the room. He carried with him what looked like a laptop and set it down on a counter on the other side of the room. He then turned to face the two men and smiled.

"This may help..." he said slowly and motioned the two men closer. The three men exchanged glances as though they expected someone to jump out of a cake, then cautiously, Eric stepped towards Rafeo followed by Christian.

On the screen was a video playback of people bringing Eric's lifeless body into the room where they now stood. Rafeo entered the room with three ancient looking containers.

"Gold, frankincense and myrrh," Rafeo listed in a low tone, pointing to each in turn on the screen.

The video went on to show Rafeo read a short incantation from a very large and very old book.

Eric's body began to glow slightly, as did the content of the containers. The glow grew in intensity until it overwhelmed the ability of the camera to record. When the bright light dissipated, Eric could see himself move.

"What the hell...?" Eric whispered in amazement.

"Yeah..." Christian matched Eric's surprise "Since when do you know how to use a laptop?"

Rafeo closed the display and turned to Eric after shooting daggers at Christian with his eyes. Christian took the hint, cleared his throat, and regained his composure.

"I guess what Christian had said earlier was the literal truth. Today the gods do show you favor and have brought you back to life," Rafeo explained, hoping that the visual would save a lot of questions.

"So, am I like a zombie, now?" Eric asked slowly.

"No," Rafeo answered. He gestured as though he was about to go into a lengthy explanation, then stopped himself.

"Through the grace of the Quies, you have been given a second chance at life, in honor of your sacrifice. You are completely fine, I can assure you, but I simply don't have time to get into detail right now."

With that, Rafeo turned on his heel and walked out. Christian put his hand on Eric's shoulder.

"Weird, huh?" he said with a smirk. "Listen, you get some rest for now and I'll check in on you later."

Eric simply nodded nervously and staggered back over to his bed.

"Oh, and uh … thanks for comin' to get us … I never said that before … guess I'm lucky to have the chance now." Christian held his hand to his chest.

Eric smiled warmly and nodded again, then crawled into bed. Christian smiled, turned, and chased after Rafeo. In the hall outside the room, he ran into Sam and Gabriel.

"Hey, you're… up," Gabriel said, catching himself mid-sentence.

"We were just on our way to see you," Sam explained.

"We're fine... well, Eric's a little freaked out, but we're fine. There's no time for that now, though, they have Mary." They all began to walk quickly down the hall, Christian at the lead.

"I'm gonna need everyone's help to get her back." Christian continued as they walked into another chamber. Gabriel slowed slightly as they walked in; Rafeo looked up, with a smile.

"There's more good news," he said as he walked across the chamber and placed his hand on the book.

"Somehow the pages we recovered from Auschwitz have been repaired. The book is whole again."

Christian didn't hesitate. "Good! Fire the thing up! You need to tell us where to go to get Mary back," he barked.

Rafeo looked taken aback, but before he could speak again Gabriel interrupted.

"Look, my friend ... we've had intelligence reports that our enemies are planning a massive attack on the peace conference. Already, several delegates are missing.

I've been ordered back to my post." Gabriel winced as he said it.

Christian stumbled slightly, as though in pain. He turned slowly to face Gabriel.

"I need... she needs your help. Are you fucking kidding me, right now? You gotta help me!"

Gabriel didn't know what to say and was thankful when Rafeo spoke up first.

"I may be able to solve this conundrum."

All eyes turned to the old man now.

"As it turns out, regardless of what else she may be, Mary is one of the delegates for the conference. She is a member of the Pope's inner council and will attend as his liaison."

No one spoke for a minute, out of disbelief. Finally, Rafeo shrugged.

"I've been around since the beginning of the Christian faith. I have made sure to keep my connections in many places," he said with a shrug.

"So, your missions are once again intertwined." Rafeo seemed pleased.

"Maybe so, but I still need to oversee my team, and we don't have a clue where to start looking for Mary," Gabriel resounded, barely hiding his feelings of defeat.

A voice from behind brought welcome news.

"Maybe your section chief can take over security at the conference while you attend to a special concern." It was Pennman; he was up, and on his feet again.

"Okay ... well, that's one problem solved," Gabriel said as he crossed the room to see his friend. "Good to have you back." Gabriel grabbed him and hugged him in relief.

"Good to be back… believe me," Eric answered with a silly grin.

"As for the other problem ..." Rafeo's voice carried. He placed his hand on the book, then reached for a lever on the wall and pulled it down. An entire section of the wall opened to reveal another chamber, deeper into the rock. The group followed Rafeo into what could only be described as a command center. There were multiple computer displays and a variety of other technologies, some of which none of the other's had ever seen. They all looked around in disbelief, then turned back to stare at Rafeo.

"Laptop, indeed," Rafeo muttered in response to Christian's earlier statement. "I may be old… but old fashioned, I am not,"

Rafeo paused to admire his own setting before he continued.

"We have placed a GPS tracking chip under the skin of every person we work with … yourselves included. This gives us the ability to find anyone we work with, anywhere in the world."

Rafeo nodded to one of the people sitting behind a computer near to him. On one of the main screens at the front of the room, a blip appeared on a map, indicating Mary's exact location. The next screen showed a real time satellite image of the area. They were able to zoom into the point of identifying people.

"Yes, we own our own satellites." Rafeo made sure to mention this.

"Quintus," Christian scowled. "I remember you." He stood atop the building marked by the GPS where Mary was.

"Eric, dispatch a squad to these co-ordinates. Have them hold on-site till we get there. Inform local officials that we will be engaging in response to a threat on the conference," Gabriel ordered. "Rafeo, please tell me you have another room like this one with some weapon's tech we can use."

With a shrug, the old man replied, "Of course. And I'll send a squad with you to assist, as well, but be careful; this is most likely a diversionary tactic. They will want to disrupt the peace talks. Mabus will want to spread as much fear and disorder as possible. He feeds on it."

They all busied themselves arming their weapons and suiting up in body armor.

"Remember, once you get Mary back, she can read from the book and assume her existence as Guardian. Perhaps we can all finally rest with this behind us," Rafeo advised as he watched anxiously. This was the closest he had been to the completion of his mission since that dark day nearly sixteen hundred years ago, although he was hopeful, he could feel the stress of his excessive years on his body.

"I will bring her back." Christian tried to reassure his old friend.

"It is nice to see your confidence return, boy." Rafeo remembered all the young man had been through. "God speed."

Christian rushed out with the others but found himself pausing for a moment to stare at the book. He couldn't help but wonder how many people had suffered or died because of it. He touched it, both admiring it and despising it, all at the same time. He lingered only a moment more, then rushed out to join the others in the transport vehicles.

CHAPTER 21

MARY AWOKE SLOWLY; SHE FELT PAIN from her wrists and ankles where she was bound. She was blindfolded but could tell she was in a horrible place. It felt damp, dark, and she could feel insects crawling over her body.

She could tell she had been raped – the pain in her chest and groin gave that away. Her head ached from where they had knocked her out. She was almost thankful for that, having been unconscious while they had their way with her.

She tried to steel her mind, remembering the night she had had with Christian. The tears rolled down her face as she realized she could hear voices.

The voice she heard was frightening, dark, and in her mind, evil. She could feel him enter the room; it grew colder and darker. She could see a little of the floor under her blindfold and noticed that this man did not touch the floor when he moved. She had experienced many things through the Garden and her time with Rafeo, and she knew that she was dealing with Mabus.

She could feel his hands run over her body; they were wet and warm. She wasn't sure if she should try to pretend that she was still unconscious or confront him.

He fondled her breasts, but it was not sexual, though it hurt. She winced from the pain as he spoke.

"I know you can hear me so you may dispense with the charade." His voice boomed in the acoustics of the room and startled her. She swallowed her fear and found her voice.

"Why are you doing this to me?" she asked, trying to project her courage.

Mabus paused and leaned in close to her face.

"Because I can." His breath smelled horrible in her face.

His response did not surprise her, until he continued.

"And because I want to destroy him." Her mind raced through the possibilities of who *He* was. After some consideration, she decided Mabus was referring to Rafeo.

"What has he done to you?" she asked in defiance.

"He has stood in my way for far too long," he yelled, his voice booming in the room; he backed away from her and spoke more softly.

"But this is merely for sport. His demise is already set in motion."

She could feel his eyes on her. Mary figured if she kept him talking, it might keep him from doing other things to her.

"You may ask me your other question."

Mabus was interrupted by another man in the doorway.

"Quintus … don't you have a job to do?" His tone was less that of a partnership, and more of a master speaking to a slave.

"Indeed," Quintus answered, stepping further into the room.

"And right now, that job is to ravage her again." She could feel him draw near, but Mabus stopped him.

"No," he commanded. "We need her in one piece for now. Go to the conference and do your duty to me."

The room fell silent as the two stared each other down. After a long moment, Mary could hear footfalls as Quintus left the room.

Quintus walked down the corridor and out of the building into a courtyard. There were dozens of men and military vehicles waiting. One man ordered the others to attention, then marched forward to Quintus.

"My Lord, what orders? We stand ready to serve Mabus and bring down the envoys of Peace." The man spat the last word, as though it was a curse.

Quintus stepped forward and struck the man, knocking him to the ground. The men in the courtyard tensed, uncertain how to react.

"You had best be ready to serve me," Quintus said quietly yet forcefully to the men. The man on the ground scrambled into a bow.

"Yes, my Lord," he replied, a slight shake in his voice.

"What orders have you?"

Quintus looked around the courtyard at the men before he spoke.

"Today, we strike for ourselves. My spy has given me what I need. You will be at the right hand of your new god before the day is out."

The men cheered as Quintus moved towards a vehicle. They filed into the trucks after him. The convoy pulled out of the courtyard, Quintus' vehicle in the middle.

Mary was impressed. Rafeo did really know his enemy. Mabus had, in fact, read her mind. He knew she wanted to ask about the conference. Her mind now raced as to why they needed her in one piece.

"Why destroy the peace conference? What do you have to gain?" She knew he already knew the question was coming.

Mabus laughed a low, quiet, and sinister laugh while he moved around the room.

"What would be easiest for you to understand?" he asked and moved closer to her.

"That I have nothing to gain, other than the knowledge that failure at this time will lead humanity to its demise ... that my only interest is evil for the sake of evil … hmm? No."

Mabus reached up and pulled off her blindfold. She saw the dark, flowing cloak that covered him from head to toe. What she could see of his face was horribly scarred and dirty. She wanted to look away but didn't.

"Or maybe you would understand that the evil that men do feeds me. I have no interest in one religion winning over another... in fact, I am a big fan of all religions," he said with a twisted smile and a giggle to himself. "More evil has been carried out in the name of religion over the millennia, than anything else in human history… indeed, a big fan. Or could it be that I have no interest in doing damage to the proceedings at all. That I am confident that they will fail by themselves. I may actually be trying to help them succeed."

Mabus circled around her and floated towards the door.

"I will leave you with that to consider whilst you hold out hope that your hero will come for you."

Mary pressed against her bonds and spat at his back.

"He will come, and you will regret it! He will bring me the book, and I will take back from you what is mine!" she avowed, with a confidence that surprised even her.

Mabus paused and turned to glare into her eyes.

"You are right about some of it. He will come… but nothing on earth can save you from your fate, girl!"

Mabus disappeared through the doorway, leaving Mary to consider what she had heard.

More than anything, for the first time, she truly hoped that Rafeo was right, and that she was indeed the Guardian. She would like nothing more than to visit justice upon this foul creature. She could not understand why he was so eager to tell her what she wanted to know. He was obviously confident that she would die, but why not kill her now?

It was obvious to her that she was the bait for a trap. But as confident as Mabus was, even he had to understand that he was taking a risk. All she needed was to read from the book, and his reign of terror would be over. All she needed was a chance, and fate may have provided her with it. Earlier, when she had pressed against her restraints, she had felt the one on her left arm loosen.

CHAPTER 22

"THE SCENE, HERE OUTSIDE LE ROYAL Hotel in Amman is one with shades of martial law. Over the past week, the U.N. security force, led by the U.S., has been present but low key as officials have seen to the final preparations for the upcoming peace conference; although the increased military presence suggests there may be something afoot.

"Political leaders from most of the developed world, as well as spiritual leaders and representatives from the world's major religions will meet here to discuss the need for peaceful co-existence. The venue is focused on a new educational initiative through the media, in an effort for the general, global population to better understand and appreciate their neighbors, and to ensure the equal share for the most basic necessities, food and water.

"The BBC has uncovered, however, that at this time, the senior leadership, including the section commander are currently unavailable, and are reported to be currently off-site. The members of the security detail are reported to be currently over-tasked, as the increased activity seems to be misdirected, a potential omen for this historical gathering.

"Sherry Landon, BBC News."

"Goddammit!" Gabriel yelled and smacked the power button on the radio hard enough to crack the display. Sam, Christian, Gabriel, and Eric had been traveling in the same SUV as their convoy made the three-hour journey from Petra to Amman, though, at the speed they were traveling, they would probably make the trip in around two hours.

"Pennman, get on the phone and tell Johnson you are enroute, and for him to get his shit together," Gabriel yelled over his shoulder. Eric did not hesitate; he pulled his phone out and began to dial.

Gabriel had a sudden flash of inspiration. A memory from their investigation they had stumbled on after finding Luke back in the U.S. the different IEDs they had found. There had been a few different designs, but the one that stuck out suddenly in his mind was the multiple brown leather briefcases. They had chosen a very common object, making it harder to identify.

"Tell him to have anyone carrying a brown leather brief case to be searched. Anyone refusing is to be detained," he continued, while Eric spoke into his phone.

Christian laughed and sat forward in his seat in the back of the SUV. It was the first sound he had made since they left the Garden, over thirty minutes ago.

Gabriel spun in his seat to face Christian.

"This isn't fuckin' funny. I'm facing charges of dereliction because of you, and you think it's funny," he spat, then almost instantly, his eyes relaxed, followed by his shoulders.

"I'm sorry," he said quietly, after Sam had reached over to touch his arm.

"What was that all about?" Sam asked, looking at Christian through the rear-view mirror.

"It's almost absurd. We're looking for people carrying brown briefcases... might as well arrest half the city," Christian exclaimed.

The SUV raced on in silence for a time after that, as the occupants considered what Christian had said. "Our task may be daunting, but it is ours none the less," Gabriel answered. His insight was not lost on the others, in fact, most of them could feel the hair on the back of their necks stand on end. He was right, and even if the fate of the world rested with the four of them, each in turn believed they would carry the day.

The emotions of the day got the best of Sam, only for a moment. She discreetly wiped a tear from her cheek, only Gabriel had seen it but knew it was no sign of weakness, simply determination. She, along with everyone else had chased any last lingering doubt from their minds.

"Eric, I might suggest a collapsible defensive perimeter with checkpoints at two blocks and one block from the facility, then at the entrance, and a final check point in the lobby," Sam said after a while. Her statement turned heads from everyone in the car; Gabriel couldn't hide his smile.

"Have you been reading my notes?" he asked her playfully.

She smiled, then looked quickly to Pennman, in the mirror. He had to nod and smiled.

"S.O.P. ma'am," he said with a smile. "You have had a good teacher."

Sam smiled and rubbed Gabriel's leg, then looked at Christian.

"Yeah, it's been the standard operating procedure every time the FBI has come and claimed one of our crime scenes," she laughed.

Mary had struggled for at least an hour but had finally managed to slip the loose bond. A few more seconds after that and she was free. The effort had emphasized the pain in her chest, though she tried to put it out of her mind.

Her captives had been both brutal and arrogant. They must have thought that she was too badly injured to get free, as they had left her in a room without a locked door, or a guard outside.

As she fled her way out of the room, she had made it to the end of the corridor and could see a door leading to the light of day and the outside world. She dared to let herself think that she could be rid of this place. She carefully peeked around the doorway of the one room she needed to pass before she could bolt to her freedom.

To her surprise, this room was also empty. As she tiptoed past, she noticed the room was smattered with maps, communiqués, and other sensitive looking material.

She hesitated for a moment and closed her eyes. After a deep breath, she decided to take the opportunity to learn of her enemies' true intensions and walked into the room.

Her eyes darted around frantically, trying to quickly discern what would be most useful to her. There, on the wall, was an aerial photo of the hotel where the conference was to be held. Around the building were red marks noting the security check points set at a two-block radius, and notes regarding the times that the *Meilich* would act. She stared at the word. It seemed familiar to her, but she put it out of her mind – 8:00 pm was the time marked on the map. She knew the time, that is all that mattered.

Her attention turned once again to escaping, set in her goal to let Christian know what time to expect the attack. She crept towards the door, still undetected, and stepped into the hall.

Suddenly, she could hear voices coming from the opposite end of the complex. It made sense for her to run to freedom, but if they caught her, they would certainly kill her. She closed her eyes for a moment. She believed in her heart that Christian was coming for her, and all she had to do was hold on until then.

Mary swallowed hard and turned back towards the room she had come from. The voices were drawing nearer as she brushed away her tears and opened the door to her cell. She raced over to the chair she had been tied to and frantically refastened the restraints, simply wrapping her wrist up in the last one and feigning unconsciousness as the door to her cell slowly opened.

She could smell Mabus as he entered the room – the rot and decay were unmistakable. She slowly opened her eyes as though just coming back to her senses. Mabus stared at her for a few moments, then chuckled, and turned to leave. Near the threshold of the door, he stopped and turned to the guard.

"Check her restraints. I'd hate to have to kill her for trying to escape," he ordered, then turned back, and smiled fiendishly.

His smile soon turned to an evil laugh as he traveled down the hall. In the echoes, Mary heard two distinctive words. "Eight o'clock," followed by louder laughter.

The guard sent to check on her discovered the loose strap. Her mind was racing, having realized she had been repeating the time from the map in her mind... had Mabus heard her thoughts?

It was the last thing she remembered as the guard hit her in the head with the butt of his rifle, knocking her into unconsciousness once again.

"10-4. Stand fast and do not engage. The section commander and his team will rendezvous on-site. Observe and advise, rendezvous in 15 minutes." Pennman closed his phone and tucked it into a pocket on his tac-vest. The convoy came to a stop as they met up with a U.N. marked vehicle.

"There's my ride," Pennman said with a grin. He had to speak up to talk over the noise from the traffic jam they had just created.

"That was the squad leader reporting from the co-ordinates we got from Rafeo's GPS. Mary's being held in an old potash plant about ten miles away." Eric had leaned in to make sure everyone could hear him.

"There is no cavalry to send if you guys step in it too deep, so be smart about it. And if you guys are gonna get into a shoot-out at the OK corral, just remember we're under a fucking microscope here!" Eric yelled as he stepped away from the vehicle. He then paused and turned back and spoke quietly, more for Christian.

"I wish I was goin' with you… bring her home safe," he said with a grin, then closed the door, and ran over to the other vehicle; the convoy moved on.

Christian smiled. He felt so determined, now that he knew, despite the odds, that he would get Mary out of there. A four-man squad had been added to the twelve men, themselves included, that they had.

"Not exactly a strike force," he said to himself, then shrugged and focused himself to the task at hand. He looked up to see Sam smiling at him through the rear-view mirror.

"I'm on-site, now, Lieutenant! We're supposed to be professionals, and from where I'm sitting, it looks like we're causing more problems than anyone." Eric keyed the mic on his radio and turned to the vehicle driver. "Stop right here, Corporal. This will act as a decent roadblock for now."

The truck rolled to a stop and Eric and the driver stepped out of the cab. Eric paused to look up at Le Royal, while the two squads of soldiers leapt out of the back of the truck. They busied themselves putting up barricades and began rerouting vehicle and foot traffic.

"Sergeant!" he yelled. One of the soldiers stopped what he was doing and ran over to Eric. Another soldier took his place without a word of instruction. "I assume I can count on you to run this check point."

"Yes, sir!" Even the sergeant's response was polished.

"Remember, we're checking IDs. Only conference personal past this point. Advise station two if you see anyone with a brown briefcase, and do not detain them here. We'll take care of it at the next point, further away from the public," Eric instructed.

"Yes, sir!" the Sergeant once again replied.

"Good. Now, if you'll excuse me, I need to go whip the rest of this place into shape." Eric turned on his heel and began, at a jog, up towards the hotel. Again, he keyed his mic and continued to give orders as he went.

"I need every platoon leader to report to me in the lobby in five minutes. We'll have this place in order by lunch time." He keyed his mic off and checked his watch; it was 11:41 AM.

They pulled the three SUVs off the road into an empty lot next to an abandoned apartment building. The potash plant was just up the street. Even before the vehicles had come to a full stop, the men were jumping out; they landed in formation, weapons at the ready.

Within a few seconds, a soldier in urban camouflage gear appeared near the corner of the building on the blindside of the potash plant. Without a word, everyone quickly made their way to his position.

"Sir," the soldier reported sharply. "We've been on station for almost three hours now since your orders came through. The place is a maze of shit, but we managed to download floor plans for the office complex where, near as we can tell, they are holding the hostage. We have eyes on at the south, east and north face of the building."

Some uneasy looks were exchanged throughout the group as they studied the floor plans. Gabriel then pointed out three two-man teams. "Join up with the men on-station." The three two-man teams disappeared in different directions to meet up with the men at the three other quadrants.

"There is some good news, though..." the soldier went on, "...about two hours ago, a small convoy of vehicles left. There was no sign of the hostage, but near as we can tell, that left their standing strength at less than twenty."

Gabriel threw a quick glance at Christian. "We'll take it," he said with a wink, then turned back to the group.

"Let's get some eyes on from above." Gabriel pointed to the two snipers standing near the back of the remaining group and nodded his head to indicate the five-story building they were standing next to. The two men drew their sidearms and rushed into the building. The five team members who remained did a final magazine check and disengaged the safeties on their weapons. Christian moved his fire selector to fully automatic. Gabriel took notice and grabbed him by the arm.

"I know you're mad, but you might hit her, ya know."

Christian stared him down for a minute, then had to concede to his logic. He moved the selector back to semi-automatic. And nodded to his friend.

"I feel like I should be sitting in the truck with a headset, but I really want in on this one," Sam said with a smile.

Christian had to think for a minute. Sam had some field experience, but nothing like this.

"It's up to you, Gabe… it's your show." Gabriel looked at Christian as if to show his displeasure at having to make the call. Finally, he looked at Sam.

"You're on me," he said plainly. Sam smiled and put her head down quickly.

"I can't wait," she said sort of under her breath, but still loud enough for everyone to hear. A hushed chuckle rippled through their group. The moment was interrupted by the radio.

"Longbow in position," the sniper team reported in. "Doors open."

Gabriel looked around. "Here we go," he said quietly. Like a flash, Christian took the lead and sprinted around the building, dashing towards the plant. The others had a difficult time matching his pace. He tucked in against the building and waited for the others. They were breathing heavier than him.

"Let's have a diversionary action; you guys sweep up this level, and I'll go for Mary," he ordered and didn't wait for conformation. He darted effortlessly up a nearby stairwell. Gabriel nodded and led the rest of the team forward.

CHAPTER 23

Rafeo tried to calm himself. He sat alone in the control room, nervously watching the monitor. The satellite image showed the team spread out and getting into position around the facility where Mary was being held.

He had not felt the Garden so empty as it was now, since his first time here. After he had lost the Guardian nearly two millennia ago, the book had led him here.

Now, only he and a few of the hopefuls remained behind to watch and wait. He had not felt so sure of having found the Guardian again, as he did with Mary. The fact that the Book had miraculously repaired itself was, to him, a sign.

He got to his feet and walked from the control room into the garden. He hoped that the serenity would bring him peace. He could see the five remaining hopefuls sitting together in meditation. He took solace in the fact that at least they were safe, but the moment was fleeting.

With a forced grin, he nodded to the group, even though they had not noticed his presence. He moved to return to the control room but stopped. He could hear what he believed to be a voice, as clear in his mind as though there was someone standing next to him.

Rafeo slowly entered the library and could see the book sitting closed on its pedestal. It awaited its master but called to him. He slowly crossed the room, tentatively reaching out his hand as he neared the sacred tome.

He carefully ran his hand across the weathered binding and caressed the faded cover. The voice in his head was only a whisper, and the words were unintelligible, but in his mind he understood.

Rafeo picked up the book and stood for a time in silence. Holding it seemed almost to heal a pain he hadn't realized he had. He took a deep breath, and in a moment of clarity, put the book back in its place.

Over the years, it had been stolen from him several times and used by some who, in turn, were used by the book. He knew that its purpose was only to be read. Though intended for the Guardian, the book itself longed to serve its purpose. If read by a mortal incapable of receiving the knowledge it contained, great disasters or horrors would follow. Rafeo, as the Magi of old, had received training to read small passages from the book, and to resist the urge to read it in its entirety. He usually chose not to touch it at all.

He stood for another moment, listening to his heart pounding in his chest, his anxiety to read the book growing within him. He tried to rationalize it, telling himself that the book would guide him to the true Guardian, that it would help his friends see the task before them to its end, that he could correct his mistake from so long ago.

He exhaled the breath he had not realized he was holding. The sound broke the deafening silence in the room and was enough to clear his head. He consciously returned his arm to his side and walked purposely from the room.

He returned to the control room with his faith renewed in his friends. They would persevere without the Book's power, and so would he.

On the display, Rafeo could see a figure burst from cover well ahead of the rest of the team. He walked closer to the screen to study the image. It was Christian. He watched as Christian allowed the rest to catch up, then bolted up the stairs on his own.

"Same angry man as you were in your youth," Rafeo said to the emptiness. He feared for the man, knowing the path his impetuous nature had led him down in the past. "Let this be the moment you defeat yourself, my friend." He touched the screen and closed his eyes, as if it would help Christian hear him.

Rafeo's eyes opened abruptly. He stared at his hand on the screen. He could feel a vibration. He moved his hand and cocked his head to the side. The vibration intensified, now dislodging small amounts of dust from the cavern wall.

"No," he said aloud and ran back towards the control room entrance, leading back to the Garden.

"To the armory!" he yelled, as he emerged from the control room. The meditating hopefuls, sitting in a group, cross-legged on the ground in the garden not fifty feet away, opened their eyes in unison, nervously looking around for a moment as they could now feel the vibration themselves.

"Now!" Rafeo ordered, as he frantically waved the others toward him.

He turned and ran ahead of them to the armory. He had enough time to choose his favorite katana and sling it over his back before the others joined him in the room. He turned to see their nervous faces.

"Arm yourselves," he said quietly, then joined them as they quickly selected various assault rifles and loaded magazines. They had just enough time to arm the weapons before an explosion rocked the room.

"They're upon us," Rafeo exclaimed, looking around frantically, as if a solution was written on the walls. "You five remain here at the entrance and do what you can. Try to hold this position at the entrance." He checked to make sure they understood and then ran out.

Quintus was the first to emerge through the hole they had blasted right through the rock of the mountain. Rafeo waited for a moment, and as suspected, several others soon joined him inside.

Rafeo shouldered his weapon and fired three times, taking out three targets. He dropped his rifle to his side, overcome with rage, as weapons fire erupted from the insurgents and those in the entrance to the armory. He broke into a sprint, unsheathing the katana as he ran.

The hopefuls were effective as they dropped enemies trying to shoot Rafeo, though not all, as he was struck at least twice by enemy fire. He was not slowed down by the gunshots even slightly and remained fixated on his target.

Quintus stood motionless, waiting for Rafeo to close the distance between them. With a grin, he unveiled his own sword, and took up a ready position.

Rafeo leapt into the air striking Quintus and knocking him back, despite him having blocked the thrust from Rafeo's sword. There was a brief interruption of gunfire, as both sides took a moment to witness the beginning of this sure-to-be-epic battle.

Quintus found his feet quickly and assumed the attack, charging at Rafeo. They exchanged blows, parrying and lunging, neither one developing a definite advantage.

Quintus managed to push Rafeo back far enough that the two paused to observe each other. Quintus held up his sword as if to display it to Rafeo.

"Good old Rafeo... old being the key word there," he said, indicating his disdain for the weapons. He quickly drew a pistol and fired. Rafeo held out his hand and quickly recited a Latin phrase. The bullets from Quintus' gun fell harmlessly to the ground in front of Rafeo.

"Okay, so you've learned a few new tricks," Quintus muttered with disgust and leapt forward to resume his sword attack. Rafeo resumed his guard as their swords clashed. Rafeo's bullet wounds closed and healed as the two continued their struggle.

Another explosive round detonated close to the entrance of the armory. Rafeo realized the hopefuls were at risk. He steadied himself and whirled his blade. Though he and Quintus were evenly matched, their weapons were not. The lighter katana enabled Rafeo to move quicker than his opponent. He knocked the other's sword aside and slashed him through the middle, knocking Quintus to the ground. Rafeo knew it was not a fatal blow to Quintus but took advantage of the time he had to break back towards the armory.

Quintus stood slowly as his wound healed, then turned to one of the other soldiers and nodded. The soldier fired another rocket. Rafeo felt it scream past him, the rumble from the engine being felt throughout his body. He was within twenty feet from the hopefuls as he watched them absorb the full impact from the rocket, killing them and knocking him backwards to the ground.

He lay still, injured for the moment, but it was long enough for Quintus to arrive where he lay. Quintus kicked Rafeo's sword away and grabbed him by the throat. He led Rafeo backwards by the throat to a nearby tree.

"I may not be able to kill you as easily," he said with a wink, his face then darkening. "But perhaps this will do." Quintus then thrust the sword through Rafeo's gut, lodging it deep into the tree, effectively pinning Rafeo there. He then bent the remainder of the protruding sword around to the side, making its removal far more difficult.

"Now doesn't this feel all too familiar... be a good lad, and stick around," Quintus said with an evil grin, then disappeared. He returned a few moments later, carrying the Book. "I believe this is mine, and you have kept it from me far too long."

The sword through his stomach may not have killed him, but the pain was nearly blinding. Rafeo pushed through it and managed to speak to Quintus as he walked away.

"That is what you fail to understand..." he gasped and continued, "...it isn't yours, but the rightful owner will come for it one day."

Quintus turned and smiled again. "On that day, old friend... it will be too late." He then turned and walked out with his few remaining soldiers.

Christian hesitated at the top of the stairs. Ahead of him lay a long, metal catwalk past the mixing silos. He knew the foot falls from his boots across the steel grated floor would give away his position before he could find cover again. He could see two soldiers standing at the far side. Seconds before he broke cover, a third soldier walked around the corner, practically on top of him.

He stood, dropped his rifle, and pulled his knife, plunging it into the stomach of the soldier. He then pitched his lifeless body over the railing. He turned, expecting to be under attack from the two at the far end, but to his surprise their attention was elsewhere. His compatriots had begun their assault on the lower level, distracting the two soldiers ahead of him, temporarily anyway.

Christian snatched up his rifle on the run and sprinted towards the others. One heard his approach and turned but was taken out by the snipers in the abandoned building. Before the sniper could fire again, Christian shouldered his weapon and eliminated the second.

Christian saw a man dressed in a long black robe further down the hallway, towards the office complex. He recognized him from Auschwitz.

"Mabus!" he yelled, louder than intended, getting the other figure's attention. Mabus turned and charged towards him. Christian wasn't sure if it was the adrenalin, but Mabus appeared to be flying. He took no further time to consider it, since Mabus had closed the distance to him very quickly. He managed to get one shot off before Mabus tackled him, grabbing him by the throat and pinning him to the ground.

He was face to face with Christian, close enough that Christian could see his dark face, and smell his foul stench. Mabus leaned in as if to smell Christian. He closed his eyes for a moment, then opened them and smiled.

"Interesting," he said slowly. Christian was very confused but was too worried that he would die before rescuing Mary.

Before Christian could respond, the sniper had refocused on Christian's position and opened fire on Mabus, hitting him twice in the head. The bullets seemed to pass right through him without doing much damage at all. As Christian looked in disbelief, he found himself covered in a dark, oily substance.

The shots to the head were enough to make Mabus retract from Christian. He stood up and turned in the direction the shots had come from. He thrust his hands forward and the entire right side of the top floor of the building exploded, consumed by blinding and powerful bolts of lightning. Christian had doubts that the sniper had survived the attack.

Christian capitalized on the distraction, picked up his weapon, selected full auto fire, and squeezed the trigger. The bullets, though not doing any real damage, were causing Mabus pain as he fled from the area.

Christian got to his feet, holding his throat. He took a moment to scan the building where the sniper had been; there was little left to see. Fortunately, the second sniper had chosen a separate room on the left side of the building. Christian could see that he had been rocked by the blast and covered with debris. The soldier quickly recovered himself and got back into a firing position. He gave Christian a thumbs up then scanned for his next target. Christian waved and continued onwards, sobered from the moment before.

Christian returned his weapon to semi-auto and changed the magazine, having emptied the last one into Mabus. He stumbled towards the office area, regaining his strength quickly as he pushed on.

He paused again, as the sound of a woman screaming caught his attention.

"Mary…" he whispered, and took off at a sprint, re-energized in his task.

At the first doorway, he broke through, quickly locating a soldier waiting in ambush, and ended him before the soldier could even react. Mary's cries grew louder as he approached, but they also sounded more desperate. Christian let his anger fuel him as he moved towards her voice.

He turned right at the next corridor and knew he had found her. There were three soldiers standing at a door in the middle of the hall. Christian opened fire and took out two before he was forced to scramble back around the corner for cover.

Sam took a deep breath as they entered the building. They came to a large, open assembly area. From her position, she could see several enemy soldiers and vehicles.

Gabriel made hand gestures, informing the other two soldiers to target the upper-level catwalk for snipers, while he and Sam would circle right, and deal with the units on the ground. After a nod for conformation, they broke cover and opened fire, their first few shots catching the enemy off-guard. Their weapons had been equipped with sound suppressers, which helped conceal their location temporarily, even after they began firing.

The corporal decided to hit and run, pausing only briefly every few seconds to fire, while his new partner covered his advance from his position near the door where they entered.

Sam and Gabriel quickly realized there were dozens of the enemy there, and if any of them made it to the vehicles, they could use them as cover, as well as deploy the vehicles heavier weapons.

"Cover me – I got an idea!" Sam yelled. She didn't wait for Gabriel's objection and sprinted from cover towards the closest vehicle. She scampered inside, fired it up, and got to the cannon turret.

"In a truck with a headset," she said to herself as she put on the ear protectors and opened fire on the crowd of soldiers still clambering for cover. From the corner of her eye, she noticed a man wielding an RPG. Sam let go of the fire controls and slumped back into the vehicle, but she did not stay there. She took two grenades from her belt, pulled the pins, and threw them towards the cannon ammunition.

She hoped that Gabriel would be ready to cover her escape and burst through the vehicle door, running back to her initial position where Gabriel was waiting.

"Fire in the hole!" she yelled and dove behind cover next to Gabriel a split second before the armored personnel carrier she had just fled exploded violently. The fireworks were enough to set any surviving soldiers on a path to retreat.

"Fire in the hole?" Gabriel inquired with a cough, choking on the smoke from the explosion. She looked up at him and grinned.

"Corporal... you clean up in here!" He yelled across the room then keyed his mic. "All units converge on the south exit to the building. We've got them on the run."

He stood up to see a quick salute from the corporal, then helped Sam to her feet.

"Let's go check on your boss," he said, pointing from whence they came.

CHAPTER 24

CHRISTIAN PEEKED AROUND THE CORNER AND drew fire from his one remaining adversary. He managed to see the soldier cross the hall and take up position in the doorway. Christian didn't want to risk using a grenade that close to Mary's cell. Instead, he pulled one out and threw it down the hall with the pin still in.

The ruse worked; the soldier darted out from cover when he heard the thud of the grenade. He sprinted towards the explosive, hoping to have enough time to pick it up and throw it back.

When he got to it, he laughed at the fact the pin was still in it. "You must be new at this," he chuckled in broken English. Christian stepped around the corner, his weapon focused on the enemy with both hands on the grenade. The soldier realized, at that point, that Christian would be able to shoot him before he pulled the pin, let alone throw the grenade. They stared at each other for what felt like an eternity. The soldier flinched to move, and Christian put him down.

The complex had grown quiet after their exchange. Christian walked carefully down the hall towards Mary's cell. In front of the door, he had to hesitate and

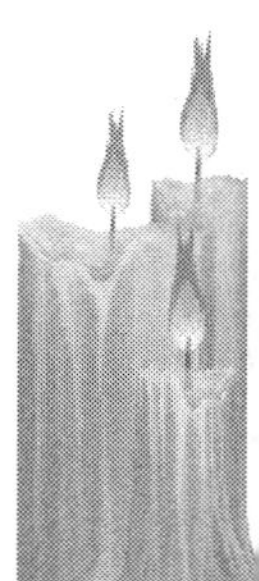

grab his weapon, again in answer to footsteps he heard approaching.

To his relief, it was Sam and Gabriel. He sighed and returned to the task of opening Mary's cell door, without so much as a greeting to his friends. Sam looked at Gabriel and shrugged, then they both moved to join Christian at the door.

Gabriel slung his weapon and began to search the dead soldiers for a key. Without any luck, he stood up again, looked at his rifle, then hesitated, deciding, instead, to grab the dead soldier's rifle. He slammed the butt into the door handle until the weapon broke, then grabbed the next man's rifle and continued.

Eventually, the doorknob gave way. Christian stuck the barrel of his gun against the mechanism and fired, disposing of the rest of the lock. He kicked the door open, and they all rushed in, freezing in the moment, caught in shock by Mary's appearance. She had obviously been tortured, beaten up and sat, slumped in the chair. For a moment Christian feared the worst, until she gasped, waking from unconsciousness. Christian reached for his knife and cut the restraints away, freeing Mary.

She slumped forward into his arms. She was weak but still in pretty good shape, all things considered. Sam gave Mary her water bottle; she drank deeply from it. After she swallowed, Mary looked up at Christian.

"I knew you would come," she said, forcing a smile.

Christian returned the smile and held her tightly. After a moment, Mary stood up a little straighter.

"Eight o'clock," Mary said in a panic. "They're going to strike at the conference at eight o'clock at the outer check points."

Christian looked at her, puzzled. "How do you know that?"

Mary didn't respond right away; she looked around, as though nervous or guilty.

"I got out of my cell." She began to cry but continued through her tears. "I tried to escape, but I found their boardroom with all their plans."

Gabriel took out his phone and contacted Pennman.

"It's coming at eight o'clock."

"I tried to escape, but I couldn't. I'm so sorry," Mary sobbed.

Christian bent down to one knee as she dropped to the floor in tears. He held her chin in his hand, and lifted her face so she was looking at him.

"It's not your fault," he said warmly. He took his vest off and removed his tunic and wrapped it around Mary, leaving him in just his T-shirt. He rubbed her arms to try and warm her up and calm her down.

"Really, it's not your fault," he repeated, and Mary began to calm down. Gabriel finished his phone conversation and put the phone away.

"And you may very well have saved the peace conference," Gabriel said with a smile, helping the two of them off the floor. They quietly began to move to the door when Gabriel's radio went off.

"Boss, the facility is clear, but I think we got media and law enforcement coming."

"Of course, we do," Gabriel said, before keying his mic. "Rally back at the vehicles. We need to get out of here, asap." He then looked at Mary.

"Are you okay to move?" he asked. Before she could answer, Mabus appeared at the doorway and blew all of them against the rear wall of the cell with the wave of his hand, showing his tremendous power. He held his captives with the stolen, god-like power of his thoughts. Each of them struggled to get free, with no luck, all but Gabriel being able to key his mic.

"I will destroy you all!" Mabus screamed, his breath and stench filled the room. Mary could only scream, frazzled as her nerves already were. Mabus began to squeeze his hands and was able to manifest the feeling of choking the life from his prisoners from across the room. Each could feel a hand on their throat, though no one was touching them physically, as their breath was squeezed from their bodies. They had all begun to black out when a barrage of gunfire erupted from the hallway to the right of where Mabus was standing. He howled, as though in pain. His physical form shifted, and his body seemed to shrink as he took flight and flew out of the room. His cloak flapped behind him, like a dark carpe, as he escaped down the hall away from the gun fire,

Christian swore he heard Mabus say "eight o'clock" as he made his escape. He was more thankful for the rescue at the moment, though. The four of them filed out into the hallway, after making their way to their feet. They came face to face with several soldiers, mouths agape.

"Thank you, corporal," Gabriel said, his voice gravely.

"What the hell was that?" the young man asked. Gabriel filed past him and slapped him on the shoulder.

"Probably best not to ask," he explained, then led them all out towards the vehicles. Christian took the opportunity to look the corporal in the eye and nod, to agree with Gabriel.

"Yeah... what he said."

They walked on in silence for a bit.

"Did I hear Mabus say eight o'clock?", Christian asked after a few minutes. Sam and Gabriel both turned and threw a glance back at Christian.

"I thought I heard it, too," Gabriel said slowly. Sam nodded the affirmative, as well.

"After I found the room, and made it back to my cell, Mabus confronted me. When he left, I swear I heard him say it, too. It was as if he was reading my thoughts," Mary added.

"So, he knows that we know..." Sam said what they were all thinking.

"There was something else, another word that doesn't make sense... *Meilich*?" she said, uncertain of its pronunciation.

"*Meilich...*" Christian repeated with a shrug.

"What the hell is that ticking sound?" the corporal asked from behind Mary. Before anyone could answer, Mabus reappeared in a whisp of smoke, howling as before, his cloak filling the room, as though it were able to grow in size at will, darkening even the lights overhead.

They dove for cover and began to fire at *Mabus*, but this time he did not try to escape. Mary yelled out in pain and Christian pulled away from the firing line to attend to her. He could feel heat coming from her and saw a faint glow from her skin. A chilled shiver washed over him as he thought back to his case in Florida that started this whole adventure.

"Ticking..." he said with horror in his tone.

"Gabriel, we need a bomb squad here, right now!" Christian screamed. Gabriel fired off a few more rounds, then crouched to see what was going on.

"They've put a bomb in her chest!" Christian shouted. Gabriel recoiled, unsure of what to do. He remembered the prisoners being booby-trapped.

"There isn't enough time... Fuck!" Gabriel answered. A strong volley of projectiles emanating from folds of his robe knocked several people down, killing the corporal. Mary looked around and saw the dead soldier lying near her. She realized that Gabriel was right. She sat up and kissed Christian long and deep.

"I said I didn't want anyone else to die because of me, and I meant it." Mary smiled through her tears. Christian was confused; he knew if they were going to save Mary, they had to act fast.

"Don't let these bastards win... Promise me!" she insisted. She grabbed the neck of his T-shirt to hold his focus. Christian nodded, and she put her trembling hand on his cheek. "I have loved you more than anyone could ever understand, and I always will."

Without another word, Mary jumped up and ran right towards Mabus. He focused his energy on her, now, but couldn't completely stop her determined strides.

The team opened fire on Mabus, breaking his concentration, and allowing Mary to get within five feet of Mabus when there was a tremendous explosion, knocking everyone back.

When they made it to their feet again, Mabus and Mary were nowhere to be seen.

Christian was in shock; he couldn't believe she was gone. Before he could say anything, the air was pierced by the sounds of emergency vehicle sirens approaching. Gabriel put his hand on Christian's shoulder.

"I'm sorry, man, you know this, but we need to leave," he said showing his desperation. Gabriel led the remaining soldiers back to the vehicles while Sam helped Christian walk.

The vehicles pulled out quickly and raced back towards Le Royal Hotel. Christian's gaze was fixed into nothingness, his breathing shallow and he did not speak a word. Even when the SUV passed through the crowds surrounding the hotel, he did not flinch.

The truck came to a stop and Gabriel leapt out. Eric Pennman fought through the chaos to join up with him. The two had a quick conversation in front of the truck before Gabriel signaled for Sam to get out, too.

"Christian, I need to go help wherever I can. Take my radio so you can call Gabriel if you need us." She paused while she handed him the radio.

"I can't tell you how sorry I am." She left it at that, knowing no words could help him right now. She placed her hand on his chest for a moment, his demeaner did not change. After another moment she turned and rushed out of the SUV.

A few moments later Christian found the strength to exit the vehicle. He was stunned by the scene that unfolded around him. The crowds were barely being held at bay at the outer check points. The noise was deafening but did help to distract Christian from his pain.

"Don't let them win!" he heard her say in his mind. He checked his watch, and it was quarter to eight. Whatever was going to happen here was going to happen soon. He stumbled down the walkway towards the hotel, not too far behind Gabriel and Sam. When he was challenged at the roadblock, he looked to Gabriel.

"He's okay!" Gabriel ordered, and Christian was let through. That one word kept running through his mind – *Meilich*. It had to mean something.

Christian stumbled closer to Gabriel and could overhear the argument he was having with Pennman.

"Look. Our intel comes right from the enemy camp. This is going to happen at eight o'clock. If these people aren't willing to surrender their briefcases, then we will shoot them and take them."

Gabriel pointed to a holding area just inside the second check point. There had to be dozens of people clutching their brief cases and yelling at the security personnel who were holding them at gun point.

Suddenly, Christian had a thought. He knew he recognized the word, *Meilich*. He ran into the hotel to the front desk.

"I need a computer with internet access, right now!" he demanded. The attendant directed him to the courtesy desk across the lobby and the computer there. Christian rushed over to the desk where a man was on the computer. He waited as long as he could, approximately three seconds, before he shoved the man out of the way.

"Believe me! I'm sorry, but I need to confirm something before a lot of people die."

Christian got little resistance from the man and set to work. He brought up a translation page and typed in the word *Meilich*. A few seconds later, he got an answer. He stared at the screen for another moment, then tore off, back outside to find Gabriel.

He checked his watch as he moved through the swarm of reporters and soldier. There was five minutes left. Christian stirred up the security forces as he forced his way through their station; he eventually found Gabriel.

"You've gotta stand down," he ordered.

Gabriel stopped what he had been doing and turned to face him.

"I don't have time right now. We've got five minutes left. I need to take these bombs and get them into those bomb disposal units.

"Decoy," Christian yelled. The word Mary didn't understand... *Meilich*... is *decoy* in Gaelic."

Gabriel froze as he heard the word.

"Think about it... how best to disrupt a peace conference? If you blow it up, you strengthen people's resolve... but if you trick the military into shooting dozens of delegates for no apparent reason…" Christian let Gabriel figure out the rest.

"Other than fear and paranoia..." Gabriel said quietly. He looked around at the chaotic scene all around him. They both realized that it made sense. "What if you're wrong?", Gabriel asked.

Christian smiled before he replied. "You just gotta have faith."

CHAPTER 25

"IN A FITTING TURN OF EVENTS here at the peace conference, an act of faith at the zero hour has changed a potential massacre into a second chance. UN security forces holding delegates suspected of transporting bombs decided to stand down rather than taking the delegate's briefcases, the suspected bombs, by force.

"There had been reports that if the delegates would not surrender the briefcases before eight o'clock local time the security forces would have to detain them further, or worse, in the interest of public safety. The delegates were adding fuel to the fire by challenging the soldiers to carry out their orders.

"As the clocks struck eight, the delegates seemed to settle down. Some have said that it was almost as if they were "waking up" from a nightmare. Though there is still concern as to whether there was some kind of mind control being applied by a terrorist group, the act of faith demonstrated by the soldiers has added an atmosphere of hope for these peace talks.

"Sherry Landon, BBC News."

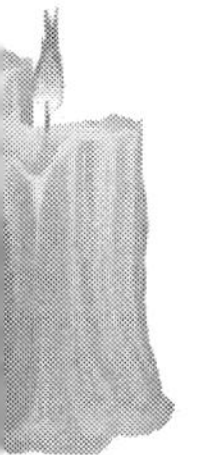

As though a switch had been thrown, every one of the delegates suddenly stopped yelling at the soldiers and began asking what was going on. Gabriel and Pennman were ecstatic with the outcome and had no compunctions of sharing their elation with Christian. He was subdued, devastated by the death of Mary, but consoled he was able to carry out her last wish.

The crowd quickly turned into a love fest – hugs and cheers were shared by everyone. He was swept up by the crowd and found himself trying desperately to focus, but just let his emotions run over him. In his state, Christian began to look for Sam to thank her for her help. She was nowhere to be found. Christian slowly began to expand his search and figured she would be with Gabriel. He worked his way back through the crowd towards the barricade where he had last scene his friend.

"Hey, where's Sam?" he yelled over the crowd. Gabriel was busy greeting and thanking his subordinates and the delegates.

"She's around here, somewhere," he answered, almost out of hand.

"No… she isn't," Christian answered, tapping him on the shoulder to try to get his attention fully. Gabriel turned to look Christian in the eye.

"She has to be..." Gabriel said, as his smile slowly faded from his face. Christian shook his head. Gabriel grimaced and keyed his mic.

"Sam, come in..." He released the radio, expecting a response. After a few moments, Gabriel began to work his way through the crowd towards the quieter confines of the hotel. Christian was right on his heals.

"Sam, come in..." he tried again. This time he could hear a faint response from the radio; it almost sounded like crying. They could make out one word… "car".

"We gotta find her," Christian said, suddenly desperate. Gabriel stopped a passing soldier and took his radio. He gave the radio to Christian.

"Let's split up," he ordered. "Switch to TAC 2; I don't wanna start a panic." He sprinted towards the parking garage.

Christian took off running around the building, hoping she was at the SUVs they had parked earlier that day. The search became frantic as Christian searched vehicle after vehicle without luck. The situation seemed surreal amidst all the celebrating people; Christian and Gabriel were desperate.

After what seemed an eternity, Christian's radio went off.

"I got her," Gabriel said quietly. She's up in the hallway, near the banquet hall… she has a brown briefcase." Christian felt a lump in his throat; he had lost Mary, and he certainly didn't want to lose his old friend.

He sprinted through the lobby and up the grand staircase to the second level, near the banquet hall. He brushed past several people mingling in the hall, unsure of which way to go until he heard a muffled scream and saw several people running towards him from the other side of the building.

"Outside people, please move outside!" he yelled as he ran against the current of people. He turned another corner and the scene unfolded before him.

Sam stood quivering in the hallway. She carried a brown briefcase in one hand and what looked like a detonator in the other. Gabriel stood in her path, holding her at gun point. Christian slowly walked up beside her. He could see the strain in both their faces.

"What's going on, Sam?" Christian asked calmly. She did not appear to be in control of her own body. Christian's mind raced and he thought back to when they first met. The years of fog and inattentiveness fell away. He could now see Quintus in his mind's eye. He had, in fact, been the leader of the cult she had been rescued from all those years ago. Quintus knew this moment would come all that time ago. The revelation may not help him free her now, but it did send a shiver down his spine.

"I don't know... I can't stop myself..." Her voice was disjointed and strained.

"She told me she had to blow up the hotel," Gabriel said slowly.

"One bomb could restart the whole thing over again," Christian said what they were all thinking.

Sam went to take another step, but Gabriel pulled the hammer back on his pistol.

"Please, don't," he begged.

"I can't stop myself," she repeated, and slowly began to raise her hand holding the detonator.

"Christian... help me... I can't do this" Gabriel pleaded. Christian looked around desperately searching for an answer, a clue, anything. There was nothing.

"Oh God, help me!" Sam pleaded. Her hands were shaking... tears welled in her eyes, and Gabriel's. Christian took a deep breath and pulled his knife out.

"No!" Gabriel screamed, seconds before Christian plunged the blade into her chest. He grabbed the detonator to ensure it couldn't go off. Her body slumped forward, but Gabriel rushed in to catch her. He held her body, rubbed her face, and kissed her cheek. He wept bitterly while Christian stood aside and watched helplessly. After several minutes, Gabriel carefully lay her body on the ground, and stood up. He turned to Christian, unsure if he was mad or thankful for his solution.

"I did what I had to do," Christian said eventually. Gabriel spun quickly and put his fist through the wall. He held himself up for a moment with his other hand, then straightened up and turned back to Christian.

"I know you did... that's what hurts most of all." He keyed his mic again and ordered a medical team to their location.

"This was that Mabus guy... wasn't it?" Gabriel asked, wiping his tears. Christian nodded.

"He will pay..." Christian grimaced through clenched teeth.

"Didn't we watch him die this afternoon? Didn't Mary…" Gabriel trailed off.

"I don't know," Christian answered, then he smiled and pulled his cell phone out.

"But we may have a friend who can tell us and can bring Sam back," he said as he dialed.

"Rafeo..." Gabriel said as he clued in.

"Hello... listen, old man, we need you and the book. Sam is dead…and what?" Gabriel could tell from Christian's changing expression that something was wrong. Christian stood silently, struggling to hear his phone, then spoke quietly.

"Hold on... you hold on; I'll send help." Christian slowly closed his phone and slipped it into his pocket. He took a deep breath, and eventually looked up at Gabriel. His face darkened, overcome with rage.

"Those bastards found the Garden..." he said, spitting out the words.

"Quintus has the book and Rafeo sounded badly injured." He pulled his gun out and check the magazine, then re-holstered it.

"I'm going after Quintus. Can you take a chopper and help Rafeo? Maybe we can still help her," Christian said, pointing to Sam.

The medics arrived and quickly realized she was dead. They picked her up and put her on a stretcher. Gabriel produced his credentials and arranged for her to be taken to the hospital and held until further notice. Gabriel picked up the bomb Sam had been carrying.

"Yeah, I'll get rid of this and go get Rafeo. Call me when you find that prick," Gabriel said, forcing his determination to overpower his grief.

Christian nodded, and without another word, sprinted away towards the exit. He dashed outside and through the crowds onto the street. He ran until he was clear of the security check points.

Looking around, he noticed traffic moving one street over and set off running again. In amongst the cars, he spotted an Aston Martin DB9 coming his way. He stepped out into traffic and ordered the driver out of the car at gun point. He leapt into the car and sped off.

Christian activated the sat-nav in the car and keyed in the Queen Alia International Airport.

CHAPTER 26

THE AIRPORT WAS MORE OF A hunch then anything. Knowing the credentials that Rafeo had accumulated over his many years, Christian was sure that Quintus would be able to board an aircraft with one of possibly many identifications in his repertoire, despite the tightened security at the airport.

He had swung the car south and was racing through the city. Christian watched as the GPS counted down the distance to the airport. He had started at thirty-nine kilometers and had closed the distance to twenty, narrowly avoiding several accidents as he drove at a break-neck pace.

The Aston Martin screamed past a local police officer, who decided to give chase. Christian saw the lights behind him, though he knew he didn't have time to stop. Instead, he pulled out his cell phone and started to call Eric Pennman. He was sure Eric could call off the local police.

As he dialed, he found himself barreling into yet another traffic circle. His car slammed into the side of a delivery truck; the truck, in turn, veered out of its lane, causing a multi-vehicle pile-up. In the collision,

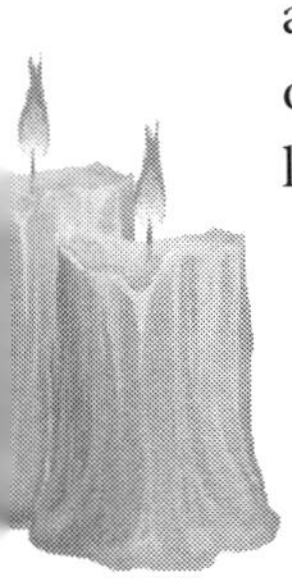

Christian's door window shattered, and he dropped his phone.

The car was still mostly functional, and Christian shrugged off the loss of his phone. He dropped the transmission into first gear and peeled away from the accident scene. The crowd of drivers from the effected vehicles were not happy with this. Christian could still see the police vehicle that was pursuing him, in his mirror, as he peeled away, the officer was caught up in the fray, but he also saw the officer yelling into his radio.

Christian had made it to the highway and opened up the car to its top speed. Now, numerous police vehicles were in pursuit but falling behind. He clenched his teeth and guided the car skillfully through the busy traffic on the highway.

The flight towards Petra had seemed lengthy, but the helicopter was able to traverse the distance in just under an hour. Gabriel could see smoke rising into the air from a section of the mountain range. He pointed to it, instructing the pilot where to go.

Gabriel was desperate; he needed Rafeo to bring Sam back the same way he had brought back Christian and Eric. He prayed Rafeo would be up to the task.

Before the helicopter had completely stopped, Gabriel rushed from the passenger compartment, followed closely by two soldiers and two medics. They approached the hole that had been blasted in the side of the mountain and Gabriel slowed to a quick walk.

"Whatever you see in here is not to be discussed..." he instructed the others. "In fact, consider it classified." He readied his rifle, shouldered it, and sighted his way through the opening. The bright garden that he had seen was gone; scorched earth was all that remained. Smoke from several small fires that remained choked the air and impaired their vision.

They checked in every possible direction for any element of the enemy left behind and continued to move, slowly, further into the garden. Soon, Gabriel saw Rafeo pinned to the tree as Quintus had left him. They cautiously approached, still scanning for the enemy. The medics broke from their position in the rear of the formation and ran to Rafeo. They scanned him quickly for bobby-traps and after finding none, began to look him over.

"This guy's dead, sir," one medic said, after a quick scan of the body stuck to the tree. Gabriel forced a small smile.

"You sure about that?" he asked, sarcastically.

"Yeah, pretty much," the medic answered, pointing at the large sword stuck through Rafeo's stomach, to emphasize his confirmation.

"Get this damned thing out of me..." Rafeo wheezed. The two medics fell to the ground in near-terror, both having been certain the man was dead.

"You want me to just pull it out?" Gabriel asked, uncertain of how best to proceed. Rafeo nodded and Gabriel grasped the sword with both hands. He was unable to dislodge the blade by himself and motioned for the medics to assist him. They were a little slow in responding but did eventually add their hands to the blade. With a grunt, the sword came loose, knocking the three pulling men backwards. Rafeo dropped to the ground in a heap.

The medics jumped to his side and cut his clothing completely away to begin treating his wounds. To their amazement, they could see the large wound begin to close before their eyes.

"It was Quintus," Rafeo gasped, the hole in his stomach making it difficult for him to breath or speak.

"I know, Christian told me. He went after him alone," Gabriel answered.

"He will need our help." Rafeo closed his eyes; he feared his young friend was in over his head.

"I need that book," Gabriel shouted, causing Rafeo to open his eyes again.

"Sam is…" Gabriel's voice faded. Rafeo lay still for a moment as the skin on his midsection healed completely. He reached up to Gabriel, who extended a hand to help the old man up.

"Then we must hurry," Rafeo exclaimed. He leaned on Gabriel as they began to move towards the entrance they had come in through. He gazed around the garden, seeing almost nothing that remained of its former splendor. His heart was heavy, but his strength was returning quickly.

"I have a score to settle." He spat as he walked, now more quickly and without aid from Gabriel.

Once they reached the entrance, Gabriel instructed the two soldiers to remain behind and secure the area from anyone trying to gain access to the garden.

"I'll send reinforcements asap," Gabriel yelled over the noise of the helicopter that was waiting.

The soldiers nodded and moved to the available cover. The others boarded the helicopter.

It quickly leapt into the air and headed back towards Amman. In the cabin of the aircraft was a very awkward silence. The two medics sat staring in shock at Rafeo. In return, the old man simply smiled and tried to make small talk. The others were either incapable, or at least unwilling, to answer. Gabriel and Rafeo shared a laugh at the other men's expense before settling into the business at hand.

Gabriel dialed his coms to monitor the local police band. After only a few seconds, he was amazed by the volume of radio chatter involving a stolen Aston Martin, and its path of destruction heading towards the airport.

"Sounds like we're needed at the airport," Gabriel yelled to the pilots over the noise of the chopper.

Christian now led an entire parade of police vehicles as he raced towards the airport. He didn't want to cause an accident or hurt anyone, but this was suppressed by rage; so much so, that he had not given much thought of what to do once he got to the airport. Once he left the vehicle, they would surely apprehend him, and Quintus would escape before he could straighten out the mess.

He caught the off-ramp exit he needed at the last second, hurtling down the ramp at near top speed, the back end of the car breaking loose. The smoke from the tires seemed to obscure the vision of the pursuing police officers. The pile-up forming behind him was a testament to the fact. Christian could not attach any emotion to it, however, as he focused too much on Quintus. He also hoped that Mabus would not be there, though his true anger was directed at him, Christian was uncertain if he could face both of them at once.

He could see the airport ahead. With his foot firmly buried in the accelerator, he closed the final distance to the terminal. He had opened a few seconds lead over his pursuers. As he approached the parking facility, he noticed a group of young men hanging out. He locked the brakes and slid to a halt in front of the men and jumped out.

"Not really my thing,", he said with a grin, pointing at the car. He shook the keys, catching the attention of one of the young men, who stepped forward and nodded. They understood each other without saying a word. Christian tossed him the keys and ran past them into the garage. He could hear excited cheers behind him, followed shortly by the squealing of tires. A few moments later, he watched the police vehicles scream past in pursuit of the car.

He stood in silence for a moment in the parking structure. He could not explain it, but he knew where Quintus was. He was here, and he was close. Another few seconds, and he bolted towards the stairwell. He ran faster than he had ever felt himself run, towards the roof. With a rage-fueled torrent, like that of an angry bull, he burst through the man-door at the top of the stairwell, onto the top level of the garage and into the dark of night. It took a few seconds for his eyes to adjust, but when they did, he realized he was fifty yards away from a limousine, next to which stood a man who had just gotten out of the vehicle.

"Quintus..." he said quietly to himself, then moved towards the car. He pulled his sidearm out of his holster and cocked it.

"Quintus!" This time he yelled, as he took aim at the man's head. The limousine driver turned, but Christian shot him before he could pull out his weapon. Several people on the other side of the parking structure heard the gun shot and screamed as they ran off, Christian paid them no attention.

"Christian, I believe..." Quintus said casually, as he stood still and grinned as Christian moved to within ten feet of him. Quintus turned to face him as he walked around the vehicle. He didn't raise his arms or try to take a defensive posture. Rather, he stood there, grinning at the man with the gun.

"Give me the book," Christian grunted.

Quintus stared at him blankly, still smiling.

"Sir, we now have reports of a vehicle chase terminating near the airport. The drivers of the car that the police apprehended say that a man fitting Christian's description gave them the car," the helicopter pilot yelled over the noise of the aircraft engine. "Also, from the local police band, we've heard reports of weapons fire at the airport parking garage roof."

Rafeo gave Gabriel a very concerned look. "We need to get to him now," he said, stating what Gabriel already knew.

"Pilot, get us there now!" Gabriel yelled.

"Yes sir, we're twenty clicks out, maybe five minutes..."

Gabriel nodded and closed his eyes. He hoped that Christian would get the book, for Sam's sake, if nothing else.

"Come now, boy..." Quintus used his most belittling tone. "You've spent enough time with that old fop. You should know that, unless you happen to have that thing loaded with bullets that have bathed in the blood of the Guardian." He paused and tilted his head to sarcastically examine Christian's gun.

"Doubtful," he smiled sarcastically, before continuing. "You could shoot at me all day, and it wouldn't give me much more than a skin rash."

Christian knew he was right but wasn't about to give up. "Be a hell of a thing to explain at the X-ray booth, though," he answered, still aiming the gun at Quintus.

A police helicopter buzzed over the roof of the garage, catching his attention for a second. Quintus went to continue his way towards the exit. Christian saw the movement and fired, striking Quintus in the leg. Quintus stopped and gripped the injury, waiting for it to heal.

"I know it still hurts, even for a moment. I'm just glad I brought a lot of bullets," Christian scoffed.

They stared at each other for a moment, until Quintus straightened up and shook the expelled bullet from his pant leg. A police team began to advance on them from the driving ramp.

"Drop your weapon!" they ordered.

"Indeed boy, give it up," Quintus said, then tried to step away again. Christian fired twice, striking him once in each leg.

"Who do you think they are going to believe? A gun wielding idiot... that's you... or an ambassador from the Spanish government... that would be me?" Quintus yelled, as he focused on expelling the bullets in his legs.

"Give me the book!" Christian repeated.

Another helicopter flew over. Christian could see Gabriel hanging out the door to get a better look. Now, Christian smiled.

"I might have influence over the leader of the UN security detail," Christian replied, his confidence bolstered by the arrival of his friends. The police had closed to within a few feet of them. Christian moved to within arms distance from Quintus.

"The next one will give you a hell of a headache, asshole, now, give me the book," he yelled, aiming directly at Quintus' head, confident that Gabriel would let the police know what was going on here.

"Drop your weapon!" the police ordered a second time.

"Might want to listen to them..." Quintus warned, straightening up again. Christian responded by pushing the barrel of his gun right against his head. "No?" Quintus was, again, full of sarcasm.

Gabriel's helicopter had landed on the far side of the roof. He and Rafeo were now running over as fast as they could.

Quintus looked at Christian and winked. "I guess you're just in the wrong place at the wrong time," he scowled.

Christian smiled.

"Right where I always am..." he answered quietly.

Christian took a deep breath and squeezed the trigger. There was a flash, and Quintus stumbled, still able to keep himself upright, despite the extra hole in his head. The blood flow stopped almost instantly, and Quintus was able to keep his footing. All the while, he glared at Christian.

A few seconds later, the police opened fire on Christian. He felt the burning as he was struck several times. In a heartbeat, he felt all his strength leave him, and began to crumple to the ground. He could see Quintus fall, as well.

The burning was quickly replaced by cold. He landed on the ground, quite softly, at least in his mind, and landing partially on Quintus. He could hear a muffled yell from Gabriel. While he lay in a pool of his own blood, his eyes growing dark, he could see Gabriel flashing his credentials to the police. Christian watched Rafeo run to him, seeing him more as a shadow.

He could tell Rafeo had grabbed him and rolled him over, but Christian felt neither the warmth from his hands nor the strength of his grip. Rafeo was trying to tell him something, but all sound was muffled, and he could barely make out the words. Another figure came to his side and Christian could tell it was Gabriel. In his mind, he was smiling, but could not tell if his face showed it or not.

Rafeo was gesturing frantically. Christian tried desperately to see what the old man was pointing at. He strained his eyes, and through the shadows he saw Quintus' body, still laying on the ground where he fell, his body was rapidly decomposing while he watched. Quintus was dead, but how?

In a burst of pain and excitement, Christian felt himself come back from the brink, but in his heart, he knew it was temporary.

"I'm sorry, son... I had you in front of me all this time, and never knew," he heard Rafeo say, his eyes full of tears. Christian struggled to figure it out. He smiled again, as he could see Mary, or a ghostly figure that resembled Mary, standing just behind Rafeo. She was easier to see and to hear.

"All this time..." she said, shaking her head. "You see, the bullets passed through you and then struck Quintus. He could have only been killed by a weapon touched by the blood of the Guardian… your blood," she said with a smile.

"Check the briefcase – it has to be in there." He heard Rafeo's muffled voice again, and he struggled to stay in this world a little longer.

"Just hang on son. I'll bring you back, and I won't lose you again..." Rafeo tried to sound soothing.

Christian could see his expression change. Then Gabriel grabbed the old man to pull him away.

"Bomb," was the only word Christian could make out. He remembered Quintus had been carrying a brown briefcase. He knew the blast would be enough to destroy his body completely. There would be nothing left to bring back this time.

"Find me again, old friend," he yelled with his last ounce of strength, before he let Rafeo go. The old man hesitated for a heartbeat, and nodded before Gabriel pulled him away.

Christian could feel himself grow colder; the darkness came for him. He smiled, finally knowing who he was. He looked into Mary's eyes and tried to speak.

"I love…"

"The standoff ended with the detonation of a small yet powerful explosive device. Casualties were kept to a minimum, as the area had been cleared by police earlier due to a reported armed gunman on the roof of the structure prior to the explosion.

"Dead is Christian Perditus, a UN security forces consultant and Spanish Diplomat Quintus Bracus.

"With the blast occurring so soon after the bomb scare at the Peace Conference, there is some speculation that this could interrupt the summit.

"Representatives from the conference are quoted as saying that they deplore the incident, and vow that they will not allow the actions of these despots to cloud the issues at hand. Only time will tell what the true fallout from these events will be.

"Sherry Landon, BBC News"

CHAPTER 27

RAFEO STOOD ON THE EDGE OF the coast looking out to the sea. From where he stood, in Essex, on the southeast coast of England, he knew he was looking across the channel towards Rotterdam in the Netherlands. He had made the voyage a few times over the Centuries.

It was late in the day, near the end of August, and he took some pleasure from the fact that the sun had come out for a change. The crops in the field around him had matured nicely and would yield a bountiful crop. He paused and smirked at the fact that these days, a good crop was almost guaranteed, but this was not always the case.

The countryside near where he now stood, at St Peter's Chapel, Bradwell-on-Sea, had changed in many ways, but in some critical ways, he was pleased that it remained familiar and remote even after all these years.

Since the loss of his refuge in the Garden of Eden, he had found it difficult to be at peace anywhere. Rafeo had helped erect this simple chapel nearly fourteen hundred years ago, and to him, it was like a homecoming, being here again.

He turned to smell the air. It was a welcome mix of the sea and the aroma of the surrounding farms. As

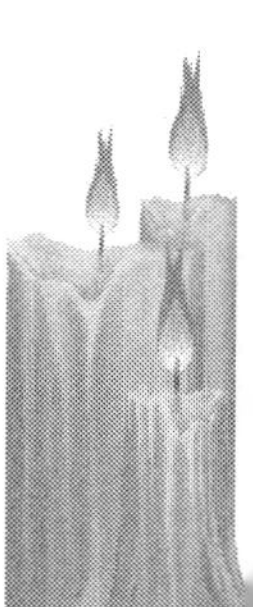

he turned, trying to calm himself, he could see in the distance two men and one woman walking up the long dirt path from the car park to the chapel. He was glad to recognize three friends as they approached.

While he waited, he turned his attention, once more, to the estuary that stretched out ahead of him towards the sea. He had laid many friends to rest here, more then he cared to count. As he held tight to the urn in his right arm, it pained him to think that, today, he was adding one more to that count.

After several minutes, he was greeted from a distance by one of the people approaching him.

“Wow. You sure can pick the spots, old man.” It was Gabriel who spoke. He was accompanied by Eric Pennman, as well as Sam.

Rafeo hadn’t seen them all since that fateful day. At the very least, he took comfort in the fact that he had been able to bring Sam back. He had wished to use the resurrection spell on the Guardian, but his body had been all but vaporized by the bomb blast, prohibiting any miraculous recovery.

Rafeo gave a smile showing he understood the affection meant by the comment. The others were close enough now to see his expression and could tell that there was still quite a bit of pain behind that smile.

“My friends...” Rafeo answered greeting them. “It has been too long.” He placed a hand on each of the men’s shoulders in welcome. In truth, it had only been two weeks since he had last seen these men in Amman, but given the circumstances, it had been too long since he had seen a friendly face.

"Sorry, we had some business to attend to," Eric answered. "But we will get to that later," he finished, with a warm smile.

"I have laid to rest many friends here over the centuries," Rafeo explained, as he turned again to face the sea. "In truth, I had almost grown accustomed to it." He turned back to face his friends with a wry smile.

"When you live forever, you come to accept the natural order of the human condition. You live and you die. I only wish the same applied to me."

As he spoke, a priest walked out from the small chapel to preside over the ceremony.

"But this time..." he said, grasping the urn with both hands. "But this time it calls for me to see how complete my failure is. I failed him nearly two millennia ago and did exactly the same when given a second chance."

Gabriel and Eric felt his pain. They may not have been searching for the Guardian for nearly two thousand years, but as soldiers, they felt as though they had failed their friend as well. Gabriel was the first to push those thoughts aside and moved to stand in front of Rafeo.

"But you didn't fail him." Rafeo looked at him in disbelief.

"From everything I heard from Christian, you loved him almost like a son for most of his life. Not because you thought he was someone special, but because he was there."

Rafeo did manage to take some solace in that.

"Christian always spoke very highly of you. I guess you could say he had a lot of faith in you."

Now they all smiled, before Gabriel continued.

"This is a setback, but it is not the end. Eric and I have both resigned from our positions, we have made new arrangements that may serve you better, and we're here to vow our service to you for as long as we draw breath." Rafeo looked at the other two and smiled warmly.

"What was it he said to you... 'Find me again, old friend?'. And I know you will, and we will help as much as we can."

"Ah faith... it is a powerful thing." The priest had overheard a little of their conversation. They all turned to recognize where the new voice had come from. They stood in silence for a time; Rafeo studied the priest that now stood before them.

To break the awkward silence, the priest smiled, looked to the sky, and continued. "I always stargaze around this time, not by sight but rather by faith. I may not be able to see them, but I believe the stars are still there."

Rafeo held up his hand to stop the priest.

"Don't I know you?" he asked slowly. He stared at the priest and took one step closer to him.

"Yes, I do. Only the last time I saw you, I believe you wore the clothes of a Muslim cleric, on the plane... and before that it was nearly a century ago, you were a missionary in Africa." Rafeo's tone grew louder.

Eric and Gabriel shared a quick glance, then without a word, both pulled out a handgun and aimed at the priest.

"Put them away, they won't do any good here." Rafeo ordered, as he grabbed the priest by his neck.

"But originally, you were a druid priest I saw on the field near Stonehenge." Rafeo walked forward, dragging the priest who offered no resistance.

"Constantine!" Rafeo spat and stared the priest down. "Where have you been? We needed you!" Rafeo was breathing hard from his anxiety and rage.

The priest regained his footing and stood back from Rafeo, who had released his grip in disbelief.

"Yes, keeper of the book of knowledge, that was my name." Constantine answered, and as he did, the expression on his face turned from fear to surprise and finally, sadness.

"I have been in hiding, afraid that if Mabus found me, he would destroy me, and absorb my half of the Guardian's power. I fear not for myself, but for all of you." He looked around at everyone standing before him. Eric and Gabriel were still unsure as to whether they should lower their weapons. Sam was overwhelmed by emotions, and she cried while Constantine spoke.

"If Mabus does find that book, he could in fact, become the Guardian. His lust for power and evil would mean an end to your world."

Rafeo looked down at the urn in his hands, then back at Constantine.

"So, I guess we should thank you for your cowardice," he said quietly, and turned and walked to the edge of the Estuary. Eric and Gabriel finally holstered their weapons and followed Rafeo, leaving Constantine alone near the chapel. Sam looked up from staring at the ground and made eye contact with Constantine before moving to join the others.

"I guess it's a good thing some of us are willing to do more than just hide," Sam whispered with such resolve that Constantine withdrew back into the small church.

They stood silently, listening to the wind, and their own hearts beating in their chests. After a few moments, a gentle breeze picked up, flowing out to sea. As if it was a signal, Rafeo opened the urn and released the ashes slowly, letting them ride the eddy out to sea.

"I will find you again," Rafeo whispered, with a new determination in his voice.

Manufactured by Amazon.ca
Bolton, ON